THE VAMPIRE WHO LOVED ME

It would be the perfect moment to kiss her, Connor thought. And he wanted to, almost desperately.

The pink tingeing her skin made her seem both innocent and sexy at the same time, which was downright irresistible. If only this table wasn't taking up so much damn space between them, he'd have his lips on her already, his hands skimming the gentle curves beneath her top and jeans.

And suddenly he wanted that. Desperately. But since he knew how skittish she was—especially around him, Lord Dracula, he didn't think he would gain any points by tossing the bit of metal aside and grabbing her like some demented creature in one of those terrible Bela Lugosi films that had given them all such a bad reputation to begin with . . .

Books by Heidi Betts

THE BITE BEFORE CHRISTMAS

MUST LOVE VAMPIRES

Published by Kensington Publishing Corporation

THE BITE BEFORE CHRISTMAS

HEIDI BETTS

BRAVA

KENSINGTON PUBLISHING CORP.
http://www.kensingtonbooks.com

BRAVA BOOKS are published by

Kensington Publishing Corp.
119 West 40th Street
New York, NY 10018

All Kensington Titles, Imprints, and Distributed Lines are
available at special quantity discounts for bulk purchases
for sales promotions, premiums, fund-raising, and educa-
tional or institutional use. Special book excerpts or cus-
tomized printings can also be created to fit specific needs.
For details, write or phone the office of the Kensington
special sales manager: Kensington Publishing Corp., 119
West 40th Street, New York, NY 10018, attn: Special Sales
Department, Phone: 1-800-221-2647.

Brava Books and the B logo Reg. U.S. Pat. & TM Off.

ISBN-13: 978-0-7582-4762-9
ISBN-10: 0-7582-4762-1

First trade paperback printing: October 2010
First mass market printing: October 2011

10 9 8 7 6 5 4 3 2 1

Printed in the United States of America

Dedicated to YOU, for EVERYTHING.

You've been in my life forever, but I don't think I ever really understood You until now. And though we've had our ups and downs over the years—more ups than downs,
thank goodness—I am better for knowing You and learning to understand You better. I'm so happy You came into my life when You did and showed me the way.

∿

And thank you to T.S., J.O.M., and J.M. for changing my thinking, helping to change my ways, and changing my life.

ACKNOWLEDGMENTS

I have been wanting to write this story for quite a while, but now that I've gotten the chance, I have to admit that it's bittersweet. You see, this is the last project my best friend and I plotted together before she passed away very unexpectedly. I remember that day as though it were yesterday. We met at one of our favorite restaurants the moment it opened and ended up closing the place down. (As usual.) We laughed, we gossiped, we plotted, we even banged our heads against the table a few times. But we had an absolute blast doing it, and I know that if she were still alive, she would be so proud and excited to see this story finally written and out on bookstore shelves. Thank you, Joanne, for everything. I miss you so much!

And giving credit where credit is due, I do not think this story would even exist without the late, great Kate Duffy, who put the Christmas vampire idea in my head to begin with and then was so excited about what I came up with. I am so sorry you're gone, Kate, and that we never got the chance to work together beyond brainstorming.

With thanks to J.R.W. for inspiring me more than you will ever know. You got me through this book in a way no one else could have, so I guess that means I owe you one. Feel free to collect any time.

THE BITE BEFORE CHRISTMAS

ALL I VANT FOR CHRISTMAS

BITE ONE

Thanksgiving Day

Despite the size of Drake Manor, Connor Drake was pleased to realize that for once the house felt cozy and warm. A fire crackled in the dining room hearth. Soft classical music played in the background. And the mouthwatering scent of roasted turkey wafted from the kitchen.

It was going to be the best Thanksgiving ever—or at the very least, the best they'd celebrated in the last eighty or ninety years.

He sat at the head of the table, admiring the delicate china and sparkling silver place settings, the cornucopia centerpiece he'd purchased himself. It was a beautiful thing, and this time, it was all going to work.

"Mr. Drake."

He turned his head slightly at the sound of the housekeeper's voice, though he'd heard her coming long before she'd reached the entryway. "Yes, Yvette?"

"Dinner is ready. Shall we set the table?"

With a nod, he climbed to his feet. "Yes, thank you. And fetch Liam and Maeve, as well."

Crossing the highly glossed hardwood floor, Connor left the dining room and headed for the cellar, where he kept a choice selection of wines. He hadn't chosen a bottle for dinner yet because he hadn't been sure what his mood would be. Now, however, he was feeling upbeat and optimistic, which called for something with a rich, hearty bouquet. Something even older than he was.

Bottle in hand, he returned to the dining room and took his seat. While he'd been gone, his staff had made quick work of laying out steaming bowls of carmelized yams, buttered beans, cranberry relish and, of course, the *pièce de résistance*, a large turkey with crispy, dark brown skin and moist, piping hot filling stuffed inside. For dessert, he knew, there would be bread pudding and thick chocolate mousse. His stomach rumbled at the very thought, and he wasn't usually one to get overly excited about normal food.

Heavy, shuffling steps echoed down the stairs and across the marble foyer, breaking into his lustful, meal-related thoughts. A second later, his siblings—younger by nearly a dozen years each—appeared in the doorway.

As usual when in their presence, Connor gave a mental eye roll. Instead of being well-dressed and neatly groomed, as he was, they seemed to enjoy flaunting their idea of independence and shocking strangers with their wild appearances.

Liam, the older of the two by a short two and a

half years, wore combat boots and ripped, faded jeans. His plain white T-shirt revealed a fresh set of brightly colored tattoos. On his right bicep, a red heart and dagger . . . on his left, a naked woman of the World War II pinup girl variety . . . and on the side of his neck, the word *chaos* in Old English block lettering.

Lovely.

In addition to the grunge-wear and body ink, Liam sported a fair amount of hardware—a small hoop in one brow, a stud at the side of his nose, and quarter-size stretchers in the lobes of his ears, making him look more like an African tribesman than the whitest white boy ever to walk on American soil. It was enough to make Connor lose his appetite.

And their lovely sister, Maeve, once a charming, delightful child, hadn't turned out much better. At the moment, her naturally dark hair was streaked with neon pink and blue and stuck up in places as though she'd just walked through a Category-Five hurricane. Something she'd apparently done intentionally, if the tiny ponytail holders at their base were any indication. She, too, had eyebrow, nose, and ear piercings, but at least her choice of jewelry was a bit more ordinary—large round silver hoops at her ears that, if solid, could easily double as drink coasters, and an armful of silver bangle bracelets.

She was wearing a hot pink top with grommets and rhinestones that spelled out REAL VAMPIRES DON'T SPARKLE, as well as a pair of skintight black leggings and a black skirt so short it reached her . . . well, it reached an area that a brother should never even know his sister possessed. And on her feet—combat boots.

Combat boots, for crissake. On a girl. On Thanksgiving Day.

He shook his head. No matter how long he existed on this planet, he didn't think he would ever understand some of the strange things people decided were fashionable. For that matter, he might never understand his own siblings.

Which was partly the purpose of this dinner, and why it was so important that it go well. Judging by the expressions on Liam and Maeve's faces, however, that was going to be an uphill battle.

"Whazzup?" Liam slurred, his arrogant slouch, white-tipped black hair, and the flash of a silver ball on his tongue causing Connor's molars to clench.

"Yeah. What's the deal, big bro?" Maeve asked, snapping her gum, and Connor's teeth went from merely meeting tightly to grinding together like a pepper mill.

A deep breath and he was able to relax. Moderately.

"Please," he said slowly, "have a seat. It's Thanksgiving." He added as his brother and sister shuffled closer, "I thought it might be nice to have a quiet, traditional holiday meal together."

Liam dropped into his chair, sending the hand-carved wood creaking. Maeve sat a bit more gently, but looked no more enthused at the prospect of sharing a fancy meal than her brother.

Connor ignored the attitudes that wafted from them in waves and forced his mouth to curve into a hint of a smile as he pushed back his own chair and rose to move to the far end of the long banquet table. "Pass the potatoes around, if you will, please. I'll carve the turkey."

"This is so bogus," Liam complained as he grabbed a nearby bowl and noisily slapped a dollop of mashed potatoes on his plate. He added a portion to Connor's plate, as well, before passing the bowl to Maeve. "Why do we have to bother with this shit?"

"Watch your mouth," Connor snapped before he could remind himself that he was supposed to be keeping his temper today, overlooking the things about his two younger siblings that normally drove him straight in the direction of the nearest garlic press.

Taking a deep breath, he let it out again through flared nostrils and counted to ten while he continued to carve the bird on the platter in front of him. Then, slowly and evenly, he said, "It's Thanksgiving. An opportunity for families to spend a bit of quality time together."

From his peripheral vision, he saw them both roll their eyes.

One. Two. Three. Four . . .

"It won't kill either of you to sit and eat a nice meal with me for once in your lives."

Liam snickered, sending a glance across the table at a grinning Maeve.

"No, it won't kill us," he retorted, "but it sure as hell ain't necessary."

Maeve giggled, even as she piled her plate higher with holiday foods.

Connor's brows knit as he transferred thick slices of moist white meat to their three plates before moving back around the table to take his seat. He took a sip of wine, letting the liquid slide down his throat, wishing it could have a calming effect on his nerves the way it did with others.

"First," he said, after returning his glass to the table, "watch your mouth. Second, just because something isn't necessary doesn't mean it shouldn't be done occasionally. Now, the staff went to a lot of bother to prepare this meal, so let's enjoy it, shall we?"

For the next few moments, they ate in silence and relative peace. Or rather, Connor ate. Maeve and Liam poked and picked at their food, making faces at each other across the table.

That lasted for all of five minutes before Liam leaned back in his chair and put his booted feet up on the table, dangling a strip of turkey meat over his tipped-back head.

"I don't know about you, but I prefer O-neg over this corn-fed crap."

"I like B-pos," Maeve piped in, joining along in Liam's inappropriate teasing.

"Feet off the table," Connor barked, feeling his blood pressure rise. "And sit up straight. Show some respect, dammit!"

Frustration boiling up inside of him, he banged his fists on the table, only to have the heavy wooden object lift off the floor at the other end by a good six inches, then slam back down, rattling dishes and silverware.

"Watch your language," his siblings singsonged at the exact same time, as though their response to his outburst had been choreographed.

But then, it might as well have been. They'd had

arguments like this a million times before. Sometimes it seemed to Connor that all they did was fight.

He thought they were flighty and immature. They thought he was stuffy and boring and—according to one recent accusation—had a stick up his ass the size of a telephone pole.

All he wanted was for his family to *be* a family, but every time he tried to bring them closer, his attempts seemed to backfire and cause them to drift even further apart.

"Is it too much to ask that we sit down as a family and have a nice holiday dinner?" Irritation tinged every word, and Connor could feel his eyes heating, beginning to glow. A sure sign he was about to go feral.

"Yeah," Liam replied, dropping his feet to the floor and tossing down his fork so that it clattered against the china plate. "It is. It's bullshit, Con. We aren't human and we don't need food to survive, so why pretend we do?"

"It is kind of stoopid," Maeve put in, abandoning her own meal and crossing her arms over her chest in a pouting show of unity with her youngest brother.

Before Connor had a chance to respond, Liam sent his chair flying and stalked from the room. "I'm out of here."

"Me, too."

Maeve stood and rushed after him, leaving Connor to storm after them both.

"Maeve. Liam. Get back here!" But they were already racing up the wide, curved staircase, his cries falling on deaf ears.

"One meal. That's all I wanted!" he shouted after them, sending the delicate crystals of the overhead chandelier tinkling, and knowing it would make no difference whatsoever.

Slamming a fist against the dining room door-frame, he charged back to the table and dropped into his seat.

A beautiful meal, a feast fit for a king, and it was wasted on his spoiled, ungrateful siblings. Worse, he'd lost his own appetite—what little there had been of it to begin with.

Reaching for his wine, he downed what was left in the glass before grabbing the bottle and pouring another. Not that it made any difference.

So many attempts at establishing a bit of tradition within the runaway Drake family. So many failures. He honestly didn't know how much more patience he had in him . . . or how many more times he was even willing to try.

"Not just a failure," Connor intoned. "An *epic* failure. A failure of magnificent, colossal proportions. If a meteorite had chosen that moment to come crashing through the roof and flatten us all, I actually would have considered that more of a success than what I tried to pull off."

Angelina Ricci, matchmaker to the stars—or the stars of the vampire world, at any rate—gave a low, throaty chuckle and crossed her slim, silk-covered legs in the other direction, taking a sip from the cut-crystal goblet in her manicured hand.

With her straight, black, waist-length hair and sapphire-blue eyes, she was a strikingly beautiful woman gifted with poise and grace and a razor-sharp intellect.

In another lifetime, she and Connor had been lovers. They'd burned very hot for a very short time before both their heads had been turned by other attractions and other, more interesting recreations.

But they'd maintained a close and valued friendship, one that was still going strong to this day.

"I've told you before that Liam and Maeve are a different breed of vamp than you and I. They enjoy living on the edge, flaunting their immortality. They have no interest in traditions or in keeping their own counsel."

Connor gave a derisive snort before taking a swallow of the thick, warm liquid in his own glass. "In other words, my younger siblings are gifted with an overabundance of sheer stupidity."

Angelina smiled gently. "Not stupidity, merely . . . a disparity in personalities and belief systems. The troubles you're having with them are no different than those of any parents with their teenage children throughout history."

"Good God, aren't we all a little *old* for adolescent games and battles of will?"

"Apparently not," Angelina told him pointedly.

Implying, Connor was sure, that he was as guilty as his brother and sister of both.

"Don't you ever miss the comfortable, cozy feeling the holidays used to bring?" he asked quietly. "That sense of togetherness, the remembrance of what's truly important as the minutia of everyday life falls away."

"You forget, love, that I'm the old-fashioned type, just like you. I still celebrate the holidays, complete with all the trimmings."

Connor took a sip of his AB-negative, then gave a weary sigh. "Only a few weeks until Christmas. It's going to be the worst one yet, I expect."

"Not necessarily." Setting her glass on the table beside her large, brocade, wing-back chair, Angelina uncrossed her legs and leaned forward slightly. "I know someone," she told him. "A professional."

Working hard to hide his astonishment, he allowed only one dark brow to dart upward. "You're offering to send me a *prostitute* to cheer me up over the holidays?"

She threw her head back, her smoky laugh filling the entire library where they sat. "Don't be silly. There are other *professions* women can excel at these days, you know. I like to think I'm a perfect example of that."

Her lips twisted in the intimation of a pout, but he knew she was really amused.

"No, I know a professional *event coordinator*. She's very good, and I think she may be able to put together a Christmas event for you that won't have you praying for Halley's comet to strike you dead."

"If only that would do the job," he muttered beneath his breath.

"Let me talk to her. If she's available, I'll have her give you a call."

"Is she also a miracle worker? Because I'm afraid that's what it will take to convince Liam and Maeve to sit still through a four-course meal and *not* burst into flames at the sound of 'Jingle Bells.'"

"I don't know about that, but I do think she'll be able to give you the holiday you're wishing for, whether your brother and sister decide to behave themselves or not."

Despite Angelina's assurances, Connor didn't hold much hope that her prediction would come true. But then, what did he have to lose?

"Fine," he replied without inflection. Then, as he lifted his glass to his mouth to drink, he added, "But I think I might be better off with the hooker."

BITE TWO

Jillian Parker tightened her sweaty palms on the steering wheel of her teal-blue Ford Focus Hybrid, wondering exactly what she was getting herself into as she drove up the long, shadowed path to Drake Manor. If ever she had seen an estate worthy of awe and trepidation, this would be it.

A tall stone wall and an ominous, spike-tipped, wrought-iron gate lined the front of the property along the main road. Large, towering trees spanned the drive and hid the house from prying eyes. And the manor itself was nothing if not imposing, reminding Jillian of every gothic novel she'd ever read, making her feel like Jane Eyre making her way to Thornfield Manor . . . or worse, a character in one of Edgar Allan Poe's horrifying stories.

Before her mind could wander too far in *that* morbid and frightening direction, she took a deep breath and reminded herself of *why* she was here.

She had a job to do, sure. And if she did it well, it could very well put her in good stead for years and years to come.

Angelina Ricci was the founder and owner of an amazingly successful matchmaking business.

So it happened to be called Love Bites, Jillian thought with a mental shrug.

So Angelina tended to cater to single vampires like herself.

Being a vampire wasn't against the law, nor was it as disreputable a condition as it had once been thought. Now that the world knew vampires existed and had come to realize they weren't the evil, bloodthirsty monsters fictional accounts had made them out to be, they were just another part of normal society.

Which wasn't to say they didn't still make people—humans, like Jillian herself—nervous, but the majority of folks weren't carrying concealed stakes or wearing wreaths of garlic around their necks. There did seem to be a rather strong trend in fashion these days for cross and crucifix jewelry, though.

Jillian didn't have much experience with vampires . . . or maybe she did, but she just didn't know it. It wasn't like they were required to wear giant red Vs on their shirts to identify them in public. With the exception of maybe being a tad unnaturally pale if they hadn't fed recently, they had the ability to blend in perfectly with humans and couldn't necessarily be branded as blood-drinkers unless they chose to be.

Though Angelina's reputation as both a matchmaker and blood-drinker preceded her, Jillian knew her only from a brief meeting several months earlier at a lavish charity event Jillian had planned. They'd only chatted for a few minutes during the soiree, but had seemed to hit it off and kept in touch afterward with the occasional e-mail.

Then yesterday, Angelina had picked up the phone and asked Jillian for a favor. Or rather, tossed a fat, juicy lead in her direction, informing her that she had a close and very wealthy friend who was interested in hiring out her services for the holidays.

The holidays. Three-plus solid weeks of guaranteed work.

The holidays were always a crapshoot in the events planning business. They could be extremely busy . . . or slow as a garden slug. Companies might throw extravagant parties for their employees . . . or they could just as easily hand out moderate Christmas bonuses. Charities might hold Christmas-themed fund-raising events in the hopes that contributors' hearts were softer during the holidays . . . or they could opt to simply send out donation request cards or assign volunteer Santas to stand on street corners and ring bells until passersby dropped coins into a bucket.

Guaranteed work for all of December was, for Jillian, a not-to-be-missed opportunity. And given the state of her personal life lately, she could use a nice, meaty project to focus on, something to take her mind off of Will and their ugly breakup.

And if that hadn't been enough to gain her immediate, undivided attention, the mention of renowned restaurateur Connor Drake certainly was. The man was famous. Or perhaps a better term was *infamous*. He owned restaurants all over the world. Five-star establishments with six- and eight-week waiting lists for reservations. Eateries that catered to the rich and famous and were a paparazzi's wet dream come true.

A man like Connor Drake could make or break a woman like Jillian. If he liked what she did for him, he could put her company on the map. If he didn't, he could put her out on the street. She would be decorating bus stop restrooms and organizing get-togethers beneath the city's most popular bridges if he badmouthed her to his friends and acquaintances.

Her chest tightened at the thought, turning more than just her palms damp. If she wasn't careful, her first meeting with the illustrious Mr. Drake would end up with him thinking she was suffering from swine flu.

In addition, if she did a good job for one of Angelina's closest friends, the professional matchmaker might send even more business her way in the future. Weddings and anniversaries and potential contacts money couldn't buy. Jillian might end up planning primarily nighttime events for the living dead, but she supposed there were worse avenues to success.

Pulling up in front of the large, gray-stone mansion, she noticed that the estate wasn't quite as daunting up close as it appeared from a distance. Snow-covered flower beds lined the walk, and other hedges of various sizes and shapes decorated the expansive landscape. There was even a pristine white birdbath in the center of a gardenlike area. No birds were showering at the moment, but in summer, she imagined it was a very popular avian hangout.

With her thick leather binder in hand, Jillian

started up the wide stone steps guarded by a pair of angry-looking lion statues. She was moderately surprised not to find gargoyles guarding the entrance, but the big granite cats were every bit as intimidating.

As was the matching lion's head knocker in the center of the thick, dark wood door. She rapped three times in quick succession, waiting only a few brief moments before her summons was answered.

She honestly expected to find *The Addams Family*'s Lurch or a similar character on the other side, but instead, the Drake Manor butler looked frighteningly normal. A middle-aged man with thinning brown hair and wearing a plain black suit opened the door and smiled in greeting.

"Hello. Can I help you?"

Jillian's own smile came naturally in response to his friendly demeanor. "I'm Jillian Parker, the events coordinator. I have an appointment with Mr. Drake."

"Connor or Liam?" the butler asked, waving her inside and closing the door behind her.

His question caught her temporarily off-guard. Though she'd done a bit of research into Connor Drake after Angelina's call—thank God for the Internet—and knew that he had a younger brother and sister, her anxiety over meeting and having to work with the family patriarch had apparently given her tunnel vision and superseded everything else.

She swallowed nervously and licked her suddenly dry lips. "Connor," she said. "Unless Liam is in need of a party planner, as well."

The minute the words were out, she felt her

face flush and wished for a bolt of lightning to flash through the ceiling or a giant sinkhole to open up beneath her feet—anything to bring about her immediate demise and put a stop to the flapping of her runaway tongue.

This was ridiculous, she thought, and ordered herself sternly to get a grip. She'd organized events for million-dollar corporations . . . weddings for local debutantes (some who made *Bridezillas* look like a very special episode of *Little House on the Prairie*) . . . and birthday parties for the richest and most spoiled Sweet Sixteens in the state.

Throwing together a private holiday gathering for one man, regardless of the size of his bank account, would be a piece of cake.

Before she could correct her minor faux pas, footsteps sounded from the far end of the foyer and a deep voice said, "Liam definitely doesn't need any help where parties are concerned. He seems entirely too proficient at them, as it is, if the amount of time he wastes in nightclubs is any indication."

Jillian turned to find a tall, darkly handsome gentleman marching in her direction.

If she'd thought the long, shadowy driveway and mysterious-looking house—both outside and in— were intimidating, they had nothing on the man now bearing down on her. To the naked eye, he appeared as normal as any other professional businessman she'd ever seen in a dark blue suit, complete with polished shoes, and a demure silk tie. But power emanated from him in waves, overwhelming everything in its path.

His hair was ink black and perfectly styled; his

complexion was smooth and, while not dark, not pale, either. She took that to mean he wasn't hungry and relaxed slightly, realizing that she'd unconsciously raised her shoulders in an attempt to protect her throat.

Oh, no, she wasn't vampaphobic.

Liar.

But it wasn't that she was a bigot. She didn't resent their existence; she just didn't quite understand it, and not knowing the details of how they lived, fed, felt, believed, apparently made her nervous. Something she would have to get over if she intended to work with this man—and with any luck, many more like him.

"That will be all, Randall. Thank you," he said to the butler, who nodded before slipping away.

He turned his full attention on her, and she felt it like a physical caress even before he held out his hand and introduced himself.

"Connor Drake. You must be Miss Parker. Angelina speaks very highly of you."

She took his hand and wasn't at all surprised by the zip of electricity that raised the tiny hairs on her arm and warmed her all the way to her core. His gray eyes were cloudy and bore through her as though he could see into her soul.

Forcing herself to wet her dry lips with the tip of her tongue, she said, "It's a pleasure to meet you, Mr. Drake. And, please, call me Jillian."

He gave an almost imperceptible nod, releasing her hand. "Then you must call me Connor. Let's go into my study where we can talk."

She followed him through the large entryway, their steps echoing on the parquet floor as they passed a wide, curved staircase and moved down a short hall lined with gilt-framed paintings.

Though it wasn't easy to drag her gaze from her new employer's wide back and head of glossy black hair, Jillian made an effort to take in her surroundings, making a mental note of what appeared to be Connor Drake's personal tastes—rich, classic, somewhat subdued. The more she knew about him or could glean from his home during this meeting, the better able she would be to fulfill his desires for a successful event.

He led her into a room lined with bookshelves and over to an ornately carved desk roughly the size of a small frigate. Taking a seat behind the desk—very lord-of-the-manor of him, but then, he *was* lord of the manor—he gestured for her to sit in one of the guest chairs on the opposite side.

Once they were comfortable and the preliminaries were out of the way, Jillian opened her folder and removed a pen, reminding herself that she was here to work.

Clearing her throat, she said, "I understand from Angelina that you're interested in throwing a Christmas party or event of some sort. She wasn't specific, but she did mention that you're looking for something traditional and family oriented."

He made a noise low in his throat that was part snort, part scoff. "That's what I'd *like*, certainly, but unless you're Jesus Christ Himself and able to work miracles, I'm not sure anything in your repertoire is capable of making our holidays *family-oriented.*"

"I'm sorry?" she said, brows dipping as she voiced her confusion.

With a sigh, Connor leaned back in his chair, linking his hands at his waist. "My brother and sister are . . . less than traditional, to say the least. Where I respect past customs, they thumb their noses at them. They would rather spend Thanksgiving or Christmas Day out with their friends, barhopping and flaunting their . . ." He paused, shooting her a curious glance. "You know we're vampires, right? Angelina was clear on that?"

Though she hadn't been prepared for the topic to come up—at least not so soon or in such a direct manner—Jillian nodded, trying not to show her surprise or unease.

With a slight tip of his own head, Connor continued. "I'm not ashamed of what I am, but I don't feel the need to advertise it everywhere I go, either. It's rather like religion—whatever your beliefs, they're your own; you don't need to go around announcing to everyone you meet that you're Catholic or Baptist or worship the sun god Ra. Maeve and Liam, however, like to use their vampirism for sheer shock value. They hang out in vampire clubs, flash fang at every opportunity, do 'tricks' as though they're part of some damn circus act."

"And you'd prefer they blend in a little more, stay home for the holidays."

His eyes glimmered and the tight line of his mouth relaxed marginally. "Yes. Is that so terrible?"

"Not at all. I'm not sure what I can do to help, though. I'm not a psychologist; I can't convince them to become more reserved in their behavior or care about the same things that are important to you."

A moment of complete and utter silence passed. Jillian wouldn't have been surprised if crickets suddenly broke into song beneath her chair.

Shortest job interview ever, she thought, sure that he was about to give her the boot. Which wasn't good for her résumé, but didn't bode well for her plans to prove she wasn't a prude, either.

She should have told him that *of course,* she could rein in his recalcitrant siblings in a mere three weeks and give him a warm, homey Christmas, to boot. She wasn't only a party planner, she was also a babysitter and part-time, out-of-control-vampire wrangler.

And afterward, maybe she would click her heels together three times and whisk herself off to the merry, merry land of Oz.

"Can you give me a Christmas *I'll* enjoy? One with all the trimmings that won't make me want to run screaming into the early morning sun? If you can do that, then you'll make me a very happy man, and I'll"—his voice lowered to what could only be described as a growl—"I'll take care of my brother and sister."

BITE THREE

Connor's level of confidence where his younger siblings were concerned was quite a bit lower than his declaration made it sound.

Did he wish he had the power to influence Liam and Maeve's attitudes and actions? Certainly.

Had he had any success in doing so thus far? Not even remotely. And nothing that had happened in recent memory made him think he ever would.

But sitting across from the lovely Jillian Parker—the events planner Angelina had sent to help keep his holiday from becoming a complete and abysmal failure—he suddenly felt the need to preen . . . or at least to act as though being the patriarch of his family carried *some* weight with his unruly brother and sister.

Angelina had told him Jillian was good at what she did. His longtime friend had apparently attended several events that Jillian's company had organized, and had been quite impressed.

What Angelina *hadn't* told him was that Jillian Parker was *hot* with a capital *H* and two *T*s.

From the moment Randall had opened the door and invited her in . . . from the moment he'd stepped out of the library and sniffed the air, he'd known she wouldn't be just another random woman drifting in and out of his life. She smelled of peaches and cream and just a hint of honey, all of which seeped into his pores and set his blood on fire.

It had been all he could do to walk calmly across the foyer to introduce himself. To take her hand instead of her mouth.

He *hadn't* been able to resist slipping his middle and index fingers over the inside of her wrist, however, to feel her pulse. To feel the beat of her heart in the one, slim vein, and the heat of her life's blood that called to his own.

Having her here, working in his home, was going to be an experience, that was for sure. And an exercise in self-control; something he'd always prided himself on . . . but now couldn't be entirely certain of.

Her blond hair was swept up in a loose knot at the back of her head, a few wisps falling free to frame her heart-shaped face and dust the pulse at her neck. He could see the gentle throb on both sides, even with the short distance that separated them.

She had bright blue eyes surrounded by light lashes and a raspberry-tinted mouth that could only be described as infinitely kissable.

Since it was winter in Boston, she was dressed more warmly and demurely than he suspected was the norm. Charcoal slacks and a thick red sweater with a deep, wide cowl neckline covered her from shoulder to ankle, but he could very well imagine the luscious figure hidden beneath.

Professional on the outside, sexy as hell on the inside. A flush of intense arousal heated his skin at the thought, moving south at a rapid pace.

Even in stylish boots with a two-inch heel, the top of her head only reached his chin while standing. But though petite, her form was lush and curvaceous, and made him feel both protective and possessive. Unusual given their short acquaintance, but not something Connor was inclined to question at the moment.

Clicking the tip of her pen, Jillian crossed her legs and adjusted the pad on her lap, ready to take notes.

"*That* I can do," she murmured, oblivious to the fact that he was nearly chewing nails on the other side of the desk, his mind having wandered to hell and gone from worries about an ideal holiday celebration to stripping her of that soft sweater and exploring every inch of her soft, white skin.

Thankfully, the wide desk hid the proof of his distraction, but if he didn't drag this out for a while, she and everyone he came in contact with in the next little while would know exactly what he was thinking of doing to his attractive new party planner.

"So tell me what it is you're looking for in a holiday event. What would make your Christmas flawless with a capital *F*?"

Exhaling a deep breath, he rocked back and forth slightly in his cushioned black leather executive chair and did his best not to picture *her* beneath the tree on Christmas morning—naked and waiting for something that definitely started with a big, hard capital *F*. And it wasn't *flawless*.

"I'm almost embarrassed to admit this, but when I think of the perfect Christmas, I imagine the end of every sappy holiday special you've ever seen. A table brimming with all of the traditional holiday fixings . . . family gathered 'round, holding hands, singing carols, sharing stories, laughing. . . ." He trailed off, reluctantly raising his head to meet her gaze. "Hokey, isn't it?"

She offered him a gentle smile that was both friendly and sensual. Or maybe he was simply reading too much into it because Jillian Parker apparently couldn't breathe without exuding sensuality like a thick, rich perfume.

"Of course not. Especially if you've never . . ." Her brows knit. "I'm sorry, I admit I don't know much about this. I don't know how old you are or how long ago you became a, um . . ."

"Vampire?" he supplied.

"Yes. What were your holidays like back when you were . . ." Again she fumbled for the right words.

"Mortal?" he offered, filling in the blanks.

She nodded, cheeks growing pink with embarrassment. It was charming, really, watching her struggle to remain polite and professional while discussing something she was either uncomfortable with or simply knew nothing about.

"My parents were peasant farmers, long, *long* ago. But even though we were dirt poor, what I remember most about my childhood is unconditional love and the closeness of our family. Christmas Day meant a crackling fire, a goose roasting over the spit, my mother baking, and my father saying grace while we all clasped hands."

"It sounds lovely," Jillian offered, her smile coming more easily now. "So you're looking for something *very* cozy and traditional, then. Very Norman Rockwell-esque."

He nodded.

"Would you like to invite extended family or friends? Are you thinking of hosting an event at another venue, outside of your home?"

Shaking his head, he said, "No. I want something here. I want the entire house to ring with the Christmas spirit. Not just one room, not just for one day—I want everyone and everything at Drake Manor to *feel* like the holidays."

"You aren't asking me to organize a simple Christmas party or dinner, then," she clarified, her pen rolling back and forth between slim fingers while her blue eyes remained intensely locked with his. "You want me to make the entire month of December feel like Christmas for you."

"Yes," he said with a sudden burst of enthusiasm as she started jotting notes, feeling hope rise in his chest for the first time since this outlandish idea had jumped into his head to begin with.

That hadn't necessarily been part of his plan in the beginning, but now that he'd met Jillian, gotten a whiff of her own unique scent, and felt the warmth of her blood heating her skin . . . well, the longer he could keep her in his employ and under his roof, the better.

"I realize it's a lot to ask. Probably not the type of occasion you're used to coordinating, either.

But if you can do it, if you feel confident that you can bring Christmas to Drake Manor . . . to this family of reluctant vampires," he added with a lop-sided grin, "I'd be willing to compensate you *very* generously for your trouble."

She tipped her head to one side, bringing the scribbling of her pen to a rest and regarding him quite seriously. "I won't lie to you. Something of that magnitude is going to be quite expensive. The cost of decorating a single ballroom would be daunting enough, but the entire mansion—"

"Inside and out," he qualified.

"Inside and out. It's going to take quite a bit of time to get it all done, and since most of my employees will be busy organizing other events, I may have to hire outside help."

"As long as you're here, running the show in person, you're welcome to hire as many people to assist you as you like."

"I can't promise anything I do will bring your brother and sister around," she said, making it clear that Angelina had filled her in on *all* of his problems, not just his lack of a Christmas tree in the foyer.

"I can hang an ocean's worth of garlands and provide the best meal money can buy, but that doesn't mean they'll suddenly be infused with the spirit of Christmas the way you might be hoping."

He inclined his head, returning her grin with a half-smile of his own. "You're not Dr. Seuss or the Ghost of Christmas Past. Understood. So I won't hold you responsible for their reactions, as long as you don't hold me responsible for any question-able behavior on their parts." Arching a brow, he tried not to let his amusement slip, even though thinking about his siblings' conduct brought out his annoyance faster than just about anything else. "They're known for being quite disrespectful upon occasion."

Jillian's only response to his veiled warning was the shrug of a slim shoulder. "Since you'll be the one footing the bill and paying my generous fees, I think I'll be able to ignore any outbursts from those who aren't."

Connor's lips quirked at her quick, yet diplomatic reply.

"Excellent response. I can see why you're so good at what you do. And why Angelina likes you so much."

"I don't really know Ms. Ricci that well, but I certainly appreciate her recommendation and confidence in me."

Hooking her pen to the top of the legal pad on her lap, she slowly closed the binder and wrapped her long, manicured fingers over the far edge. "If it's not too much trouble, I'd like to take a look at the house and property. If you can give me the tour yourself, it might help me get a better idea of what you'd like to see, decoration-wise. But if not, a member of your staff would work just as well."

Pushing up from his chair, Connor rounded the desk and held his hand out to her in a silent offer to help her to her feet. Once again, he got a sweet whiff of peaches and cream, and more than his stomach growled with hunger.

"It would be my pleasure to give you the grand tour," he told her, his voice lower and huskier than intended as he tamped down his inner beast. If he wasn't careful, he'd give her more of a lesson on vampires than she'd bargained for—one centered on sexual preferences and extreme staying power.

As it was, she was going to get a bit of on-the-job training soon enough . . . provided he could convince her to take the position he was prepared to offer.

"It will give me a chance to show you the room where you'll be staying for the rest of the month."

Jillian nearly choked on her own tongue at Connor's out-of-the-blue pronouncement. Her fingers tightened reflexively in his hold before she quickly loosened them, afraid he might take the automatic gesture for a deliberate—and suggestive—one.

He wanted her to stay? Here? For the entire length of her employment?

Heart beating in her chest like a conga drum, she tried desperately to regain her bearings. She was used to demanding clients making outrageous requests, but "move in with me" had never been one of them.

"No. No, no." *Okay, take a deep breath, Jillian. No need to start babbling like an idiot.* "I won't need to stay here."

The very idea sent a shaft of cold fear skating down her spine. Stay at Drake Manor? Sleep under the same roof as a family—nest? coven? gaggle?—of vampires?

She knew she was overreacting, but she didn't particularly care. Not when she didn't know enough about their race of undead (technically, anyway) to know how they lived, how they functioned.

Did they sleep in coffins? Did they need blood from a fresh source? Did they possess the ability to mesmerize their prey . . . er, victims . . . er, human sippy cups . . . into thinking they were donating willingly?

She didn't know, and she didn't care.

But visions of herself in a long, flowing, Mina-like white nightgown, traipsing through this big, cold house in the dead of night to the silent, hypnotic call of Connor Drake did not sit well. Neither did the thought of sprinkling holy water around her bed or sleeping with a necklace of garlic around her neck.

Apparently unaware of the panic coursing through her veins—or perhaps unaffected by it—Connor released her hand and started out of the study.

"Don't be ridiculous," he said, clearly expecting her to follow. And darned if she didn't do it, racing after him like some needy puppy dog.

"You said yourself that there's much to be done and not much time to do it. This is a big place, with a lot of square footage in need of transformation. Not to mention the meal to plan."

They were at the base of the stairwell now, and he started slowly up the thickly carpeted steps. "Though I have no intention of working you around the clock, you will be putting in long hours, and it won't make sense for you to go all the way home only to get a few hours' sleep, then turn around and come all the way back."

At the top of the stairs, he stopped and turned to wait for her to join him on the landing. That whole "Mina walking like a zombie into the night to meet Count Dracula" image flashed through her head again, and she felt the pulse at her throat pick up its beat.

Not such a good thing to have happen when she was within biting distance of a self-professed bloodsucker. Resisting the urge to lift a hand and cover her throat with the cowl of her sweater, she took that final step onto the landing so that she was standing eye-to-eye—well, eye-to-eye if she tipped her head back forty-five degrees—with him.

"I've organized any number of large-scale events without having to stay on the premises. I assure you, you'll have my undivided attention, and your Christmas will go off without a hitch."

"Of that, I have no doubt," he answered smoothly. "But I still prefer you stay here while you work. Consider it a condition of your employment."

Without giving her a chance to respond, he turned on his heel and continued walking.

Connor was being unreasonable, and he knew it. There was no logical reason a party planner would ever agree to move into a client's house. No reason a client would ever even request such a thing.

But something primal was driving him to keep this woman close. Frankly, she was lucky he hadn't grabbed her up already and kissed the reluctance right out of her, as his hands and lips and cock were itching to do.

He had four weeks until Christmas. Only four short weeks in which he would have an excuse to keep her around, get to know her a bit better, hopefully find out what made her smell so much like a basket of fresh-plucked fruit. After that, she would be off planning some other event for some other person—some other man, perhaps, who would find her just as desirable as he did.

A streak of possessiveness had his fangs throbbing and his lips peeling back in a near-growl. He tamped it down quickly, diverting the green-eyed monster by clenching and unclenching his fists at his sides, not wanting to alarm her—or worse yet, scare her away.

So he would have to use his time wisely, taking advantage of every moment he had her to himself.

And what better way to ensure that she spent the majority of those forty-thousand-odd minutes in his company than to demand she move in with him?

It had nothing to do with his being a vampire, and everything to do with the fact that he was a very wealthy man, used to getting what he wanted. In situations like these, at least, it was good to be filthy rich.

"Mr. Drake. Connor," she said, rushing to keep up with his long strides. "You can't require me to live with you while I organize your holiday."

"Of course I can. The customer is always right, isn't that the general consensus?"

He stopped, turning to face her. "This is the east wing, where you'll be staying. And rest assured you'll have it primarily to yourself. There's a library in this part of the house, as well as a gym and media room. Our suites—Liam's, Maeve's, and my own—are located in the west wing. We also employ a full staff who will be at your disposal. If you need anything, either personally or to complete your job, don't hesitate to ask for their assistance."

The longer he spoke, the more Jillian's gaze narrowed. When he finished, she crossed her arms beneath her breasts—potentially lovely breasts, from what he could see of them—and did her best to stare him down.

"I haven't said I'll stay here, and I think it's extremely unprofessional of you to even suggest it."

Without a doubt. But that didn't sway him one iota from his objective. Nor did it stop him from using his trump card.

"Let's be perfectly honest," he said in a calm voice, reaching up to straighten and smooth his tie. "You're running a very successful business on your own, I'm certain. But you're here because you know having me on your client list is a cachet that could lift your company to the next level. Angelina's recommendations, too, could bring you untold sums in future profits."

One light brow winged upward. "You're *black-mailing* me?" she demanded.

"Of course not. I'm simply trying to make you see reason. I'm also a man used to getting what I want, and am not above playing dirty when necessary."

"So what you're telling me is that I have to move in here for the next month while I work to give you your Charlie Brown Christmas, or you'll take your business elsewhere."

That hadn't been what he was saying at all; the thought of hiring another event organizer in her place had never crossed his mind. But if it would help to sway her to go along with his obscure demand, he wasn't above letting her think that was the case.

"I'm afraid so," he intoned with a sharp nod, drawing his own brows together in the hint of a scowl he hoped she would see as a sign of his dogged, if haughty, resolve.

Haughty and determined, *not* salivating and nightmare inducing. He had to be careful, when attempting to intimidate humans, that he didn't let too much of his vampire disposition slip through. Glowing eyes and dripping fangs tended to send people running rather than simply getting them to see things his way.

He also had the power to persuade by climbing into a person's mind and gently nudging them where he wanted them to go. But while other vampires might use those powers freely and without remorse, Connor felt it was an invasion of privacy, and the last thing he wanted to do was hold Jillian against her will.

Manipulating her slightly when she knew exactly what was going on was one thing; jumping into her head and forcing her to do something against her will would make her nothing more than a zombie, brainlessly doing his bidding. And he liked this woman too much as she was now, standing in front of him, to want to turn her into some stiff, mannequinlike version of herself.

Seconds ticked by while Jillian seemed to weigh her options. It was clear from the dip of her lips and the daggers sharpening in her eyes that she wasn't the least bit happy about being faced with such an ultimatum.

And used to getting what he wanted or not, Connor was already envisioning the phone calls and explanations he would have to make to Angelina and Jillian both after she told him to seek sunlight and stomped off the job.

Maybe he had gone too far. Maybe forceful arrogance was not the best route to take with Miss Jillian Parker. Perhaps he should have hired a different event firm to plan his holiday, then invited *this one* to Christmas dinner in an attempt to wine and dine her.

Or maybe he should have simply done the whole grab-and-growl-and-kiss thing that had been churning through his brain ever since he'd first laid eyes on her. It certainly couldn't have gone over any worse than this.

But before he could backpedal and attempt to climb out of the hole he'd dug for himself, she dropped her arms, shoulders slumping slightly as she released a breath.

"Fine," she said, her tone clipped and rough, and he knew it must have taken all of her effort to force the single word up her throat and past her pink-tinted, heart-shaped lips. "I'll stay here through Christmas. And I'll give you the best damn holiday you've ever had. But after that, you'd better come through with *your* end of the bargain, Mr. Drake."

She said his name as though it were a particularly foul curse, and he almost chuckled. He'd gotten his way, which of course made him happy. But more than that, he'd gotten the chance to see Jillian with her hackles up, which he thought might be one of the sexiest things he'd ever experienced—

and he'd been around for a while, so he knew what he was talking about.

"You have my word, Miss Parker."

Spinning on his heel, he continued down the long hallway to show her exactly which suite of rooms she would be occupying during her visit. But even without his exceptional hearing, he clearly heard her mutter, "Fat lot of good that will do me, coming from a vampire."

BITE FOUR

Jillian stood in the self-help aisle of her local bookstore, skimming spines and covers to find what she was looking for. Not that she was entirely sure what that was. All she knew was that she needed *something* to bolster her courage and point her in the right direction.

Connor Drake had played the Rich, Arrogant Jerk card, demanding she move into his home while she worked to give him the Christmas of a lifetime. Which, given his immortality and how long he'd likely been wandering along the (im)-mortal coil already raised the bar pretty damn high.

But as annoyed as she'd been with his high-handedness, she was now over it. Sort of. At the very least, she'd decided that taking up residence with a tall, dark, and handsome vampire might give her the opportunity to do something she'd been thinking about for a while now . . . if she was brave enough to follow through.

It was kind of a crazy plan, and could even jeopardize her position with Connor Drake, but she was just so tired of thinking of herself as boring and timid and—worst of all—frigid. None of which she'd ever *actually* thought about herself until Will had tossed them in her face as the reason she didn't hold his interest . . . the reason his eye had started to wander . . . the reason he'd apparently found it necessary to start humping everything that moved.

Jillian didn't believe for a minute that *she* was the reason her ex couldn't seem to keep it in his pants. That was on him, one hundred percent. But he'd said enough—enough cruel, hurtful things— that a couple of them had hit their mark, and she had begun to wonder: *Was he right?*

Was he right that she lacked a sense of adventure? She'd never been skydiving or bungee jumping, didn't have a tattoo or piercing below her earlobes, had never even signed up for something as mundane as an online dating service.

Looking back, she couldn't think of a single thing she'd done in her thirty-three years that would qualify as "wild" or "daring" or "courageous."

Which basically meant she was a thirty-three-year-old bore. A pathetic Holly Hobby type whose most exciting exploit to date was agreeing to let her hair stylist give her layers. A coma victim on Valium was more exciting than she was.

It bothered her enough that she wanted to do something about it. She wanted to wake up and have some actual *fun* for a change. She needed to prove to herself . . . and, yes, maybe a tiny bit to Will, even if she never saw the cheating bastard again . . . that she *wasn't* a complete and total snooze fest.

Unfortunately, it wasn't just her recessive boredom gene keeping her from jumping out of a plane or climbing Mount Everest . . . it was stark, pants-wetting terror. So those got crossed off her list right away, as did anything else categorized as remotely life-threatening. No speed racing, no racing toward the ground with nothing but a rubber band or shower cap to keep her from going *splat*.

Being adventurous perhaps required practice and more of a buildup to the truly dangerous stuff.

She also wasn't in any hurry to have her skin punctured or abused, but a tattoo or body piercing was on the list of possibilities. Not high on the list, but there, somewhere around line . . . oh, nineteen or twenty.

Yes, something like that would mark her as a bit of a rebel, but then she would have to live with it for the rest of her life. And what if she decided a week too late that she didn't really want a dolphin on her ass or a silver hoop in her va-jay-jay? (Yeah, even if she went for a below-the-neck piercing, it was *not* going to be that low. Belly button maybe; hoo-ha, no way in hell.)

Then Connor had insisted she move in with him. Well, not *with him*, but into his big, giant hulk of a mansion for the better part of a month.

It had seemed hugely boorish of him at the time, but after she'd allowed herself (possibly against her better judgment) to agree, she had gotten to thinking.

She was human. He was a vampire.

She would be living with a vampire.

Will—a human—had cheated on her with a vampire, and then accused her of not being woman enough to satisfy him. (Apparently it took razor-sharp fangs and a hundred-year-old pussy to get him off.) And to add insult to injury, he'd also had the nerve to say *she* would never have the nerve to sleep with a vampire herself. She was too bland, too boring, too vanilla.

Vanilla! Her least favorite flavor of ice cream, hands down.

So wouldn't he be surprised—if he ever actually found out or she ever bothered to actually tell him—to learn that she'd been plenty bold enough to sleep with a vampire. A sexy, powerful vampire who could buy and sell a schmuck like Will ten times over—not to mention rip his cheating, lying, tiny-peckered throat out.

It certainly would be a tidy little bit of revenge on her part . . . if she could find the courage to go through with it.

That was where her inner Holly Hobby reared her sun-bonneted head and caused butterflies to break out of their cocoons and flap crazily in her belly.

But she had a month to poison that freaking Lack of Adventure Barbie and prove that she *wasn't* a frigid, boring, pathetic cold fish of a woman.

Grabbing a bright yellow, oversize paperback off the shelf, she studied the title: *Vampires for Dummies*. Couldn't get much simpler than that, she decided, tucking it into the crook of her arm. Then she reached for one called *Living Amongst the Undead* and another titled *So You're Dating a Vampire.*

If these didn't give her at least a glimpse into the secret lives of vampires and how to get closer to Connor Drake without losing all of her bodily fluids, there probably wasn't much hope, and she would just have to learn to live with the idea of having a dolphin on her ass.

After making her purchases and trying *not* to look the clerk—who probably thought she was some kind of sick vampire groupie—directly in the eye, she left the bookstore and stood for a moment at the edge of the mall common.

Glancing first in one direction and then the other, Jillian told herself the smart thing to do would be to turn right and head back to the parking lot, get in her car, and drive home, since she still needed to pack for her enforced stay at Castle Dracula. That's certainly what old, boring, Will-Era Jillian would do.

New, bolder, post-Will Jillian, however, forced herself to turn left and walk resolutely in the opposite direction. Her heeled boots clicked in time with her rapid footsteps all the way to the entrance of P.S. I Want You, a Victoria's Secret–like shop that specialized in sexy, skimpy outer- and underwear.

While she didn't limit herself to plain white bras and undies on an everyday basis, she didn't own anything really nice or va-va-va-voom, either. Definitely nothing that said *P.S. I Want You.* Probably more along the lines of *P.S. We're out of milk, can you pick some up on your way home from work?*

But she suspected that it was going to take a little voom and at least one va to catch Connor Drake's attention.

If she could actually work up the courage to wear any of it in front of him.

But just in case, she heated up her credit card with a few sleek, slinky numbers for both inside and out, struggling not to blush as the young lady behind the counter rang her up, and then finally made her way to her car before she could chicken out and return everything for a full and speedy refund . . . including Connor's hefty deposit for her party planning services.

The minute Connor stepped out of his bedroom, he smelled fruit—peaches, to be precise—and knew Jillian was in the house. He took a deeper breath, holding the delicious fragrance in his lungs for long minutes. Very long minutes, since technically he didn't need oxygen to survive.

Vampires breathed for the same reason they ate—because it was normal; because it was a habit learned after decades of being mortal; because humans expected it and it was hard to blend in (if that was one's intention) if you didn't. In actuality, Connor could be dropped to the bottom of the ocean for centuries and still not die. Oh, his craving for blood would likely drive him insane and send him as close to the brink of death as a vampire could get, but the lack of oxygen would make very little impact one way or the other.

It was times like these, though, that he enjoyed breathing. Appreciated the fact that being a vampire heightened *all* of the senses, and made him feel as though Jillian were in the room with him rather than in the next room, or down the hall, or even downstairs.

It was hard to pinpoint exactly where she was at the moment. The scent of ripe peaches surrounded him, coming from both the other wing, where her suite of rooms was located, and the stairwell, where she'd likely passed recently.

Starting down the stairs himself, he used one of his other senses—his exceptional hearing—to track her down. Not because he had business with her, not because he wanted to check on her progress with the house, but simply because he wanted—perhaps even *needed*—to see her again.

The sound of humming reached him well before he reached her. "Winter Wonderland," if he wasn't mistaken.

He found her in his study, and the minute he cleared the open doorway, his heart—newly flooded with the blood he'd consumed for "breakfast"—thudded against his rib cage at the sight of her. She was perched on a small stepladder, facing the other direction as she stretched on tiptoe to tack a full, lovely pine bough garland interspersed with groupings of gold bows and shiny, round, red and gold glass ornaments along the topmost edge of the bookshelves lining the walls.

For a moment, he simply watched her, enjoying the view. She was wearing a pair of jeans that hugged her butt like a second skin—like *he* wanted to hug her butt—plain but for a few glittering silver grommets decorating the rear pockets, and a long-sleeved, lightweight white top. The outfit was casual, not nearly as dressy or professional as the slacks and sweater she'd worn the first time he'd seen her in this very room, but he definitely liked these clothes better. What man wouldn't, when they were snug enough to display her lovely figure and comfortable enough to invite a man to touch?

Doing his best to get his libido under control, and making sure his blatant desire for her didn't show in his eyes—in more ways than one—he cleared his throat and took a step into the room.

In the process of reaching about three feet away from her center of gravity to measure the distance between tacks along the string of the garland, Jillian jerked her head around at the noise, lost her balance, and started to fall. Arms pinwheeling, she gave a little yip of fear as her feet slipped from the metal rung of the ladder, and she went over backward.

Before the first tack pulled free, before she could even go vertical or finish her yelp of alarm, Connor was there, catching her, plucking her from the air and saving her from a broken neck— or at the very least, some very nasty bruises.

"Are you all right?" he asked, letting her slide slowly down his body and to her feet. Her breathing was raspy, panic making her heart race and her pulse pound, every beat of which he felt like a hummingbird's wings under his touch.

"I-I think so," she said, her hand going to her throat as she swallowed hard, and then slowly sliding lower, as though she was checking all of her extremities for broken bones.

Then she lifted her head, meeting his gaze with

round, fully dilated blue eyes. "How did you do that? How did you get to me so fast?"

One corner of his mouth quirked up in amusement. "Just one of the more useful side effects of being a vampire. Super hearing, super sense of smell, super speed . . . able to leap tall buildings in a single bound."

If possible, her eyes widened even more. "Really?"

"Yes to one, two, and three. No to four. I could possibly *lift* a tall building in a single bound, though. Or maybe a small to mid-size vehicle."

"Wow," she murmured, sounding stunned. Whether in awe or trepidation, he didn't know.

"You're sure you're okay?" he asked again, realizing that his hands were still wrapped around her arms and she was still touching him—however lightly—from chest to hip.

"Yes, thank you. And thank you for catching me. I can't imagine hitting the floor from that height would have felt very good."

"You'd have probably broken something— preferably not your neck." The thought had him frowning, especially since he could think of much more enjoyable things to do with her neck than trying to realign the bones and sticking it in a brace.

"Why are you up on a ladder at all?" he wanted to know, aware that his tone came out rougher and more accusatory than intended.

One of her pale brows arched and she took a step back, breaking his hold. He lowered his arms, already missing her warmth against his fingertips.

"I'm decorating your house, the way you asked me to," she informed him. Her own tone was a cross between annoyance and patience with a very small child or . . . someone with a very low I.Q.

"Don't you have people to do this sort of thing for you? I didn't know *you* were going to be the one hanging from the rafters and risking your life to hang tinsel."

Taking another step back, she leaned down to retrieve the end of the fallen garland, looping it a few times in her hand and resting it on the top-most step of the ladder.

"No hanging from the rafters," she said. "I'll leave that to you."

Slanting him what could only be described as a wicked glance, she added, "You can turn into a bat, can't you?"

Before he could stop himself, he laughed. An honest to goodness laugh filled his chest and diaphragm. He couldn't remember the last time he'd laughed out loud or been so genuinely amused.

Damn, she was refreshing.

"Sorry, no. Shape-shifting is only the stuff of myths and legends. If we all turned into bats, we probably wouldn't last very long. Too many people are afraid of bats and are quick to call in exterminators."

"And people aren't afraid of vampires?" she asked.

"Not *as* afraid. Not scream-at-the-top-of-their-lungs-and-hide-under-the-furniture afraid. Or if they are, they simply stay out of known vamp hangouts and make sure they're home before dark."

"I'll have to remember that," she murmured, crossing her arms and leaning back against one of the lower rungs of the ladder.

He chuckled, mimicking her crossed-arms stance. "Isn't it a little late for you to be planning how you're going to avoid coming into contact with the undead?"

"Maybe. But then, I assume there are good vampires and bad vampires, just like there are good humans and bad humans," she said, feeling suddenly like Glinda in *The Wizard of Oz. Are you a good witch, or a bad witch?*

"True. But just like humans, they don't wear signs on their foreheads, so you have to be careful and trust your instincts. And stay away from some of the rougher parts of town, the vamp bars, et cetera."

No problem there, she thought. She didn't make a habit of spending much time in rough *human* hangouts . . . or the subdued ones, either, for that matter. Coffee with a friend or the occasional margarita at Señor Sombrero's with some of the girls after work was more her speed.

Had been more her speed. She was working to change that. Maybe not by walking into the first biker bar she ran across—human or vampire—but she was taking baby steps . . . if moving into Drake Manor and planning to seduce Connor Drake could be considered a baby step.

"Look," he said when she didn't respond, "I have to get to the office, but do me a favor—stay off of ladders. And chairs. And step stools, for that matter."

"How, exactly, am I supposed to get your house

ready for Christmas without being able to hang decorations? By osmosis?"

"No," he said slowly, dragging out the word, "you can hire assistants, as I suggested. Or get someone from my own staff to help."

"But I don't need assistants yet. And if I ask someone from your household to help, I'd just be standing there, issuing orders."

"So what's wrong with that?"

She tipped her head and fixed him with an assessing stare. "I'm not that kind of decorator. I have no problem hiring extra people when the situation warrants, but when I can just as easily do the work myself, I prefer to do it myself."

It was Connor's turn to cock his head, but rather than annoyance, his lips were curved slightly in amusement. "And you're adamant about this?"

"Absolutely," she replied, rather than telling him that there was actually a lot of wiggle room to her position.

For a second, he remained silent, narrowed dark eyes studying her. Then he uncrossed his arms, letting them drop to his sides as he rounded the corner of his desk, opened a black leather briefcase, and started filling it with folders and papers.

"All right, have it your way," he said, closing the attaché and flipping the latch. "You don't have to ask anyone else to assist you, but I still don't want you climbing things or doing anything that could be potentially dangerous. So as soon as I get home, *I'll* help you."

He straightened to face her, case in hand. "How does that sound?"

Jillian wasn't sure how it sounded because she was still trying to figure out if she'd heard him correctly.

"*You're* going to help me?" she asked, hoping the shock wasn't too clear in her voice.

"Yes. Why is that such a surprise to you?"

Maybe because he was Connor Drake. Connor Drake, vampire, sure, and she didn't think vampires did home improvements. (Not that she knew enough about them to be sure.) But also because he was Connor Drake, mega-mogul restaurateur. He didn't have to do *anything* himself. He could hire people to brush his teeth for him, if he wanted. (Did vampires brush their teeth? She didn't know that, either, but she hoped they did; blood left some nasty stains.)

"I'm not in the habit of putting my clients to work on their own party plans," she told him instead.

He shrugged one broad, well-tailored shoulder and moved back around to the desk toward the door. "There's a first time for everything."

Yes, there was, she thought as she watched him leave. A first time for a client to decorate his own house, and a first time for her to try to lure that client into bed.

Hopefully neither of them would end up costing her her job.

BITE FIVE

Stifling a yawn with the back of her hand and resisting the urge to rub at her dry, tired eyes, Jillian double-clicked on yet another bread pudding recipe and began comparing its ingredients to the other dozen she'd perused already. She wasn't even sure bread pudding was the way to go for Connor's Practically Perfect Christmas Dinner, but that hadn't stopped her from opening sixty-seven different tabs on her laptop's browser.

"Found her, Maeve! She's in here!"

The raised voice, ripping through the silence without warning, made Jillian jerk and sit up straighter behind Connor's wide desk. She hoped she wasn't about to get in trouble for working here. She hadn't asked if she could use his desk while he was gone, but she wasn't using his computer and hadn't touched a thing on his desk other than the blotter, where she'd set her own wireless notepad.

Doing a quick save of some of her searches, she

stood and tried to look as though she *hadn't* been making herself at home, just as a heavily pierced young man with white-tipped, spiky black hair appeared in the doorway. He was dressed in black denim and leather from head to toe, had a tattoo of a small, black widow on his cheek just below his right eye and one of a skull and crossbones on his forearm. They looked so fresh, they might have been a real spider and someone's actual skull resting on his flesh. *Ugh.*

He stood there, hands on hips, looking more than a little menacing as he studied her with intensely curious hazel eyes.

A second later, a girl of about the same age, with the same dark hair—though hers sported a bright stripe of magenta rather than peroxide tips— came to stand beside him. She, too, had multiple piercings, but her clothes were a bit more animal friendly: bright yellow spandex skirt, ratty blue high-top tennies, and a white T-shirt that said: LOVE SUCKS . . . AND SO DO I.

Pulse slowly returning to normal, Jillian closed the lid of the laptop and carried it around the desk to rest on the seat of one of the striped armchairs.

"You must be Liam and Maeve." Though she hadn't met either of them yet, she'd heard enough to make an educated guess at their identities.

Brushing her hands nervously against the denim of her low-rise jeans, she moved forward and offered her hand. She aimed for Liam first, but he made no move to shake . . . and neither did Maeve when she made the attempt.

Ohhh-kay, Jillian thought, tucking her fingers into the back pockets of her pants instead. *So much for a warm vampire welcome from Connor's brother and sister.*

"You're the balloon blower Connor brought in to make us celebrate Christmas, huh?" Liam asked, hands on hips in as cocky a pose as she'd ever seen. "Sorry to disappoint you, A-pos, but hanging a few wreaths and piping carols through the manse isn't going to turn us into the Cratchits."

"I'm sorry," she said with the shake of her head, wondering if the young man had taken a guess at her blood type . . . or knew in some eerie, possibly intrusive vamp way. "Your brother didn't mention the two of you when he hired me. If you'd like to be involved in the preparations, I'd certainly love the help and input, but Connor only asked me to fix the place up and plan a traditional Christmas dinner for him."

Not entirely true, but from the back-off vibes these two were giving off, as well as what Connor had told her about their rebellious streaks, she figured they would enjoy a good argument. And if she remembered anything from her own teenage years, it was that the more her parents had told her she *had* to do something or *couldn't* do something, the more she'd wanted to do the exact opposite.

Better, Jillian thought, to ignore all the things they did to attract attention—the piercings, the tattoos, the questionable fashion sense . . . and the argumentative spirits.

At her announcement, Maeve's face went slack and Liam's brows knit.

Not wanting to lose the momentum she'd managed to build with them, Jillian added, "Come to think of it, if you want to join your brother for Christmas dinner . . . well, I'll have to clear that with Connor first, of course, and then you'll need to let me know in the next week or so because it will affect the size of the meal." Also not entirely true, but they didn't need to know that. "I hope that's not too short notice."

"You're not gonna try to convince us to get all *The Night Before Christmas* with you?"

"Nope. You can be as Grinchy and *Scrooged* as you like. I'm just here to get the house ready for your brother's Christmas."

Maeve leaned close to her brother and whispered in his ear, "I thought you said she was going to try to make us help and go along with Connor's stupid idea."

Liam shrugged, but he looked annoyed that his carefully staged confrontation wasn't going as planned.

"Actually, there is something you could help me with," Jillian told them.

Liam's mouth twisted and he shot his sister a smug I-told-you-so smirk.

Brushing past them, she started down the hall toward the front entrance, waving them to follow. Her car was parked out front and she still hadn't brought in all the boxes of decorations she'd brought along. Shrugging into her coat, she stepped outside, went around to the driver's side door, and leaned in to pop the trunk.

To her surprise, the two kids were there to meet

her. The two kids who weren't really kids. They looked—and acted—so much like teenagers or young adults that she had to continually remind herself they were older than she was. Older than any other living, breathing human she knew, most likely. Maybe even older than dirt—literally—for all she knew.

And maybe that was part of the problem Connor was having with them. He was potentially older than dirt, too, but rather than embracing his immortality with an outlook of perpetual youth, he was serious and mature and very obviously an adult-adult in both appearance and state of mind.

Liam and Maeve, on the other hand, seemed to be milking their conditions for all they were worth. They looked young and knew they were never going to age another day, physically, so they acted even younger than they really were. Not only by staying out all night at parties and nightclubs or by their choice of clothing and hairstyles, but by acting out against their older, more solemn brother.

Connor wanted them to settle down.

They wanted to do everything *but* settle down.

And that sort of antagonism did not make for a cozy, conflict-free holiday. No wonder the Thanksgiving Connor told her about had been such an unmitigated disaster. No wonder he'd had to call in reinforcements.

The question now became whether or not she could pull this off. It wasn't her job to change Liam and Maeve's minds; Connor had said he would take care of them and bring them around to his way of thinking by Christmas. But she imagined even the attempt to do such a thing would simply end up adding to the level of holiday stress Connor was already experiencing, not lessen it. And it *was* her job to make sure things were as flawless and peaceful as possible for her client.

Leaning into the trunk, she lifted out a large, bulky cardboard box. "You wouldn't mind carrying this inside, would you?" she asked Liam as she handed it over. "Be careful, it's heavy."

His eyes widened in surprise as the box hit him square in the chest, but just as she'd hoped, he took it—and added a small smirk to show that it wasn't too heavy for *him*. Muscle boy and vampire extraordinaire.

She took out another, smaller box and passed it to Maeve, who was standing with her arms up, ready for what was coming now that her brother had been put to work.

Jillian grabbed the last one for herself and trailed behind the other two back into the house, wondering if she should say something to Connor about his intentions with these two. His brother and sister didn't seem all that bad. A little mouthy, a little rebellious, maybe, but not *bad*. If they were, they wouldn't have followed her out to her car when she'd asked them to. And when she'd handed them the boxes she needed carried, they'd have dropped them on the ground at her feet and told her to take a flying leap. Or worse.

Since she was still relatively insult free, she had to assume that Maeve and Liam tended to be more insulting than usual around their older brother just to get a rise out of him. Many of their exploits were probably more for show than anything else.

She hoped that was the case, anyway. Lord knew she was far from qualified to be a family counselor, especially when it came to a family of vampires. Dr. Phil for the Fanged, she was not. But from what little she'd seen so far, she liked Liam and Maeve and wanted to think the best of them, give them the benefit of the doubt.

And if they wouldn't come around to celebrating Christmas the way Connor wanted them to, then maybe Connor should think about letting them go off to do their own thing while he invited other, more willing friends or family in to spend the holiday the way he preferred.

It was worth mentioning, at least. Now all she had to do was work up the courage to broach the subject when she wasn't entirely comfortable being in the same room with him to begin with.

Then again, since she intended to approach him about other, much more intimate topics one of these days, perhaps a nice, cozy talk about his domestic situation would be a good icebreaker. Something along the lines of *Your brother and sister don't seem quite as rebellious as you led me to believe. Oh, and by the way, is there any chance you might like to rock my world before you climb into your coffin for the day?*

Connor arrived home later than he would have liked. His habit was to put in long nights in an attempt to make up for certain things he couldn't get done during the day. But now that Jillian was living under his roof, he found himself thinking about her, unable to concentrate. Sniffing the air for a hint of peaches and cream from anyone, any-*thing* else. Wanting to cut everything short and put off as much as he could until tomorrow or the next day so that he could hurry home and see her again.

Now. Tonight. Preferably in the same tight jeans and snug top she'd been wearing when he left.

And he *had* promised to help her hang the rest of that garland, after all.

The minute he entered the house, through a rear entrance leading from the six-car garage at the back of the house, he knew something was different.

For one, there was music playing. Not the soft, classical music he sometimes piped through his of-fice or library. Not the loud, ear-splitting junk Liam and Maeve played at full volume just to piss him off. Not even beautiful, traditional Christmas carols that would be appropriate to the season.

No, this was . . . Christmas music with a twist. For several long minutes, he stood, briefcase in hand, and simply listened, realizing that he was hearing holiday tunes that would be right up his brother and sister's alley.

The final notes of "Christmas at Ground Zero" soon led into something that sounded entirely in-nocent but turned out to be about chipmunks roasting over an open fire.

Holy stakes on fire, he thought, not knowing whether to be amused or offended. Who on earth came up with this stuff? he wondered.

Since vulgar parodies were definitely not *his* idea of appropriate listening material, especially at Christmas, his first instinct was to find the radio or CD player responsible for spewing out such irreverent nonsense and turn it off immediately.

But then he heard voices. And laughter.

Laughter was definitely not something the walls of Drake Manor were used to—from him or anyone else. He almost didn't know what to think . . . had he walked into the wrong stone mansion at the top of the wrong long, sloping drive? had his home been taken over by a happy, cheery Brady Bunch–like family? . . . but he *did* want to find its source.

After dropping off his briefcase in his office and shrugging out of his suit jacket, he wandered past the wide curved staircase to the other side of the house. The closer he came to the dining room, the louder the music and voices grew, so he knew he was headed in the right direction.

Inside, the long, bare, highly polished mahogany table was covered with Christmas paraphernalia. He couldn't make heads or tails of it himself. And even more confusing to him, his brother *and* his sister were seated at the table with Jillian, all three of them smiling and laughing and enjoying themselves.

It had been so long since he'd seen anything but defiant scowls on either of his siblings' faces that he was surprised to find they still had teeth other than fangs.

Any intention he might have had to demand they turn off their questionable choice of music disappeared as surprise and . . . appreciation? . . . replaced any initial annoyance he may have felt.

Liam and Maeve were actually laughing. They were home before sunup—apparently willingly— and they were sitting in a room with a woman they'd known less than a day, helping her to prepare decorations for a holiday they purported to despise, and they were *laughing*.

Connor wondered if this remarkable turn of events could be considered a Christmas miracle.

It was certainly a minor Drake family miracle.

He stood somewhat mystified in the doorway, not sure whether he should go in or slip quietly away. He definitely didn't want to disturb whatever camaraderie was growing between his younger siblings and Jillian.

Before he could decide on a plan of action, however, Jillian raised her head and spotted him. The moment their gazes met, he felt a stab of heat bloom in his chest and head at warp speed down to *le petit général*. The rogue appendage didn't offer a full salute, but it did stir inside his BVDs and consider standing at attention.

He couldn't remember the last time he'd had such an instant, visceral response to a woman . . . unless it was the first time he'd seen this *same* woman standing in the foyer or sitting across from him in his study.

Oh, he'd enjoyed his fair share of lovers. And there was a faction of women in the world—also known as fang-bunnies—who considered banging a vampire a major coup. Not often, but occasionally he let himself be lured in by their overt sexuality and willingness to share a few minutes of fast, anonymous sex.

But Jillian was different. She wasn't coolly sophisticated like the businesswomen he interacted with on a regular basis. Nor was she brainless, bubbly, or over-eager.

If anything, she seemed almost nervous around him at times. Was she simply trying to keep a professional distance between them, or was it possible she was attracted to him and didn't want him to know?

He liked that explanation best, and made a mental note to test the theory as soon as possible. And if she wasn't secretly attracted to him . . . well, he'd just have to do his best to change her mind about that.

"Mr. Drake," Jillian said, breaking into his wayward thoughts. Then she quickly corrected herself: "Connor."

Liam and Maeve both twisted in his direction, their former happy, lighthearted expressions sliding into blank faces and dark, angry eyes.

Sigh. At least he knew they were *capable* of fun and enjoyment, just maybe not around him.

"Come on in," Jillian invited, gesturing for him to take a seat at the long table.

There were several empty chairs at the far end, closest to the doorway where he was standing. But there was also one on Jillian's immediate left, and he decided *that* would be a better spot for him to occupy.

Footsteps sounding on the hardwood floor, he crossed the room to sit between Jillian and Maeve, not entirely sure what they were doing or what he was supposed to do now that he'd joined them.

"We're decorating wreaths," Maeve provided, apparently taking pity on him.

Slanting a glance in her direction, he noted for the first time in a very long time that she wasn't sneering or rolling her eyes at him.

"I want to hang them on all the doors in the mansion, but Maeve and Liam thought it might be fun to decorate a few of them differently from the others instead of having them all look exactly alike."

Almost as though she was afraid he'd balk at such an idea, she rushed to add, "The ones downstairs and outside will all be the same and very traditional. But upstairs, I thought it might be nice to relax a little, especially with the ones for your brother's and sister's doors."

Connor raised a brow, not because the idea of having non-uniform wreaths spanning the property bothered him, but because he'd never known his siblings to be agreeable about much of anything.

"You two are letting her put wreaths on the doors of your suites?" he asked, not bothering to mask the astonishment in his voice.

It took a moment to get a response, but finally Liam shrugged, head still down as he concentrated on the project in front of him. "She said we could decorate them however we wanted, so they won't be completely bogus like the rest."

Whether Liam's accusatory comment was meant to rile him or not, Connor let it go. This was as

close to family time as they'd spent i̶
closer to getting them to do anything ho̶
lated than he'd ever expected to see.

"I think that's great. Good idea, Jillian," he said,
sending her an approving smile. "Wish I'd thought
of it. But then, I guess that's why you're the professional."

She smiled somewhat reluctantly in return before ducking her head and going back to work on
the wreath in front of her. She was stringing it with
thin strands of red and gold ribbon, and given the
glue gun slowly dripping hot wax on a plastic
placemat at her side, it looked as though she
would soon be adding small round ornaments in
the same two colors.

He liked them; they were just the sort of thing
he thought of when he imagined classic Christmas
decorations. One more reason to be glad he'd
heeded Angelina's advice and hired an expert. Especially *this* particular expert.

"So what did you two find to decorate your
wreaths?" he asked turning his attention—or part
of his attention, at any rate—back to his siblings.

One corner of Liam's mouth turned up. It was
his Billy Idol impression, but this time the sneer
seemed to be all show, without the usual cynicism
behind it.

"Skulls and crossbones, and lots of black ribbon," his brother announced proudly.

Looking closer, Connor could tell that the tiny
plastic images he was seeing upside-down were indeed gruesome white skulls with bone-shaped *x*'s
beneath. It suited Liam's tastes to a T.

u?" Connor asked Maeve.

wreath up to show him a circle
en shrubbery dotted with red and
Interspersed between the hearts were
d crossbones . . . but hers were pink and
of cute instead of ugly and menacing.

Connor almost sighed. Even though they were more suitable to Valentine's Day than Christmas, the little hearts in bright, festive colors had gotten his hopes up.

But he supposed he couldn't have everything all at once. He had to consider what was taking place right now as progress. Both the fact that Liam and Maeve were sitting here, helping Jillian to decorate at all, *and* that they were allowing him to join them instead of getting up and storming off the minute he entered the room, most likely tossing creative epithets over their shoulders as they went.

"Very nice," he told them. And he meant it. It might not be Santa Claus or Frosty the Snowman, but if this was their idea of Christmas and they were willing to celebrate with him in *any* way, then he supposed he should be grateful.

"I realize I'm late to the party, but is there anything I can do to help? Maybe a wreath I could take a bit of artistic license with for my office door?"

Three sets of eyes lifted and locked on him in incredulity.

"What?" he asked after a moment of dead silence. It wasn't often that someone could make him squirm, but he was certainly feeling twitchy under their intense, joined stares filled with a mix of curiosity and awe.

"You . . . never do anything yourself," Maeve put in, her voice low and small.

Connor wasn't used to hearing his sister sound so meek . . . or to having Liam look at him as though a matching pair of Venus flytraps had just sprouted out of his ears.

She had a point, of course. He'd gotten used to having a large staff on hand. There were servants who catered to his every need and whim at home, and a staff who happily did his bidding at work.

But he'd volunteered to help Jillian hang garlands, and fully intended to follow through with the offer—as well as anything else she needed help with that would put him even remotely in contact with her lovely feminine curves.

Holding a ladder steady . . . catching her when she fell . . . carrying her to his bed and showing her exactly what put the *vamp* in vampire. . . .

Maeve was one to talk, though. She and Liam were just as spoiled by their wealth and station as he. Not that he thought now was the best time to point that out.

Given their shock at his offer to help with what they probably considered menial labor, though, Connor realized that perhaps he hadn't been setting the best example for his brother and sister all these years. Instead of giving them everything they'd ever wanted, making sure they were not only provided for, but extremely *well* provided for, maybe he should have made them work for a few things. Even put them to work. The devil knew he owned enough restaurants that he could have placed them both into any number of positions rather than allowing them to spend all of their time partying and playing at being adults.

It was food for thought, and he intended to chew it thoroughly over the next few weeks.

"There's a first time for everything," he told his sister decisively.

Loosening the knot of his tie, he slipped it off, then unbuttoned his cuffs and rolled the sleeves of his shirt up to his elbows.

"Hand me a wreath and show me what to do," he said to no one in particular.

Glancing at Jillian, who had paused in the act of gluing a round glass ornament strategically to her wreath, he found her studying him with glittering blue eyes and a pleased, almost happy expression on her face.

The idea that she approved of his participation and his interaction with his brother and sister made him shift slightly in his chair, pride straightening his spine. He'd never realized before that such small gestures could act as an aphrodisiac. That relaxing his normally rigid attitudes and rolling up his sleeves to help with something as mundane as putting together Christmas decorations could make a woman smile.

And when she smiled, he got hot, both inside and out.

Clearing his throat to keep his brother and sister from noticing the desire that was probably wafting from him in waves, he clapped his hands and rubbed them together.

"It's Christmas," he said, starting to reach for miscellaneous items spread across the table that he thought he would probably need if he was really going to do this wreath-making thing. "If the two of you can be Santa's helpers, then so can I."

Flashing Jillian a grin that showed teeth but not fangs (no sense scaring her back into her shell, if he could help it), he added, "Right, Santa?"

BITE SIX

Jillian couldn't believe how quickly the next few hours passed. Or how much she enjoyed them.

And actually having fun wrapping ribbon around two dozen wreaths while surrounded by vampires was not something she ever would have thought possible.

On top of that, Liam, Maeve, and Connor seemed to be enjoying themselves, too. After getting off to a bit of a bumpy start, the two younger siblings had not only warmed up to her, but apparently been willing to put whatever issues they had with their older brother aside long enough to let him join in the decorating process.

They'd passed him a bare, artificial-pine circlet and all the supplies he would need, giving him blow-by-blow instructions on what to do, the same as she'd instructed them earlier. Then they'd teased him about his lack of imagination when he'd opted to follow Jillian's lead and put his wreaths together the exact same way so that they would match when hung around the inside and outside of the mansion.

Connor had handled it well, though. Rather than taking offense, he laughed along with them, then tossed back a bit of their own medicine, ribbing them about the skulls and crossbones they'd chosen for theirs. He wanted to know what Christmas special had given them the idea . . . or if there had been a pirate ship flying the Jolly Roger somewhere in the story of Jesus's birth that he didn't remember. Maeve had stuck her tongue out, and Liam had flipped him the bird—good-naturedly, Jillian hoped—but the mood in the room had remained light.

By the time Jillian started to yawn in earnest, they had nearly fifty wreaths perfectly decorated and ready to go. Liam, Maeve, and Connor helped her pack them all into boxes to be dealt with later. Then Liam announced that there were still a few hours left until dawn, so he was going to hit the clubs.

Jillian noticed a small frown marring Connor's brow at that, but he didn't say anything, merely watched his brother and sister shrug into their almost matching black leather jackets that made them look like something out of *The Matrix* trilogy and leave the house.

"Well," Connor said slowly a moment later, "that was nice while it lasted."

She chuckled. "Considering how surly they both were earlier when I first met them, I'd say it was a smashing success."

He gave a small *hmph* from the back of his throat.

"I think you handled things quite well, too," she told him softly, knowing it probably wasn't her place to comment on his conduct one way or the other.

But he didn't seem to take offense. Instead, he offered a small smile and said, "I nearly bit through my tongue a couple of times, but it's been a while since the three of us were in the same room without snapping at each other, so I thought it would be wise to keep my mouth shut."

Nodding, she crossed her arms first beneath her breasts and then more loosely at her waist. She wasn't cold; the entire house was toasty warm. There were even fires burning in each of the many hearths scattered throughout the mansion. But being suddenly alone with Connor in the doorway of the giant dining room, silence echoing all around them, caused a chill to snake down her spine. One caused by nerves or trepidation, she wasn't sure.

"I know Maeve and Liam can't possibly be in their teens, but they do come across that way sometimes."

Connor cocked his head and fixed her with dark, fathomless gray eyes. "Are you familiar at all with vampires and the details of their turning?"

Okay, now she *was* cold. "No," she answered, swallowing hard and hoping he wasn't about to give her a lesson a la '*Salem's Lot* or *The Lost Boys.*

"It's simple, really, and not nearly as gruesome as you might expect."

Good, because right now she was envisioning massive bloodletting and Chinese take-out containers writhing with worms and maggots.

No more horror movies, she decided. No more books or films that looked even remotely spooky. She wanted only to read and watch things that were light and fluffy, with no paranormal creatures in sight and nothing that was likely to induce nightmares. *Pollyanna. Anne of Green Gables. Kung Fu Panda.*

Well, maybe not *Kung Fu Panda.* Bears scared her, too, even the animated ones.

Her stomach chose that moment to rumble, and her cheeks flushed with embarrassment. Either she was hungry—it had been several hours since her last meal—or it was her body's way of telling her to run. Maybe through the kitchen, where she could grab a sandwich, and hide in her room before Connor started regaling her with the gruesome details of how one became a member of the undead Army of Darkness.

She tightened her arms around her waist, trying to stifle the sound before Connor noticed. Of course, he was a vampire, with superior hearing, so he probably heard the growl before she did.

"You're hungry," he said, as though she wasn't aware of that fact. Brows knitting, he asked, "When was the last time you ate?"

Since she wasn't wearing a watch and hadn't paid much attention to the hours as they ticked by, anyway, she honestly wasn't sure. She did have the vague recollection of a gummy raspberry breakfast bar that tasted like cardboard while she'd packed up her car that morning, but that was it.

"A while ago," she admitted with a small shrug. "Around lunch," she lied.

In vampire time, "lunch" probably meant somewhere around midnight, anyway.

Connor muttered a low curse before grabbing her hand and dragging her from the dining room entryway into the long hall leading to the foyer.

"Randall!" he called in a near-shout. "Randall!"

A second later, the butler appeared on the other side of the wide staircase. "Sir?"

"Jillian is desperately in need of sustenance. Bring something filling and delicious to the upstairs solarium as soon as possible. I'll eat with her, so enough for two."

"Yes, sir," Randall replied with a curt nod, then turned on his heel and headed back to the kitchen.

"You didn't have to do that," she insisted, surreptitiously trying to tug her hand out of Connor's strong grasp. "I could just as easily have made a sandwich for myself or grabbed a quick bowl of cereal."

"Cereal?" Connor repeated, his mouth turning down as if she'd suggested eating snails . . . and not fancy French escargot, but the flower garden variety. "Why would you do that when my cook can whip you up plate of pasta or chicken parmesan in under twenty minutes?"

"Because asking your cook to prepare something for me in the middle of the night is an inconvenience for her, and fixing a bowl of Count Chocula for myself isn't."

He gave a low chuckle, his fingers tightening around hers for a brief second. "Count Chocula?"

"It was the first thing that popped into my

head," she admitted somewhat sheepishly. Gee, wonder why.

Still holding her hand, he started up the stairs, pulling her along beside him. "No Count Chocula. You're a guest here, and guests don't resort to cold cereal at Drake Manor."

"You're used to getting exactly what you want exactly when you want it, aren't you?" she asked, more amused than anything else.

"Of course."

They'd reached the second-story landing, and he led her off to the left, to the end of the long hallway where a beautiful glass-paned solarium looked out over the pristine, snow-covered landscape.

"But I forget that you're human, and that humans need to eat every few hours."

"And you don't?" The question slipped out before she even realized she was curious.

At the small, wrought-iron patio set arranged amidst the junglelike plants and flowers filling the room, Connor held out a chair for her and waited for her to sit before taking the opposite seat for himself.

"You don't know much about vampires, do you?" he asked.

Jillian felt her cheeks heat and looked down at the intricate leaf-and-vine design of the tabletop, unable to meet his gaze. "No, I'm afraid not. Does it show?"

He chuckled. "Just a little. But at least you're willing to learn, which is more than can be said for the majority of mortal society."

Randall appeared in the solarium then, providing them with place settings and wineglasses. He poured a glass of Chablis for her and a glass of . . . well, she assumed it was blood, since it was much redder and thicker than any wine she'd ever seen . . . for Connor.

After adding a low, crystal hurricane lamp with the tealight already burning as a centerpiece—a rather romantic one, Jillian thought somewhat nervously, given that the only other illumination in the room came from scattered pockets of moonlight shining through the overhead window panes—he silently disappeared, leaving them alone once again.

"Most of the humans I work with either think they know about vampires or pretend they do, faking it enough to get through meetings with me and hoping I won't call them on it."

"Give them a bit of a Vampire 101 pop quiz, you mean?"

"Exactly," he said, flashing her a wide smile.

Jillian could have sworn she saw the tip of a fang in that grin, and quickly grabbed her wine, taking a sip to cover the fact that her heart was suddenly beating faster and she was trying hard not to stare.

"Would you like a lesson in what makes us tick, Jillian?" he inquired softly.

She set her glass aside, licking her lips before replying. Did she? Was she brave enough to listen?

"Will I be tested on the information later?" she asked.

Tipping his head to one side, he murmured, "I don't know. I guess you'll have to wait and see."

The soft, low timbre of his voice slithered through her like hot melted butter, turning her insides out.

"Okay," was the only thing her overheated brain could think to say.

Randall reappeared to place two steaming plates of food in front of them. The simple scents of grilled flounder, steamed vegetables, and potatoes au gratin wafted up from the table, making her stomach growl again. But at least this time she could do something to appease it.

"First, what we were discussing downstairs about Liam and Maeve," he said as they each lifted their forks and began to eat. "How vampires become vampires to begin with. It's simple, really. If a vampire bites a human, drains them of blood nearly to the point of death, and then allows that person to consume their blood, the human becomes vampire."

"What if a vampire bites a human, but doesn't give that person their own blood?" she asked, her curiosity winning out over her uneasiness with the topic they were discussing.

"Then the person doesn't become a vampire, and it's like any other bite one might receive—from a dog, a mosquito, or a rabid toddler. It might bleed and hurt for a while, but eventually the wound will heal. Vampire blood and saliva also contain an enzyme that speeds healing, so if the immortal doing the biting takes the time to . . . *treat* the wound, for lack of a better word, it heals that much faster. Almost instantaneously. That's why you don't see more donor humans walking around with bandages taped all over their bodies, looking like Egyptian mummies."

Jillian had heard the term *donor* before and knew it didn't apply only to those who agreed to sacrifice their organs after death or voluntarily walked into the Red Cross to give blood. She'd also heard the term *blood boy/girl* to describe groupielike humans who willingly became regular blood donors to vampires for the chance to be a part of their inner immortal circles.

"Unfortunately, becoming a vampire brings with it a bit of arrested development," Connor continued when she didn't respond. "That's why you don't see vampire children. It's . . . not forbidden, because we don't exactly have 'rules,' but it is *extremely* frowned upon to turn a child. Whatever age a person is when they're turned, that's the age they remain forever—perhaps not when it comes to calendar years, but mentally and maturity-wise. And nobody wants to deal with a bunch of vampires going through their 'terrible twos' into infinity."

Pausing with a bite of fish halfway to her mouth, her eyes widened slightly. "So Liam and Maeve are . . ."

"Perpetually twenty-one and nineteen—respectively," Connor finished for her, the corners of his mouth tugging downward. "They've existed for over a hundred years, but they've never really grown up, and likely never will."

So much of the younger siblings' attitudes and behavior suddenly made sense to her. It was a difficult concept to wrap her mind around—living in a state of permanent adolescence. Recalling some of the more traumatizing portions of her own youth, it sounded like a fate worse than death. Poor Maeve and Liam.

And Connor. Though he didn't look that much older than his brother and sister, he was so obviously more adult than they were.

"So how old are you? Were you?" she wanted to know. Realizing how rude the question sounded, she cleared her throat and lowered her gaze to her plate, where she stabbed negligently at the potatoes. "I'm sorry, I shouldn't have asked that. Women don't like to be asked their age; I imagine men aren't fond of it, either."

"It's not a question I get very often, I admit," he said, a devilish half-smile spreading across his face. "But I was thirty-six when I was turned."

Not counting the century or so he'd been immortal, he was only four years older than she was.

"That's quite an age gap," she commented. "I can understand why Liam and Maeve get on your nerves sometimes . . . and why they might think you're a bit of a stick in the mud."

Connor made a noise that was somewhere between a snort and a chuckle. "Did they say that?"

They had said a lot of things, not all of which she remembered verbatim—or would be willing to repeat to Connor or anyone else. "It was more the impression I got."

"I'll bet," he replied wryly, obvious humor in his tone.

"But tonight went well," she was quick to point out. Pushing her near-empty plate a few inches away and leaning forward to cross her arms on the edge of the table, she said, "You were good with them, and they were good about not acting out."

Taking a sip of . . . she would just think of it as A-positive, since the word *blood* still gave her a bit of the willies, and she remembered hearing one of the younger siblings mention it was one of Connor's favorite . . . flavors? Types?

Sigh. Learning to coexist with vampires was complicated. She almost felt as though she was touring a foreign country, having to stumble her way through learning a whole new language, a whole new culture.

Lowering his glass, Connor's stormy gray gaze locked on her, holding her attention like a hypnotist's watch.

"*You* were good with them," he told her softly.

Warmth suffused her body and climbed up her throat to her cheeks.

And then that low heat burst into blue-white flames as he added in a near whisper, "I think you may be good for all of us."

BITE SEVEN

It would be the perfect moment to kiss her, Connor thought. And he wanted to, almost desperately.

The pink tingeing her skin made her seem both innocent and sexy at the same time, which was downright irresistible. If only this table wasn't taking up so much damn space between them, he'd have his lips on her already, his hands skimming the gentle curves beneath her top and jeans.

And suddenly he wanted that. Desperately. But since he knew how skittish she was—especially around him, Lord Dracula—he didn't think he would gain any points by tossing the bit of metal aside and grabbing her like some demented creature in one of those terrible Bela Lugosi films that had given them all such a bad reputation to begin with.

Oh, yeah, that would go over well. Like pulling the beard off a mall Santa in front of a hundred expectant little kids.

"Are you finished with your dinner?" he asked,

knowing she was since she hadn't taken a bite in the past five minutes.

Glancing down at her plate as though she'd forgotten it was even there, she nodded.

"Good." His chair legs scraped against the flagstone floor as he pushed back and got to his feet. He held out a hand to her, waiting until she slipped her fingers into his. Reluctantly, he noticed, but not quite as reluctantly as before they'd sat down to dinner.

He started to lead her away and was encouraged when she didn't ask where they were going or what he was up to. She simply trusted him. Or perhaps now that her hunger had been satisfied, lethargy was beginning to set in and she was too tired to protest.

Either way, he would take what he could get.

"You never told me about vampires and food," she remarked as they walked slowly out of the solarium and back down the hall. "You eat, but you don't get hungry. So do you need food? Do you even like it?"

Since she was feeling so complacent, he switched from merely holding her hand to slipping her arm through his and pulling her a few inches closer. In a pair of flat-soled, comfortable-looking tennies, the top of her blond head came to just over his shoulder. Not that he minded; it made him feel big and strong and very Me-Tarzan, You-Jane—or whatever the vampire/human equivalent might be—and he realized he liked the sensation. Wouldn't half mind feeling it more often.

"You're right that we don't get hungry for food

or need it to survive, but we can appreciate the flavors and textures just as much as anyone else."

"Which means that you enjoyed dinner well enough, but if I hadn't been here, you probably would have gotten a glass of . . ."

"Plasma?" he supplied when she trailed off. She bumped against him from shoulder to calf all along his left side as they strolled toward the second-floor landing—something else he didn't think he would mind growing used to.

"I was going to say A-positive. I think Liam and Maeve mentioned that's your favorite." She tipped her head up to glance at him, her nose crinkling adorably. "Do you really have preferences when it comes to blood?"

"Of course. All vampires do. Humans may not realize this, but each type has a unique flavor. Sort of like the difference between Coke and Pepsi, or root beer, Mountain Dew, Dr Pepper. They're all carbonated beverages, but also very distinctive. Which is your favorite?"

"Diet Cherry Coke," she responded, almost without thought.

"Ah. You're a woman of discriminating tastes. That would be something along the lines of AB-negative in the vampire world."

She surprised him with a quick, lighthearted laugh. "Good to know. In case I ever run into a vampire in a dark alley."

Connor paused at the top of the stairs, pulling Jillian to an abrupt stop. Startled, she turned to look at him, putting them face to face.

Moving his hands to her shoulders, he gave a

gentle squeeze and tugged her close, forcing her to tip back her head in order to retain eye contact.

"You don't need a dark alley," he told her, his voice lowering to a dark, dangerous rasp. "There's a vampire standing right in front of you."

And then he lowered his head, taking her mouth to kiss her the way he'd been fantasizing all night long.

Katy Perry's "I Kissed a Girl" spun through Jillian's head, only in her version, it was "I Kissed a Vampire."

I'm kissing a vampire.

Oh, my God, *I'm kissing a vampire!* she thought, a lance of anxiety spiking through her system.

Then she thought, *I'm kissing a vampire, and I think I kind of like it.*

For a dead man, Connor's lips were surprisingly warm, and both soft and firm at the same time.

Though the kiss had started slow, with just the gentle press of his mouth against hers, it didn't stay that way for long. As soon as he knew she wasn't going to scream or bolt or try to stake him with a sharpened number two pencil, he pulled her closer, flush with his body, and wrapped his arm around her waist like a vise. His lips parted and his tongue began to probe, seeking entrance and reciprocation.

And while her brain forgot her earlier plan to seduce him and prove she was a wild woman, it now shrieked, *No! Don't do it, he's a vampire!*

Her body, however, wasn't nearly as discerning. Her body, especially those rapidly warming erogenous zones, was writhing in ecstasy and moaning, *Yeah, baby. He may be a vampire, but he's a hot vampire.*

Brain, body. Brain, body. The battle warred within her for all of three seconds before she decided she didn't care if Connor was immortal. These days, death seemed to be a technicality, anyway. And at the moment, this particular corpse (*eep!*) felt and smelled and tasted very much alive . . . and she wanted more.

Sliding her hands up the length of his strong arms and broad shoulders, she linked them behind his neck, fingers playing with the silky strands of his midnight hair. She opened her mouth beneath his and let him in.

Or maybe she dragged him in. It was hard to tell at that point who was kissing whom, who was in charge, who was more in control.

Jillian definitely didn't feel in control. If anything, she was spinning out of it faster than a racecar at the Indy 500. But there were times when Connor's touch lightened, was more passive, and when that happened, she tugged him closer and deepened the kiss. Then there were times when Connor's hold was so tight, his mouth so possessive, that there was no doubt he was behind the wheel, steering her exactly where he wanted her to go and keeping them very much on track.

But no matter what, he was always careful with her. She felt the scrape of his sharp fangs against her lips and tongue, but he never let them pierce her, hurt her, draw blood.

She didn't know how long they stood there, raising the temperature on the landing by a good twenty-five degrees; it could have been five minutes or five hours. But by the time she broke away—or perhaps he pulled away from her—the world was spinning around her. The dark paneled walls, the oriental carpets, the brightly lit chandelier with its million tiny bulbs sparkling like diamonds and lighting the entire mammoth foyer . . . it all whirled around and around her, blurring her vision and making her dizzy.

As though he knew she was none too steady on her feet, Connor kept hold of her elbows, anchoring her so she didn't slide down his body in a puddle of raging hormones.

"Come to my room," he whispered, his voice little more than a sandpaper rasp.

His eyes were dark, fathomless orbs that threatened to swallow her whole, and she shivered at the need, the desire, the passion reflected there. They were emotions she knew were written clearly on her own face.

"There's only an hour left until dawn. Let me take you to bed and finish what we started."

Oh, it was tempting. If he could set her on fire and burn her to embers in the middle of the hallway with a mere kiss, she wasn't sure she could handle what he was capable of without clothes involved.

She pictured him naked and nearly came right where she stood. She pictured them both naked, writhing together on silken sheets, and whimpered with longing.

But as much as she wanted to throw up her arms and say, "Yes, yes, take me, I'm yours!" she couldn' help but remember what he was. The amazing, mouthwatering image of Connor in the buff suddenly sprouted immense, dripping fangs.

The toe-curling fantasy of having him over her, under her, wrapped around her like a string of blinking Christmas tree lights was all well and good—and turned her knees even weaker than before—but now his eyes glowed red, and his teeth were dripping with blood. Her blood.

She shivered again. This time, however, it wasn't with yearning, but with fear. Or at the very least, extreme apprehension.

This was what she'd wanted, what she'd *planned*, for heaven's sake, but now that the moment was here, she felt frozen in place, unable to go through with it.

She was supposed to be brave and bold, throwing herself at the first attractive male vampire she saw. . . . Well, all right, she'd seen Connor first, *then* decided luring him into bed might be a fun way to prove she wasn't the dullest woman in Boston proper. And while she hadn't quite had the chance to throw herself at him, she wasn't going to split hairs on how they'd ended up here.

But her pulse was pounding, her heart racing a mile a minute inside her chest, and her head was filled with doubts and fears. As much as she wanted to backtrack a few seconds to the part where Connor was kissing the misgivings right out of her, now that her brain *was* engaged, she couldn't seem to stop the horror movie clips flashing through her brain.

"I'm sorry," she said, shaking her head and tearing her gaze from his. Tugging at her arms, she broke his grasp and retreated a step. She just couldn't do it. Not yet.

"I'm sorry," she said again, her voice breaking over the words because of how sincerely she meant them. "I can't."

And then she turned, brushing past him as she ran down the hall to her suite of rooms and slammed the door behind her.

BITE EIGHT

The minute Connor woke the following evening, he wanted to go to Jillian and take up where they'd left off just before dawn.

Her scent was in his nostrils, in his very blood, just as it had been hours before, and he knew without checking that she was still in her room. Also just like last night, he wanted to go there and break down the door. Anything to be closer to her again.

But she was wary enough of him as it was, and barging into her room with eyes glowing and nostrils flaring wasn't going to allay her fears. If anything, it would earn him a stake straight through the heart.

He wanted her, and with a little magical Christmas fairy dust—or whatever the hell was supposed to be floating in the air at this time of year—he would have her. But he had to be patient, go slow, and not do anything to spook her.

So instead of barreling down the hall and pulling a Jackie Chan on an innocent panel of wood, he got out of bed, showered, dressed, and downed the liquid breakfast Randall had delivered to his room on a silver platter. Literally.

He also asked the butler to call his office and have his secretary reschedule the evening's appointments. It was Friday, and though he'd never taken one off before—and, in fact, often worked Saturdays, as well—there was a first time for everything. A long weekend wouldn't hurt anything, and it would give him more time with Jillian before he had to work again.

That done, he made his way slowly but determinedly out of his suite and down the hall to the opposite wing. At his sides, his fingers clenched and unclenched, and he realized he was nervous. Nervous, for Christ's sake, when he hadn't been anything close to that since . . . well, ever, to the best of his recollection.

But he was anxious about Jillian.

Apparently because she mattered to him. She was the first woman—human or vampire—to catch his attention this strongly in a very long time. To seep into his pores, get under his skin, invade his every waking thought.

The sleeping ones, too. He'd spent a fairly restless night, dreaming of having a naked, willing Jillian in his arms, in his bed, writhing beneath him. Of her damp skin sliding along his, her nails grazing his back . . . his teeth sinking into her soft, warm jugular.

In addition to a hard-on that just wouldn't quit, the erotic dreams had brought about his current state of mild apprehension. If Jillian knew he was fantasizing about biting her, about drinking her blood, then licking the wound closed . . . his cock gave a twitch of longing at the thought . . . she would run screaming into the night, likely leaving a hole in his wall the exact size and shape of her fleeing form.

Which meant he would have to work on calming her fears, helping her to become more comfortable with the fact that he was a vampire, and seducing her as simply a man instead of a . . . man with something more.

A few feet from her door, he inhaled deeply and knew she was still inside the suite of rooms. The scent of peaches was tinged now with something else, something spicy, he thought perhaps cinnamon, making his mouth water for more reasons than one.

Reaching her door, he took another deep breath, this time to steady his nerves, before tapping gently with the back of his hand. From inside, he heard what he thought was a squeak, followed by a light scraping sound, a thud, and quick footsteps crossing the carpeted floor.

A second later, from the other side of the door, Jillian's shaky, breathless voice asked, "Yes?"

"Jillian," he said, as softly and calmly as he could manage, "it's Connor."

She didn't respond, but he could hear—*feel*—her pulse jump and her already rapid heartbeat kick up a notch.

"Are you all right?" he asked, reminding himself to tread carefully. "I know you were upset last night, and thought you might like to talk about it."

"No. No, thank you," she responded, half an octave higher than usual. "I'm fine."

All right, patience was one thing; walking away was something else entirely. If he left her alone with her fears and unsubstantiated beliefs about his kind, the distance between them would only grow. In a matter of hours, she would have herself convinced that he was some sort of John Carpenter monster who made a habit of attacking children and performing human sacrifices.

No, walking away was not an option.

"You know," he told her gently, "if I wanted to, I could turn myself into a cloud of smoke and come in under the door."

Stark silence met his claim, along with a kick of panic that sent her blood pressure spiking. He heard her lick her lips and swallow hard.

"Can you really do that?" she asked tentatively.

His lips quirked up in an amused grin. "No," he admitted, letting his gaze fall to the spot where door met floorboards. "But I do have a key." Not on him, but she didn't need to know that.

Her heartbeat slowed and he heard her give a low chuckle. Nothing the average human would be able to detect, but he could feel her stress levels evening out.

And then there was a *click* as she turned the lock and twisted the knob. The door opened a crack and blue eyes peeked out, her head cocked so that he couldn't see any more of her face or body than that.

"May I come in?"

An indecisive moment passed, and then she released a breath, stepped back, and let the door swing open.

In addition to a head of sleep-tangled hair, Connor noticed she was still wearing the jeans and top from the night before. Every light in the suite blazed brightly, as though she'd lit the place up in an attempt to scare away the bogeyman—i.e., him.

A silver cross the size of a small tarantula dangled from her neck and fell in the very center of her chest. Her right hand held a wooden crucifix, her left a strand of whole garlic bulbs, skins and roots and all.

He cleared his throat to cover a gurgle of laughter. Apparently she had spent a rather restless night anticipating his violent return. He wondered exactly what she'd planned to do with her makeshift weapons, useless as they were.

Shifting his attention back to her face, he said, "I take it you didn't sleep well after we . . ."

He trailed off, and she supplied, "Kissed?"

"I was going to say 'parted ways,' but 'kissed' works just as well." And told him clearly that she hadn't been able to get their steamy encounter out of her mind any more than he had.

Good. He didn't want her to forget it, or to be able to forget him. Not that easily.

Careful not to frighten her, he lifted a hand and brushed a stray blond curl behind one ear. "I'm sorry if I overstepped my bounds, but you need to know that I'm attracted to you, Jillian."

Understatement of the millennia.

"Very attracted. And if I get the chance, I intend to kiss you again."

Longer, deeper, and hopefully more than once.

The tip of her tongue darted out to wet dry lips, while her fingers fidgeted around the items in her hands.

"It wasn't the kiss that made me run off," she admitted in a small voice. "It was . . . what might have come next."

The letters, big as a skyscraper and flashing a blinding neon, hung in the air: S-E-X.

"What was it, exactly, that scared you?"

"I didn't say I was scared," she quickly corrected, chin lifting to a defiant angle. "Just . . . apprehensive."

He smothered a smile. "All right. Then what were you . . . *apprehensive* about?"

She licked her lips again, something he was coming to recognize as a nervous gesture. Her eyes darted everywhere but his face, and she tucked her hands—still holding her vampire-repelling weapons—behind her back.

"Well," she said slowly, easing into her admission, "you're a . . ."

"Vampire?" he offered.

She nodded. "And I'm a . . ."

"Not a vampire?"

She nodded again. "And I'm not sure how . . ."

"Things work between a vampire and a not-a-vampire, sexually speaking?"

Her head bobbed up and down. "My mind started racing, my imagination ran wild, and I let my nerves get the better of me. After I calmed down, I looked through the books, but I couldn't find anything."

He arched a brow. "Books?"

"They were all I could find when I knew I would be staying here and wanted to . . ."

She trailed off, and a hint of pink colored her cheeks. Rather than finish that thought, she spun on her heel and headed out of the sitting area into the bedroom, careful to tuck the garlic and crucifix in front of her and away from him as she went.

In the bedroom, she set the "weapons" on the bed, which was made with a soft, sage-green coverlet, but had obviously been slept upon, if the wrinkles and lopsided pillows were any indication.

She pulled a stack of books from the nightstand and set them beside her as she hopped up on the raised mattress of the wide four-poster. When she glanced in his direction, he took it as an invitation to join her.

"They touch on some of the things you told me yesterday, and make suggestions for how humans and vampires can learn to 'live together in harmony'—"

She rolled her eyes at the last, which he took to mean she was quoting a phrase directly from one of the colorful tomes. He plucked a title from the top of the pile and nearly swallowed his tongue at the bright red title that jumped out at him, dripping one-dimensional blood drops: *There Goes the Neighborhood: How to Deal with the Undead Next Door.*

Jesus, no wonder people were so afraid of his kind, if this was the kind of garbage they were using as a guide to get along with vampires.

"What is it you were looking for in these?" he asked in a low voice, skimming the rest of the titles and the information printed on a few of the back cover flaps. Some of it sounded logical, but some was downright alarming.

"Stuff about . . . you know, the mechanics."

Her eyes darted away as she murmured the explanation, and Connor felt a rush of warmth suffuse his chest. In a word, she was adorable. Gorgeous, and sexy enough to rival any of Hollywood's most beautiful starlets, but also sweet and innocent in a world where there wasn't much sweetness or innocence left.

He wanted to grab her up and *show* her the mechanics of vampire-on-human sex, but knew that would only send her reaching for her garlic and crucifix again. As much as the stake in his pants might wish otherwise, he needed to go slow, put her fears to rest before jumping her like some crazed and horny rogue bloodsucker.

"Are there any questions I can answer for you?" he asked politely, even though he felt anything but polite.

Her mouth opened, but only a strangled squeak came out as her eyes widened in embarrassment and twin circles of red filled her cheeks.

"Or how about this," he suggested, resisting the urge to tug her close and kiss the uneasiness right out of her. "What if I simply tell you how it works, and you can stop me if you have specific questions."

She didn't look as though she loved that idea, either, but she was apparently curious enough— and he hoped *eager* enough—to jerk her head in the affirmative.

Taking a moment to organize his thoughts, he returned the stack of books to the nightstand, then moved the crucifix and string of garlic bulbs to rest beside them. When his skin didn't begin to smolder and he didn't shriek in agony, her eyes went wide.

With a grin, he said, "Those things don't work quite as well as television would have you believe. Vampires aren't evil, so we don't have much to fear from God or religious articles—including holy water, in case you have any of that tucked away somewhere."

From her guilty expression, he assumed she did and gave a low chuckle. "If you want to kill one of us, go with a very sharp stake through the heart. Wood, metal, whatever. Of course, that's something that will kill mortals and immortals alike. But with immortals, you're going to want to leave the stake in there. . . . Remove it and we begin to heal, just like from any other wound. And then you'll want to remove the head and burn it and the body well away from each other."

At that, her blush disappeared, taking the rest of the color in her face right along with it. Okay, maybe that was too much information. But she'd wanted to know about vampires enough to start her own library on the subject, so she might as well learn the truth from someone who knew it firsthand.

And somewhere during his acquaintance with this woman, he'd decided not to lie to her—about anything. Good, bad, or ugly, if she asked a question about his kind, he intended to answer it frankly and with no beating around the bush.

To lighten the mood, however, he said, "But you're not planning to kill me, are you?"

She shook her head almost violently, eyes wide and finally centered on him instead of darting all around the room.

"Good. I'd hate to think you had despicable plans for me and I just gave you a how-to guide on how to follow through on them."

Her mouth turned down in a frown. "That's *not* what I was going through the books for."

She looked so horrified that he would even think as much, he couldn't tease her any longer.

"I'm only kidding," he told her, reaching out to brush the pad of his thumb across her warm, rosy pink lips. "I know you aren't interested in murder. You're interested in sex."

His voice grew thick and gravely on the last word, and his body turned hard, envisioning that act with this woman. Preferably several times and in several different positions.

She swallowed, her own anatomy quickly following suit. He could hear the leap of her pulse, sense the rise of her temperature, and smell the thick, ripening scent of her arousal. Outwardly, her breathing grew shallow, her nipples beaded beneath the cotton of her shirt, and she shifted on the bed, hinting at the ache building between her legs that he hoped matched his own.

"The most important thing for you to know is that humans and vampires are extremely compatible. We don't sprout horns or transform into monsters or possess abnormal appendages. And we don't need to bite to achieve orgasm."

"Well, that's candid enough," Jillian muttered, staring down at her feet.

"I want you to understand that when we make love, nothing is going to happen that you don't *want* to happen. I won't hurt you. We like to bite during sex, that's true. And piercing our lovers' flesh, sipping their blood, can heighten the sexual experience. But it's not necessary, and most of us only do that sort of thing if it's mutually agreed upon, both partners willing."

Instead of moving away from him, as he would have expected, she moved closer. Just an inch, a slight shifting of her legs on the mattress, but it brought them into the lightest of contact from hip to thigh.

"So how does a human know if she likes being bitten?"

The question, along with her matter-of-fact delivery, hit him square in the solar plexus. Damn, but he loved this woman. She kept him on his toes like no one else he'd ever met, blushing one minute and shocking him with her brazenness the next.

"I suppose the only way to find out is to give it a try," he replied honestly.

"I don't like being bitten by bugs or my cat," she told him.

"I'm not a cat." Or a bug.

"No," she agreed. "Your teeth are bigger."

"Other things, too, one would hope," he felt the need to point out.

There was that flush again that heated his blood and made him want to claim her in every way possible. With his fangs, as well, but only once she was weeping with need, begging him to give her all that he had, all that he was. Then, and only then, would he sink his teeth into her neck and show her how satisfying such a thing could be—for both of them.

"Bug bites are itchy. And I assume your cat bites

you because he's angry or afraid. During sex, vampire nips and bites are sensual, erotic. An added form of pleasure."

"Like extra-special bonus sex."

He arched a brow. "What's extra-special bonus sex?" He might have been around for hundreds of years, but that was a new one, even to him. And wouldn't he have known if he'd ever experienced something remarkable enough to be termed *extra-special bonus sex*?

Jillian cocked her head and gave him a look that had the blood pumping through his veins like oil through a well-tuned engine. Good thing he'd filled up this morning, or his appetites would have been out of control. *He* would have been out of control.

As it was, he was hanging on by a thread. A very thin, very tense, very frayed thread.

And then that thread broke, snapped clean in two as her blue eyes darkened to navy and her lips parted to whisper, "Anything you want it to be."

BITE NINE

Now that Jillian knew Connor wasn't going to morph into some kind of demonic monster or come at her with some freaky bit of snapping male anatomy, any anxiety she might have felt drifted away, leaving her achy and weak . . . and flushed with the same keen desire as the night before when he'd been kissing her senseless in the hall.

She wanted him to kiss her again. Kiss her, and touch her, and . . . everything.

She didn't care anymore if she seduced him or he seduced her. Hell, she hoped they were working at seducing each other.

Whatever spell he cast over her, it was working. And she could see by his smoky expression, the heat flaring in his eyes, that she had captivated him at least a little, too.

And all it took was a single suggestive remark to send him over the edge. One minute she was looking at him through lowered lashes, wondering if her attempt at flirting was going to have the right impact. The next, she was flat on her back, pressed down into the soft mattress by his heavy, solid weight.

The air whooshed from her lungs, and he caught it with his mouth, his lips searing like a brand as they covered hers. Not that she minded; she didn't need air when she had Connor's strong body scorching her from head to toe and filling her lungs with something better than oxygen. He was filling her nose with the scent of sandalwood and a hint of pine, and the rest of her with passion and longing.

His kiss consumed her, picking up where they'd left off the night before. Hours had passed between the two encounters, but it felt like less than a second. And this time, she had no intention of running away.

To make sure he knew she wouldn't be calling a halt to anything . . . and he should think carefully, if he had any notions about stopping before the sun was well up in the sky and threatening to turn him into a crispy critter . . . she wrapped her arms around his neck and her legs around his waist, holding him tight.

He growled low in his throat and ground his pelvis into hers, making her muscles clench. She lifted her hips, meeting his downward gyration and smothering a laugh over the fact that such a short time ago, hearing Connor the Vampire growl at her over anything, would have made her wet herself. Now, it simply made her wet—in a very good way.

He tasted of mint, like freshly gargled mouth-wash, reminding her that she hadn't had a chance to brush her teeth yet this . . . evening. *Eep*. But he didn't seem to mind, didn't even seem to notice, if the fervor of his tongue tangling with her own was any indication.

She sucked gently, reveling in the click of teeth on teeth and the occasional nip of his fangs running along her lips. Again, the idea of kissing someone with fangs, of having those fangs scrape against her mouth hard enough to possibly draw blood would have freaked her out only a short while ago.

Even through the daylight hours, she'd tossed and turned, fighting *Dark Shadows*-like images of very bad things happening to her if she let Connor get too close. But now, being afraid was the farthest thing from her mind.

She ran her hands down the firm plane of his back, over the soft knit of his thick, coffee-brown sweater. Thank goodness he wasn't wearing another one of his stuffy suits. As appealing as they were—and Connor Drake filled out dress clothes like no one else she'd ever seen—he looked even sexier in casual clothes. And these were going to be much easier to get off of him.

Hooking her fingers beneath the ribbed waistband of the sweater, she pushed it up, going slowly enough to enjoy every inch of his smooth, warm skin. He moaned into her mouth, then released her lips to skim her cheek, her jaw, the lobe of her ear. His stomach went concave as she ran her nails along the muscles there, and he shifted, moving however she needed to best aid the removal of his sweater.

Yanking it up over his head and off his arms, she

tossed it aside, not much caring where it landed. She fell back against the pillows with Connor hovering above her, braced full length on his long, muscular arms.

Did vampires work out? she wondered. Did they need to? Because no one, not even a preternatural being with super strength, super hearing, and a super sniffer, could be born with a body like this.

His skin might be a shade paler than sunbronzed, but Connor was far from pale. And beneath that golden skin were hard, bulging muscles. Beautifully sculpted biceps, taut forearms . . . and a chest that would have made Michaelangelo rethink his vision of *David* as the epitome of male perfection.

As thick and black as his hair was, there was only a smattering of crisp dark curls on his chest. Just enough to have her licking her lips and imagining the wicked thrill of those rough hairs rubbing against her swollen nipples.

Wanting that, possibly more than her next breath, she latched on to his shoulders and pulled him down. Unfortunately, she was still wearing her shirt *and* bra, and though her nipples were beaded behind the silk cups, pressing against the wall of his chest didn't have quite the effect she'd been hoping for.

As though reading her mind, Connor grabbed the hem of her top and tugged. "Off. Now," he growled, wrangling the material up her torso, over her arms and head.

She shook the wild tangle of her hair away from her face in time to see him going for her bra. The hooks were in the back, and she cursed underwear makers world 'round for their apparent lack of vi-sion when it came to easy access during bouts of sweaty, mindless sex. Maybe they were Shakers and didn't want *anybody* getting lucky.

Connor, however, didn't waste so much as a nanosecond worrying about her choice of under-wear's design flaws. He leaned forward, licked a slow path from the hollow of her throat to be-tween her breasts, and then bit through the thin stretch of lace holding the bra's underwires to-gether.

"Holy razor blades, Batman," she breathed, and couldn't decided if she should be shocked or aroused. Maybe a little of both.

Lifting his attention to her face, he met her gaze with eyes that glowed a bright orangeish-red around the black irises.

"I'm sorry," he said, his deep voice both gravel rough and breathless at the same time. "I didn't mean to frighten you."

Jillian laughed. Or at the very least, a huff of air burst from her lungs.

"You didn't," she assured him quickly, tracing her palms lightly up and down his bare arms. "I thought it was kind of hot."

He raised an eyebrow, as though he wasn't sure whether or not to believe her.

"So are your eyes. Do they glow like that when-ever you're turned on?"

"Or angry," he said after a confused, speechless moment.

She let one corner of her mouth quirk upward. "Nice," she told him. "I guess I'll know any time you're thinking dirty thoughts, then, won't I?"

The opposite corner of his mouth lifted in a mirror image of her own. "Where you're concerned, I'm *always* thinking dirty thoughts."

Her half-smile turned into a full-blown grin as pleasure coursed through her. "I think dirty thoughts about you, too," she admitted barely above a whisper, even as her cheeks flared with heat.

Connor, of course, wasn't the least bit embarrassed by the topic of conversation. If anything, he looked wolfish, especially with the sharp tips of his fanged incisors showing between curved lips.

"Really?" he said, a wicked lilt to the single word. "What kind of dirty thoughts?"

Too many to count, and definitely none she was willing to share. She might be half naked, with a half-naked man lying on top of her, but she didn't know him *that well* yet.

Maybe someday she'd have the courage to share a few of her more X-rated secret fantasies with him, but it wasn't going to be here or now. Besides, she'd used up her daily quota of bravery just letting him into her room . . . and into her bed.

She had to tell him something, though, so she went with the truth.

"This is one," she said softly. "You, here with me. Looking at me like that."

"How am I looking at you?" he wanted to know in a tone just as low, just as laced with barely restrained longing.

"Like you want to devour me."

A sound somewhere between a growl and a strangled groan rumbled in his chest and throat.

"I do want to devour you. But only in the very best ways."

She lifted a hand and ran her fingers through his silky black hair, smiling when a few unruly strands fell forward over his brow, making him look boyish and charming. Ironic, considering those were two words she never would have expected to use to describe a vampire.

"But no biting unless I ask you to, right?" she said, half teasing, half wanting to be sure.

"No biting unless you ask," he promised, running his wide, warm palms along her sides, over her ribs, and up to cup her breasts beneath the parted halves of her torn—bitten?—bra. "Though I intend to make it my mission in life to get you so hot, you not only ask, you *beg* for it."

The very notion of having him pierce her flesh—her delicate throat and ever-important jugular vein, no less—scared her silly. But it also intrigued her, aroused her, made her heart beat double-time in anticipation.

Only a few short days ago, she'd been afraid of vampires, and look where she was now. Pinned beneath one, chest heaving and blood rushing while she waited for him to ravish her. *Wanted* him to ravish her.

Licking her lips, she trailed her fingertips over the thin line of dark hair that led in a pleasure path down the center of his abdomen, feeling her own stomach tighten when he sucked in a sharp breath. Curling her fingers into the waistband of his khakis, she slowly started to work loose the top button.

"I'll consider myself warned," she said, feeling like some brazen, worldly coquette when she'd never thought herself capable of such behavior. It certainly wasn't an aspect of her personality that she was overly familiar with.

Now that she was experiencing the power of being a wanton woman, though . . . of the freedom it brought, and the reaction she could extract from Connor simply by batting her lashes and lowering her voice to a smoky whisper . . . she kind of liked it.

Responding to her statement just as she'd hoped he would, his lips pulled back in a snarl, revealing the same sharp incisors he'd used to slice through the material of her bra, and his hands went to the front of her own jeans, tearing them open and yanking the stiff denim down her legs.

When he got to her feet, he tore her boots off with the jeans and let the entire pile of balled-up clothing fall to the floor with a thump. Then he kicked off his own slacks, slipped an arm under her waist, and lifted her off the bed just enough to whip back the covers and set her down again on cool, pale green cotton sheets.

He moved so fast, he made her dizzy, but she suspected his speed had less to do with his being a vampire and more to do with his being simply a man eager to get lucky. Not that she minded; she was pretty eager to get lucky herself.

As he came down atop her, covering her from chest to ankle, her brows knit and she felt her mouth turn down in a frown.

"What's the matter?" Connor asked.

He was strangely attuned to her every mood or change of expression, she was learning. Was *that* a vampire thing, or just another natural trait of the handsome, charming man?

"Nothing," she said, giving her head a weak shake. When he arched a dark brow and continued to stare, she rolled her eyes and let out a sigh of surrender.

"Nothing's *wrong*," she told him truthfully. "I'm just sorry you got into bed so fast. I would have liked to look at you a while longer."

Admire his amazing physique, get a better glimpse of the rigid length that had been pressed against her for so long. And that she would soon—please, God—have inside of her.

A devilish glint sparkled in his kohl-gray eyes as he grinned down at her. "We'll do the show-and-tell thing later. I've got a few fantasies that involve you being stark naked and swinging around the bedpost like it's a stripper pole, too."

He shifted so that his body was better aligned with hers, sending shivers up her spine at the friction of skin on skin.

"Right now, though, my self-control is at a minimum." He nuzzled her throat, making her purr and wiggle beneath him in an effort to get closer. "I'm not sure how much longer I'll last, and if I have to stand still while you ogle me like a particularly juicy steak, it will be over much, *much* too soon."

She nearly chuckled at his creative descriptions. "I don't know about a steak," she told him, lifting first one leg and then the other to wrap around his narrow hips. She followed suit with her arms, letting them drape so that she could cup the globes of his tight, bare butt.

Mm-mm. If Will could see her now, he wouldn't call her boring or frigid. He would probably be picking his tongue up off the floor.

"Maybe an ice cream sundae with hot fudge and caramel, whipped cream and a big, succulent cherry on top."

She could have sworn she felt his teeth—the fangs or just his regular teeth?—nip the side of her neck, but he licked the spot so quickly after that she couldn't be sure.

"Food doesn't usually interest me all that much," he murmured against her skin, "but you're making a simple dessert sound like ambrosia . . . and making me very, very hungry."

"Hungry for food?" she wanted to know. "Or hungry for something else?"

He lifted his head, his gaze boring into her while she raked her nails suggestively along his buttocks and lower back.

"For you. Only for you."

BITE TEN

Connor couldn't believe the intensity of the feelings coursing through his veins for this woman. He'd known Jillian barely a week, but already he couldn't get enough of her: her beauty and her wit, her equal parts innocence and brazenness.

He wanted to know everything about her. What made her laugh, what made her cry. What frightened her—other than vampires, anyway—and what infuriated her.

But that would take time—time he was looking forward to spending with her, but not time he cared to take right this minute. Right this minute, the only thing he wanted to learn about her was where her sweet spots were and what made her scream like a banshee.

While he continued to nip and lick and suckle the soft skin of her throat and along her collarbone, he slipped his hands down the sides of her slim waist to cup her buttocks. Her legs were already wound around his hips like ivy, holding him close, burning him with her intimate warmth.

And all he could think about was getting inside of her. A battery of foreplay options raced through his head. All very good, very enjoyable acts that he fully intended to perform on and with her . . . later.

He hadn't lied when he'd told her his self-control was running out. He felt like a rubber band stretched to its absolute limit. His skin tingled, blood was pounding hot and heavy in his veins, and if his cock grew any harder, he was afraid one touch would snap it off like an icicle.

He needed her, and all the petting and stroking and flowery, seductive wooing would have to wait.

Not that he was worried about *her* level of readiness. Her nipples were pointy little diamonds in the centers of her full, luscious breasts, her breaths were coming in tiny, shallow pants, and he could feel the dampness between her legs just from where they pressed together like Twinkies inside their cellophane wrapper.

His penis twitched at the thought of rubbing against her moist curls, of sliding home and feeling her slick walls engulf him with heat and sensation.

Raising his mouth from her throat and the tops of her breasts, he waited until her eyes fluttered open to meet her gaze.

"Tell me you want me," he demanded in a rough whisper.

He didn't know why he needed to hear her say it, why he was risking the possibility that she might come to her senses, realize she *didn't* want him, and kick him out faster than he could say *sun's comin' up.*

But when she didn't hesitate, when her response came immediately—albeit slightly out of breath—something in his chest loosened at the same time it filled with relief and no small amount of possessiveness.

"I want you," she said, running her hands up his sweat-slicked back to his shoulders, the nape of his neck, and finally into his hair, where her fingers tangled and tugged and ratcheted his pulse rate up by another dozen beats per minute.

"I want you," she said again, canting her hips so that she brushed even closer to his heavy, aching arousal. "I need you. Now. Please."

He didn't have to be asked—at least not twice. He needed her just as much as she needed him . . . and even now seemed too far away.

Taking her mouth, he tried to show her with his lips and tongue all that and more. He kissed her like a dying man clinging desperately to life while his hands stroked her breasts, her rib cage, her navel, and lower until he reached the neat triangle of curls at the apex of her thighs.

His fingers caressed them, playing there for just a second before sliding into her cleft, finding her soaked with her desire for him. It was like the stroke of a hand to his cock and balls, and his scrotum drew up, tightening with need.

Parting her tender folds, he toyed gently with her clitoris and was rewarded by the sharp arch of her back, the bite of her nails at his scalp, and a low mewling from deep in her throat. He didn't release her mouth, instead absorbing her moans into his own.

Then he centered himself at her opening, nudging forward with the tip of his penis. He was only in an inch and already he had to clench his jaw to keep from coming undone. Having her writhe beneath him, struggling to pull him in even farther, didn't help matters, either.

Though he didn't require oxygen himself, Jillian wasn't as lucky, and he figured she could probably use a bit of fresh air by now. Reluctantly, so very reluctantly, he released her mouth, holding himself carefully above her while still covering her from chest to hip and then some.

She gasped, sucking air into her lungs. Her cheeks were flushed a rosy pink, her lapis blue eyes heavy lidded and glowing with passion.

"Don't stop," she panted, tugging at his ears in an attempt to pull his head back down to hers.

He couldn't help but grin at the concern on her face. As though he had any intention of stopping. Her bigger worry should have been that once he started he would *never* stop. He wasn't even fully inside of her yet and already felt as if he couldn't get enough of her.

Unable to speak past the lump in his throat and the pulse pounding in his ears, he shook his head and kissed her again, lighter this time. Short, quick bites at her lips and tongue.

And even though her legs were already wrapped around his hips, he lifted them higher, opening her wider so that he could settle more firmly in the cradle of her thighs. He pressed forward, slowly, enjoying the sweet friction as she closed around him.

They were both panting now, doing their best to hang on and postpone the inevitable. But there was no holding back. They'd come too far, and he wanted her too damn much.

His incisors throbbed, wanting to sink into the tender flesh of her neck and suckle gently on the warm flow of her blood. He could smell it in her veins, coppery and sweet, and he itched to taste for himself.

He wouldn't, of course, not only because he'd promised to keep his fangs to himself, but also because she wasn't ready. Not yet. But with luck . . . someday.

In the meantime, simply making love to her—in the plain old no-bloodletting sort of way—was just fine with him.

Nipping at the side of her neck—because he couldn't resist a teeny-tiny bit of a taste, even if it was only of her salty, sweat-slick skin—he started to slowly pull out and then surge forward. Out and in, out and in, a building rhythm that had his jaw clenching and his muscles pulling taut.

"Connor," Jillian breathed in his ear and against his skin. Her lips grazed his cheek, her nails scoring his back and buttocks as she twisted beneath him, urging him on.

Together, they increased their pace, rocking, pumping, grinding until the room filled with their moans, groans, panting breaths, and the staccato crash of the bed's giant wooden headboard against the wall. She murmured his name over and over, begging him for harder, faster, more. And he gave it to her, wanting it just as much as she did.

Fingers clutching the soft flesh of her hips, he yanked her to him with each thrust of his own. Blood rushed through his veins, making him lightheaded and pooling in his groin until he knew he was about to explode.

He lifted Jillian closer, holding her tight. So tight, her breasts flattened between them, the hard little beads of her nipples digging into his chest and making him crazy. The vampire in him wanted to taste her, drink from her, devour her. The man in him wanted to crawl under her skin, find more than just her G-spot, and make her scream.

It was that last thought that sent him over the edge. The pressure in his throbbing dick reached its boiling point, sending shards of ecstasy flying in every direction as he exploded, spilling into her for what seemed like forever.

Beneath him, Jillian shuddered and cried out as her own orgasm hit—just in time to let him know he hadn't dropped the ball or been entirely selfish in his lovemaking. Her inner muscles clenched and rippled around him, dragging out the pleasure, he hoped for both of them.

Finally, he collapsed, boneless, drained, and more sated than he could ever remember. With the last bit of energy he possessed, he circled her waist and rolled them to the other side of the bed so he wouldn't crush her. And then he was out, as dead to the world as though the sun were high in the sky and he hadn't fed for weeks.

BITE ELEVEN

Seconds, minutes, maybe hours later . . . Jillian really had no idea how much time had passed while their hearts slowed, their breathing returned to normal, and the sweat dried on their skin . . . she shifted beneath the cool sheets, Connor's body warming her in all the right places.

"So that was sex with a vampire," she murmured, almost to herself.

"Mmm. So what did you think?"

"I don't know why any woman would bother with a human lover ever again," she answered honestly.

His chest rumbled against her cheek with his laugh. "And you didn't even let me bite you."

Goose bumps broke out along her arms and a shiver skated down her spine. She felt like a ghoul for the sensual images that were racing through her mind and the pulse-pounding feelings they evoked.

What kind of person *wanted* to be bitten? How

could she suddenly find the idea appealing and be thinking, *Maybe next time?*

She wondered if this was why Will had cheated on her with a vampire. If he'd let her bite him. Maybe he got off on that more than anything else.

But even without the fang-play, what had happened between her and Connor was extraordinary. At least for her.

"Is it always like that?" she wondered aloud, then found herself holding her breath, afraid of what his response might be.

"No," he said, quickly enough that he didn't have time to think about it, and she could only hope he was telling her the truth. "At least it never has been before."

Her head slid from his shoulder to the pillow as he rolled to his side, propping himself up on one elbow. He gazed down at her with soft gray eyes, toying with the ends of her hair, which she was sure looked like she'd been through a wind tunnel. Twice.

"In a hundred years, I've been with a lot of women, vampire and human both." He said it matter-of-factly, not bragging, but not apologizing, either. "I've never felt the way I do when I'm with you. And I've never had sex like that in my life, which—as I mentioned—has been quite extensive."

One corner of his mouth quirked up, and she couldn't help mirroring the expression. He was just too cute when he was sated and relaxed, not nearly as stern and intimidating as usual.

It didn't hurt, either, that he was whispering

words every woman dreamed of hearing. Her heart clenched, wanting so much to believe him.

"Maybe it was a fluke," she said, her pragmatic side rearing its head and reminding her not to be swept away by a handsome man and pretty words.

Nodding sagely, he agreed, "You're right. We were probably both due. I'm sure it couldn't possibly be that fantastic the second time around."

Her brows rose in surprise even as her stomach plummeted. Okay, so that wasn't quite the response she'd expected.

"Of course, there's only one way to find out for sure," he continued.

She opened her mouth to ask what that was, but he silenced her with a kiss. And then with so much more.

Sometime in the middle of the night—which was really day for her now, she supposed—Jillian felt herself being lifted from bed and carried as carefully as a child out of the room. She stirred enough to open her eyes, and saw Connor's strong countenance above her, dark hair ruffled, jaw squared with determination.

It registered, somewhat belatedly, that she was wrapped in a sheet but otherwise naked. And Connor, as best she could tell, was entirely naked. He was marching down the hallway in the buff, carrying her near-buff self, without a care that someone might see them. Not that Drake Manor was brimming with activity, but at any moment, Liam, Maeve, or more likely Randall could pop out and kill her with embarrassment.

"Where are we going?" she asked, voice raspy from disuse. Or too much use, maybe, given how often she'd screamed his name over the past few hours.

"My room," he told her. Firmly, definitively, brooking no argument.

Yeah, like she was in any mood or condition to fight. If the house was on fire, she wasn't sure she could work up the energy to care. But she was curious.

"Why?"

"Because I want you there. It's where you belong."

Gloria Steinem be damned, his caveman routine made her weak in the knees. No man had ever carried her off to bed before, especially from one bed to another, simply to lay his claim.

"Do you have a problem with that?" he asked when her only response was to let her eyes drift closed again as she rested her head on his broad, solid shoulder.

"That depends. Is staying in your room with you a part of my job requirement?"

She was teasing, and she felt certain he must know it, but his expression didn't soften. If anything, he turned more serious.

"About that," he said as they reached the thick, carved wooden door leading to his suite. Without loosening his grip on her, he twisted the knob and let them in, kicking the panel closed behind them.

He was quiet for so long as he carried her through the sitting room and into the large master bedroom, that she thought he wasn't going to finish what he'd been about to say. She caught a glimpse of dark, masculine colors—maroon, hunter green, touches of dark wood and gold trimmings here and there—before he set her in the middle of the neatly made bed and stepped back.

She finally got the chance to see him, every inch of him, fully, blessedly naked. She tried to swallow, but found her mouth dry as the Gobi. He was . . . impressive, to say the least. Magnificent.

And obviously aroused, regardless of the fact that they'd had hot, sweaty monkey sex not so long ago. More than once.

While she hugged the sheet from her bed to her chest and was grateful for the covering, he didn't seem the least bit self-conscious of either his nudity or his growing erection.

It must be nice to be a man, she thought. All that confidence without the numerous hang-ups women had about their physical appearance. Her face flamed at the very thought of standing at naked attention as he was doing now.

Then he drew her concentration back to his face and his previous, unfinished comment with two little words.

"You're fired."

Her eyes widened and her mouth fell open. "Excuse me?"

Okay, so the caveman thing had grown old fast. And now she was thinking she might have to give Gloria Steinem a call to complain about her employer giving her the boot after he'd gotten what he wanted from her—a good, quick roll in the hay.

"You're fired," he said again, eyes dark and locked on her like heat-seeking missiles.

"I don't want you here because I'm paying you.

I'd still like you to help me plan for a traditional family Christmas, if you're willing, but not as an employee."

She opened her mouth . . . to say what, she wasn't sure. Either she was still half asleep or that double dose of incredible sex had zapped her brain cells, because her thoughts were jumbled and she couldn't seem to form a logical retort.

He held up a hand to stop whatever argument she might have made. "I'd like you to celebrate the holidays with us, but not as my events planner. As my . . . lover."

Swallowing hard, she felt her heartbeat kick up and her chest grow tight.

"And where would I stay until then?" she asked in a quiet voice. "Here or at my place?"

"Here," he answered firmly and without hesitation. And then somewhat more uncertainly, "At least I would hope so, if you're comfortable with the idea."

"I have a cat," she told him. "If I'm going to be away from my apartment for that long, and it's not business related, I should probably bring him with me."

He gave a quick nod. "I like cats. I think."

She almost smiled at that. "Do they like you?"

His mouth twisted wryly. "I don't know. It's been a while since I've been up close and personal with one. But I'm not going to *eat* him, if that's what you're worried about. And even if yours doesn't like me, this house is certainly big enough for the two of us to keep our distance from each other."

"True. But are you sure you want me here?" Was she sure she wanted to *be* here when she didn't have the job to use as an excuse? "Don't you think things are moving awfully fast? What if we're blinded by lust? What if one of us wakes up next week and realizes we can't stand the other?"

Connor strode forward, reaching her almost before her eyes had time to readjust. Grabbing her arms, he hauled her up off the bed and flush to his broad, bare chest.

"I'm not going to change my mind," he said, his warm breath fanning across her face. "The one thing I can promise you is that I've been around long enough to know my own mind . . . and my own heart. To know that whatever this is sparking between us, it doesn't happen every day. And it isn't going away anytime soon."

Loosening his hold slightly, he let out a pent-up breath. "I understand if you're nervous and want to take things more slowly. I'll understand if you want to move back to your apartment or continue on in a strictly professional capacity until you're feeling more sure of the situation." A muscle in his jaw jumped as he clenched his teeth together. "I won't like it, but I'll understand and go along with it, if that's what you need to feel comfortable about being with me."

For a long moment, she said nothing, letting his words sink in, weighing her own thoughts and feelings.

"I don't usually do this sort of thing," she told him, needing him to know the truth so that *he* could make an educated decision about *her*. "I got it into my head that I should sleep with you only because my last boyfriend was a jerk. He cheated on me—with a vampire—and then tried to convince me it was my fault because I was cold and boring and inhibited."

Connor raised a brow and she gave a small smile.

"What better way to prove I'm none of those things than to seduce a man I'd just met. And an immortal one, to boot."

"*You* seduced *me?*" he murmured, more a question than a statement.

She tipped her head. "Didn't I?"

"I thought I seduced you. I was going to apologize for rushing you into something you might not have been ready for."

Her lips quivered as she chuckled. "Well, don't we make quite the devious pair."

Connor's own mouth curved, but the smile didn't reach his eyes. "Are you sorry?"

She shook her head. "Are you?"

"You can ask me that," he said, his tone a cross between shock and annoyance, "after what happened in your room and my asking you to stay here?"

She felt guilty for teasing him. But then, it wasn't every day a mere mortal woman had a big, bad vampire wrapped around her little finger.

"A girl needs to be sure about a guy's feelings for her before she agrees to move in with him," she told him with a shrug of one bare shoulder, the sheet slipping half an inch to reveal the topmost curve of her breast.

Going statue-still, his voice lowered and he said, "Does that mean you will? Move in with me, I mean."

"Yeah. I think maybe I will." Her reply sounded

flippant, but inside, her stomach was trying out for the Olympics' American gymnastics team. She could only hope she was making the right decision and not letting her desire to shed her inhibitions supersede her common sense. "I'm willing to give it a shot, anyway, at least through the holidays."

Shooting her a wicked, satisfied grin, he doubled his arms around her waist and lifted her straight up off the ground. She laughed, his enthusiasm contagious.

He carried her the few steps to the bed and toppled them both down in the center of the wide, soft mattress. His mouth covered hers, and for the next several minutes, all she could think about was his kiss, his weight, his warmth.

The sensation of being wrapped in cotton candy and safely cocooned by this magnificent man washed over her. Even if moving in with him so quickly turned out to be a mistake, she knew it would be of the Sheryl Crow variety—her *favorite* mistake.

And if things between them worked out . . . Oh, her future was looking rosy, indeed. Learning to work through the night and sleep during the day was nothing compared to waking up in Connor's arms. And any other differences they had . . . well, they'd work them out.

Unless, of course . . .

She pulled back slightly, already out of breath and feeling the heat of arousal pulse between her legs where his growing erection nudged.

"What about your brother and sister?" she asked, her fingers toying over his shoulders distractedly.

He frowned. "What about them?"

"Do you think they'll mind if I move in with you? That you're involved with"—she arched an eyebrow—"a human?"

"My romantic life is none of Liam and Maeve's business. And if they don't like it, they can move out. It might be time for that, anyway," he added, almost as an afterthought. "But for the record, they both seem to like you, so I don't think they'll mind one bit."

That made her feel moderately better, but just to be safe: "Okay, but I think I'll let you be the one to tell them."

Connor chuckled, his lips lifting enough for her to see the sharp, white tips of his fangs. She must really be gone on him, she thought, because the sight of them didn't bother her at all. Not anymore.

"Fair enough," he agreed, lowering his mouth to kiss her again.

Just before their lips touched, she whispered, "Connor?"

"Hmm?"

"About that biting thing . . ."

A Vampire in Her Stocking

TYPE A

The intercom on Vivian Harrison's desk buzzed, followed a second later by her favorite voice in the entire world. Deep and masculine, it poured over her like warm honey and sent her belly flopping like a barrel of fish.

"Vivian, could you come in here for a minute?"

"Yes, sir," she responded automatically.

It was two weeks into December, and everyone was clearing out of the offices for holiday vacation. A temporary staff would be moving in, because, of course, the news never slept—or took a holiday—but regular employees of DNN who had been with the news network long enough to deserve a few weeks off were more than happy to tidy up their inboxes and vacate the premises.

And though the rest of the eighteenth floor's nightly news staff had already cleared out, she was still here because Sean was still here, and it wouldn't be right for an assistant to take off before her boss. Not that she'd want to.

Since they had no work pending, she didn't

bother grabbing a notepad and pencil. Instead, she pushed open the heavy wooden door separating his corner office from her work area and stood just inside, waiting.

Sean Spicer was behind his desk, a wide glass-and-chrome monstrosity that she knew for a fact had cost a bundle; she'd been the one to put through the paperwork. Boxes littered the surface, filled with items he apparently planned to take home with him over the holidays.

As always when she saw him, a jolt of longing struck her, making her breath catch and her knees go weak. He'd long ago shed his suit jacket, standing now in dress slacks and a simple white button-down, open at the neck, sleeves rolled up, leaving his forearms bare. His blond hair was ruffled after a long night of work and running his fingers through it probably two dozen times, as was his habit.

She only wished she could be lucky enough to share the practice so she could find out if the short strands were as soft as they looked.

"Is there something I can help you with?" she asked when he didn't immediately tell her what he needed.

He stopped loading up yet another box, straightened, and finally met her gaze. His green eyes looked sad, reluctant, and a sudden wave of apprehension washed over her.

"No. Thank you," he told her, moving around the desk to stand in front and lean against the opposite edge. He gestured to one of the matching black-and-chrome visitor chairs. "Come sit down for a minute."

She did as he asked, the dread in the pit of her stomach growing with each passing second.

Oh, God, please don't let him fire me.

Her mind raced over the past few weeks of work.

Had she done something, said something to necessitate her termination?

Was he moving to another network where he would be assigned a fresh, perky new assistant?

Vivian was no slacker, but she would also never be some bleached-blond, twenty-year-old intern with plastic boobs and more dark roots than brain cells.

Sean took a deep breath and blew it out, the hands resting on his upper thighs fisting and unfisting in an uncharacteristic show of nerves.

"There's something I need to tell you," he said in a low voice. "I've put it off as long as I could, but now . . ."

She swallowed, her heart banging in her chest like a child with a pot and a wooden spoon.

"I won't be coming back after the Christmas holiday."

Oh, no. He *was* moving to another network. And he wasn't taking her with him.

She blinked rapidly, trying to hold back tears of bitter disappointment. She could work for anyone, she knew, and was sure she'd get along well enough with her next boss. Even if she had to leave DNN and find a new job. But never again would she find a man like Sean, who gave her a reason to wake up in the evening, a reason to smile her way through her job every single night.

"I don't understand," she said, embarrassed when her voice wobbled.

How could he leave her when she'd been so good to him? The perfect assistant. A woman willing to give up nearly everything else to be there for him, on the job and off.

"I know. I'm sorry to break it to you this way, but I couldn't seem to bring myself to say anything before."

Reaching out, he took both her hands in his, their warmth comforting even as the touch of his skin on hers sent a different kind of heat to pool in a much lower spot.

"We've had a good run here, you and I," he continued, his lips curving into a poignant half-smile. "I couldn't have asked for a better partner in crime."

She gave a watery laugh at the inside joke. He'd started referring to them as "partners in crime" a year ago when they'd worked on a story against his superiors' wishes and done everything they could to gather the facts and get it on the air without losing their jobs.

"The truth is, Viv, that I'm, um . . . sick. Have been for quite a while, but I didn't want anyone to know, so I've done my best to hide it. Rather than wasting away in the public eye, I'm leaving while I still look healthy and normal, and the official story will be that I'm 'pursuing other interests.'"

Vivian heard him talking, heard his explanation of why he was leaving and not coming back after the holidays, but nothing past the word *sick* registered in her consciousness.

How could he be ill? He looked fine. More than fine, he looked amazing, just like always.

Well, all right, he'd lost a bit of weight in recent

months and his pallor was less than tanned and robust, but she hadn't thought it was anything to worry about. It was winter in Boston, after all; everyone looked like they could use a week in the Bahamas and would remain that way until high summer unless they went for the tanning beds or spray-ons.

And a man was allowed to change his diet and shed a few pounds without everyone immediately jumping to the conclusion that he was ill, wasn't he?

How could he be sick without her knowing about it? She scheduled his appointments, took his calls. He'd had more out-of-office appointments lately, had been going out to lunch and dinner more often without specifics, taking more time here and there for himself. And there had been a few calls that had seemed odd, but nothing had set off blips on her radar as being terribly out of the ordinary.

Licking her lips, she forced her brain to slow down, to clear, to process what she was hearing and put it into some sort of neat, organized package that she could understand.

"How sick?" she asked, her voice barely squeaking past a throat tight with fear.

For a brief, tense second, he didn't answer, but his eyes darkened and his jaw clenched. "I'm dying, Viv, of a brain tumor. There's no coming back from this one."

She knew she should ask what and how long and when, but the only thing going through her head at that moment was a gut-wrenching *Noooooooooooooooo!*

Her heart twisted, shattering into a million

pieces inside her chest. The tears that had merely been pricks of concern behind her eyes when she'd thought he was leaving DNN for another network spilled over to roll down her cheeks in a waterfall of emotion.

"Oh, come on, Viv." Sean went down on one knee in front of her, their hands still clasped together and now resting on her lap. "It's not so bad. I've had a good life. I've accomplished a lot. And I got to spend the last few years eyeing a very pretty assistant while she worked hard to make me look good on camera and off."

He was trying so hard to put on a brave front, even as anguish and regret shone through his forced smile, filling every line of his beautiful, clean-shaven face. Which only made her cry harder.

"Oh, Sean," she sobbed, throwing her arms around his neck and hugging him tight.

She felt pathetic, weeping onto his shoulder and feeling sorry for herself when he was the one who was dying.

Dying. How could this be happening? *Why* was it happening?

Sean was such a good man. Thick as a redwood when it came to what was right under his nose, but smart and funny, decent and kind.

She'd been pining after him for ages, loving him from afar. Biding her time until he realized she was the perfect woman for him—well, almost perfect, anyway—and decided he couldn't take another breath without kissing the red right out of her hair.

And now she was going to lose him. Not to another news agency, not even to another woman, but to the Grim Reaper. That cruel, fickle son of a bitch.

"Shhhh," he whispered in her ear, making her shiver even as guilt and despair flowed like acid through her veins. "Don't cry. It's going to be okay."

She lifted her head, certain her eyes were a swollen mess, and that she looked even worse when she wiped her running nose on the sleeve of her lavender satin blouse.

"It's not okay," she keened. "It's never going to be okay."

"It will," he told her with a calm she couldn't comprehend. Running a hand through her hair, he tucked a long strand behind her ear and offered a gentle, courageous smile. "It really will, Viv. You'll come back after Christmas to a new boss with new ways of doing things, and pretty soon you'll forget all about me."

Whaaaaaaaaaaa!

"No, I won't!" she cried, angry now. At him and his cavalier attitude . . . at whatever dread disease was taking him from her . . . at the whole horrible, godforsaken world. Oh, how she hated them all!

"I could never forget you," she vowed, holding his soft green gaze and pouring her entire soul into the heartfelt words. "I could never forget you, Sean. I love you."

His smile widened, but even through watery eyes, she could see that he was just humoring her. Trying to placate the crazy woman who was staining his clothes and carpeting with her tears.

"I love you, too."

He didn't mean it, not the way she wanted him

to, but at the moment, she didn't care. She only cared that this was her last chance to be with him, to show him how she felt before . . . before there were no more chances. Ever.

Launching herself against him, she smashed her mouth to his and kissed him for all she was worth. She tasted her own tears on his lips, but also coffee, a hint of what she thought might be scotch, and something else . . . a flavor that went with the scent that was distinctly Sean.

It took a second for him to absorb her weight and the shock of her sudden assault, but once he did, his arms lifted to circle her waist and he was kissing her back.

Her fingers tangled in his hair, her skirt scrunching up around her thighs as he settled between her legs and she used them to pull him closer. Next thing she knew, his hands were at her blouse, slipping the buttons free, separating the silky material, and sliding it over her bare shoulders to reveal the lace and satin of her matching lavender bra.

His thumbs toyed with her nipples through the material for a moment before delving inside. She gasped at the sensation of skin on skin, of the rough pads of his thumbs bringing the tips of her breasts to achingly rigid peaks.

He kissed her throat, trailing his mouth down, then up again, licking, nibbling, blowing softly on the damp flesh. Lower, his hands pushed her skirt even higher, running his palms along the outside of her thighs and up to squeeze her buttocks. Fingers curling into the waistband of her panties and pantyhose together, he tugged them down. Down her legs, past her knees, and off her feet, right along with her three-inch, patent-leather pumps.

Then he was lifting her, swinging her around, and sweeping an arm across his desk, sending boxes clattering to the floor. Thank goodness everyone else had already gone home, otherwise the noise would surely have brought their coworkers running and given them quite an eyeful.

He laid her back across the flat surface, his mouth going immediately to her breasts. Pleasure shot through her and she wiggled against the glass, wanting more, wanting everything.

She tore at his shirt, opening it the same way he'd opened hers—except for a few lost buttons— so that she could get to his magnificent chest. It was as warm and smooth as she'd imagined, her fingers tracing the hard planes of his pectorals, his rib cage, his abdomen. She teased his tiny male nipples, giving him a taste of the sweet torture he was working on her.

And then she reached for his belt and zipper, pushing his pants and underwear down just far enough to free him to her touch.

He groaned as her fingers closed around his engorged sex, squeezing, stroking.

"Enough," he panted, tearing his mouth from her breasts to part her legs and draw her closer. Grasping his throbbing cock, he lined himself up with her opening and pressed home.

One long, hard thrust and he filled her, leaving them both gasping for breath. For a moment, neither of them moved, absorbing the sensations of their joined bodies, trying not to go off like rockets too soon.

Sean kissed her neck, nibbled the lobe of her ear. "If I'd known you'd feel this good," he whispered, "I'd have bent you over my desk a hell of a lot sooner."

She chuckled, the sound coming out breathless and strained. She'd only been hinting for him to do just that for going on two years now. Too bad it had taken a terminal illness and her emotional breakdown for him to open his eyes and see that she was more than willing and not the type to file a sexual harassment complaint. On the contrary; she'd wondered if she could report him for *not* sexually harassing her.

But all she said now was, "You feel good, too." Better than good. And better than in any of her many fantasies, which had been pretty darn amazing at times.

"It's about to get even better."

He drew her up, hands at her back under her blouse, his tongue sweeping inside her mouth to tangle with her own. She clutched his shoulders, rubbing her breasts against his chest, locking her ankles at his hips to hold him where she wanted him most.

But that didn't keep him from moving, from pulling back slightly and then sliding back in. Withdrawing even farther, then filling her again.

Each movement sent frissons of pleasure radiating out in every direction, making her hungry for more and more and more. Harder, faster, deeper. Please.

And he gave them to her, all of them.

Their mingled moans and heaving breaths filled the room. The edge of the glass-topped desk cut into her bum, but she couldn't have cared less. Especially when Sean canted her hips at such an angle that he began to hit her clit with his pelvis on every downward stroke.

"Oh, my God," she cried out as the pressure built, as ecstasy coursed through her with each thrust of his hard length into her body. "Yes. Oh, Sean . . . *yes!*"

Orgasm washed over her in a flood so intense, her vision went black and she screamed his name. Her climax seemed to give him permission to find his own release as he drove into her one last time, burying himself to the hilt before stiffening with a shout and spilling himself inside her.

TYPE B

Vivian didn't know how long she lay there beneath Sean, her bones liquid, her heart rate slowly returning to normal, her brain a well-shaken Etch-a-Sketch. And if it weren't for the wall-to-ceiling windows lining his corner office on two sides, reflecting the end hours of a starless night sky, she wouldn't have had a care in the world.

Sean lifted his head, perspiration still dotting his brow. "Are you all right?"

All right was the understatement of the century. She was so much better than all right, they hadn't invented a word for it yet.

She nodded, incapable of intelligent speech just yet.

"Well, you can't be comfortable," he said, levering himself off of her to tug up his slacks and straighten his clothes.

But, oh, if only he knew. Granted, her position on the glass-topped desk might best be described as contorted and better left to those with a bit of gymnastics training or pretzel DNA, but she'd never been so comfortable. He could have twisted her into a sailor's knot, hung her by her ankles from the nearest chandelier, and she wouldn't have minded a bit as long as he was about to join her and do those wonderful things to her that he did with his mouth and hands and the rest of his body.

Just thinking about them made her hot and wet all over again.

Still, she sat up and began to rearrange her own clothes. Her legs weren't quite steady enough to hold her, so she used the edge of the desk to prop herself up.

"I should get you home," he murmured, coming to stand in front of her and wipe a smear of lipstick from her cheek with his thumb.

She nodded dumbly. It was the last thing she wanted, even though she knew it was absolutely necessary.

"I can drive myself," she said, her voice a near-croak scraping up from her dry, ravaged throat. "My car is in the parking garage."

Sean unbuttoned the top two buttons of her blouse and rebuttoned them properly, an amused grin turning up one corner of his mouth. "I'll have someone drop it off for you later. But for tonight, I insist on taking you home myself. Never let it be said that I seduce my assistants on my desk, then send them on their way without a backward glance."

His comment was meant to be funny, a little joke about the impulsiveness of their actions. To Vivian, though, it hit too close to home and made her stomach seize in pain—for so many reasons.

That he might have had affairs with other of his female assistants before she came along. . . . That he'd finally made her dreams come true by making love to her, only to tell her on the same night that he was dying and would likely never see her again. . . . That he could be so sweet and witty and charming, even in the face of so much despair, when she felt like crumpling to the floor and sobbing her heart out.

She swallowed hard, refusing to break down in front of him. Again. If he could be strong, then so could she.

When he offered his hand, she took it, following him across the office.

"What about your boxes?" she asked as she paused to retrieve her shoes. She didn't bother with her discarded panties or pantyhose, instead slipping her shoes on bare feet.

The underwear she balled up and held behind her back until she could stuff them into her purse. Better that than leaving them for the cleaning staff to find. She would die of embarrassment if that happened, even if they didn't have her name embroidered at the crotch.

"I'll pick them up later. Or have them packed up and delivered. There isn't much in them I'll be needing, anyway."

His words made her chest tighten and tears prick behind her eyes. How was it possible that she could be having the best night of her life and the worst night of her life both at the exact same time?

With her hand still clasped in his, she let him lead her out of the office and down the hall to the elevator. They walked out of the DNN building and to his car in silence, drove through downtown Boston traffic in silence, pulled up in front of her apartment without saying a word. Sean cut the engine and made a move to get out, but Vivian stopped him with a hand on his arm.

"You don't have to see me up," she told him quietly. And wasn't sure she could handle it if he did. Inside, she was shaking and didn't know how much longer she could hold back a complete breakdown.

"You're sure?" He sounded reluctant to agree, as though his chivalrous side balked at putting a woman out of his car at the curb and letting her make her own way home.

"I'm sure," she answered, mortified when her voice wavered. She sniffed and did her best to tamp down the emotions threatening to burst free.

As though he knew how close she was to losing it, he gave a curt nod, fingers flexing on the steering wheel. Her own fingers clutched the door handle, resisting the urge to yank it and bolt.

"I'm so sorry, Sean," she murmured, unable to remember if she'd said as much back at the office when he'd first told her about his illness. "I wish there was something I could do."

He gave a sharp, self-deprecating laugh. "Yeah. Me, too."

"If you need anything . . ." She trailed off, knowing the offer sounded feeble and predictable.

"Thanks," he muttered in return.

Then he turned his head, meeting her gaze. Even in the dark of the car and the surrounding night edging its way toward dawn, she had no trouble seeing the warmth and sincerity in his greenish-brown eyes.

"I'm going to miss you, Viv. You've been a great assistant, and an even better friend."

She sucked in a breath, her throat snapping closed as the tears behind her eyes broke free to roll down her cheeks. Her chest lifted and fell, lifted and fell, and she wondered if she was on the verge of a panic attack.

It took all of her strength, every fiber of her being not to throw her arms around him. But if she did that, she knew she would never let go. She also knew that if she didn't get out of the car *right this second*, she would do just that, which would only make the situation worse.

So without a word, she leaned forward to press one last, heartfelt kiss to the corner of his mouth before springing the door, leaping out, and racing as fast as she could for the front of her building. She didn't look back. Wouldn't have been able to see anything through the flood of her tears even if she had.

And then she was out of the cold night air, pulling herself up the stairs to her apartment, unlocking the door. Once inside, she collapsed in a heap on the carpeted floor, not bothering to kick off her shoes or coat or anything else. And there she remained, sobbing uncontrollably while the dark gave way to light, the light back to dark, and the world as she knew it ceased to exist.

"Honey, you've got to hush. You're going to make yourself sick if you keep this up."

Vivian lay curled up on the sofa, knees pulled to

her chest, face buried in her folded arms. She hadn't stopped sobbing since Sean had dropped her off two nights before. She was only even in her bathrobe now and on the couch instead of the floor because Angelina had come by, kicked in the door, and hauled her to her feet.

The stripping and shower Angelina had forced on her hadn't helped. The hot tea and then cocoa Angelina had attempted to pour down her throat by the gallon hadn't helped. And the dose of plasma Angelina had insisted would make her feel better had only made her sick to her stomach.

"He's dying, Ang. I love him, have loved him since the moment I met him, and now he's dying. I'll never see him again."

Never see him, never touch him, never be touched by him. And even though she fought them, she couldn't seem to clear her head of images of his imminent death. His cold, stiff, lifeless body laid out in a satin-lined coffin. That coffin being lowered into the ground. Worms and other assorted flesh-eating insects turning his beautiful form into a zombielike corpse.

Her friend stroked a hand through her hair, stringy from being left to air dry after her involuntary dousing and damp again at the temples from her tears.

"Maybe," Angelina murmured softly. "Or maybe not. It all depends on how much you love him."

How much she loved him? She'd been carrying a torch for him for years. Taken a job she didn't need and would never even have considered just to be near him. Showed up early, stayed late, sometimes staying at the office 'round the clock, if she couldn't get home before sunrise.

"I love him more than anything," she asserted in a watery, hiccupping voice.

"Then turn him, sweetie."

Vivian's chest hitched as she lifted her head and tried to slow her tears. It was a testament to her grief that she hadn't thought of it herself. The idea had never even crossed her mind.

But . . .

"No, I couldn't," she said with a shake of her head. "He wouldn't want that."

"How do you know? Have you asked him?"

Another shake. "I know him. He wouldn't want to live like that. He's too proud, too human." And had made more than a few questionable remarks about vampires along the way.

Another reason she hadn't declared her undying love for him sooner—she hadn't been sure how he would react to the knowledge that he was working with a vampire. And worse, one that had the hots for him. For all she knew, he might have fired her on the spot, then called security and had her escorted from the building.

"You never know unless you try. And talking big is always easier before one is standing eye-to-eye with the great abyss. If this fellow of yours is truly dying, facing his own mortality, he may be more than willing to consider eternal life. At least talk to him about it."

Oh, how she wished she could. But that would mean admitting to him that *she* was a vampire, and she couldn't stand the thought of having him look at her with horror or hatred or disdain. He would see it as a betrayal, the fact that she'd worked with him for so long and never told him the truth of who—*what*—she was.

"I can't," she said miserably.

Her wracking sobs had subsided into silent tears trailing down her face and the occasional hitch of her chest. She was sure she looked like something the cat had dragged in. Dragged in, batted around, chomped on, devoured, and then puked back up a few hours later.

Angelina, on the other hand, looked model perfect, as always. She perched on the edge of the sofa in a soft, copper-colored knit dress that hugged her curves like a second skin. Her jewelry was expensive but tasteful, her shoes designer and high-heeled. Her raven hair fell sleek and straight to the middle of her back, framing high cheekbones and dark, doe-shaped eyes.

If it hadn't been for her friend's pure heart and kind disposition, Vivian might have been jealous. Especially at moments like these when she didn't stand a chance of holding her own next to the Italian beauty.

"Suit yourself, darling," Angelina told her, still stroking her hair like a mother comforting a child. "Just know that you have options. Choices. You and he both."

TYPE O

Two days later, Vivian awoke in her own bed, under her own covers. The curtains were drawn to block out any sunlight, but even so, she knew it was nighttime; she could feel it.

A glance at the digital clock glowing red on the bedside table told her it was a little after nine. Much later than she normally rose, but she'd had a rough couple of days. And it wasn't like she had anywhere to go. Not anymore.

Head throbbing, stomach queasy from being empty for so long, she pushed to her feet and forced herself across the room to the bathroom, then down the hall to the kitchen. She started a pot of coffee, not even sure she would be able to drink it, before going to the refrigerator and pulling out an unopened bottle of B-positive.

The weakness in her limbs, dryness in her eyes and mouth, and throbbing in the gums around her elongated incisors all told her she needed to feed, but darned if she could work up the appetite for it.

Fate was too cruel, she thought, twisting the cap off the bottle of synthetic plasma and bringing it reluctantly to her lips. Here she was, completely immortal, with no chance of dying in the near future unless she fell on a stake or opened her blinds at high noon. While across town, an all too mortal man was facing a certain death, and there was nothing anyone could do about it.

Well, she could, as Angelina had suggested before leaving her alone with her misery and heartbreak, but he wouldn't thank her for it if she did.

Tipping back the bottle of blood, she made herself swallow. Gulp after gulp, the thick metallic liquid slid down her throat. And it did make her feel better, relieving a bit of the dizziness and lethargy pulling at her.

When the bottle was empty, she moved to the sink, gave the bottle a quick rinse, and added it to the recycle bin. The coffee was almost ready now, and she would drink a cup of that, too. After all, in higher doses, caffeine had the same effect on vamps as it did on humans, and she could use a touch of artificial pick-me-up.

She had a mug in one hand, creamer in the other, when a sound from the other room caught her attention. Her mind, sluggish as it was, raced to identify the noise.

She lived alone, so it wasn't a roommate. And she spent so much time at work that she didn't even have a pet—though maybe she should consider getting one now that she was short on both a job and a romantic obsession.

Could it be Angelina? Had she come back? Or perhaps she was still here and only Vivian's scattered state had made her think her friend had left at all.

The noise came again, lower and longer this time. It sounded like . . . was she imagining things? . . . a moan.

Setting the mug and creamer on the counter, she started slowly for the living room, tugging the edges of her robe tighter together and retying the sash.

The room was dark except for the glowing lights of the Christmas tree in the corner. She'd decorated it herself just after Thanksgiving, taking absurd pleasure in the placement of each ornament and every flosslike strand of tinsel.

But she didn't need light to see. Thanks to the vamp in her, her vision was twenty-twenty, and even better in the dark.

The problem was, she didn't *see* anything. Just her living room . . . thick mauve carpeting, rarely used fireplace, sofa and matching armchair, and the wall of windows lining the entire west side of her apartment.

Yes, she knew it was odd—a vampire living in a penthouse, surrounded by glass that increased her chances of sun exposure by about eighty percent. But even though she had to keep the shades tightly drawn throughout the day, the view at night was spectacular.

Living here also made her feel more normal, more a part of the human race instead of one that was thought to spend most of its time underground or sleeping in coffins.

That same low moan came again and she stepped farther into the room, rounding the end table at the foot of the sofa—and jerked to a halt. Her eyes widened, heart speeding up in her chest.

"Oh, my God," she breathed. She felt frozen in place, unable to move.

Sean lay sprawled on the sofa, taking up every inch of the off-white space. His eyes were closed in what she *hoped* was simply deep sleep. His clothes— a pair of worn jeans and a dark green sweater— were rumpled and his sandy blond hair stuck out in every direction.

And draped across his chest like a beauty pageant sash was a wide red ribbon, complete with giant bow.

One corner of a large white envelope was tucked underneath, just over his heart. She slid it free, careful not to disturb him. Inside was a card with Snoopy and the rest of the Peanuts gang standing around Charlie Brown's legendary twig of a tree, singing a Christmas carol.

Vivian opened the card. Scrawled in large, flowing script were the words: *Merry Christmas. Enjoy your present.* It was signed simply *A.*

"Oh, no," she murmured, closing the card and dropping it to the coffee table in front of the couch. "What did you do?"

She wasn't sure if she was asking an invisible Angelina or herself, but a sinking feeling was beginning to churn in her gut.

Kneeling down beside the sofa, she ran her gaze over Sean's still form. He looked all right. Unconscious and slightly the worse for wear, but his lips were rosy instead of blue, and his skin still retained a hint of color rather than being the porcelain white of someone no longer shuffling along the mortal coil.

Though shallow and slow, his chest *was* rising and falling as he drew air into his lungs. Which didn't exactly allay her fears. On the one hand, breathing was good. On the other, it only meant he wasn't dead, not that he wasn't *undead*.

Vampires breathed in and out the same as everyone else. It wasn't necessary; they could go a millennia without oxygen, if circumstances warranted it. But it was as easy to continue breathing as to stop, and it allowed them to blend in more easily without looking like mannequins or drawing sometimes unwanted attention to themselves.

Taking a deep breath herself—one she really did feel she needed to brace herself—she lifted a hand and carefully turned his face away from her. A low moan rolled past his lips, and she paused, waiting to see if he was about to wake up. When his jaw remained slack against her fingers, she reluctantly lowered her gaze to the side of his throat.

And there they were. Two perfectly round puncture marks just over his jugular. The holes were still tinged red, but well on their way to being healed.

With a long, heartfelt groan, she released his chin and dropped her head to the edge of the sofa.

"Dammit, Angelina," she muttered into the thick cushion. "What the hell am I supposed to do now?"

Sean felt like hell, but couldn't figure out why. He didn't have a hangover because he hadn't gone on a bender since college. And it couldn't be the chemotherapy, even though the doctor had warned him the treatments would be rough—vomiting, exhaustion, and becoming a sickly version of Mr. Clean were just some of the fun side effects he'd been promised—because he'd decided against it.

There was no point. He'd been diagnosed too late, the tumor in his brain too large and deeply embedded, rendering it inoperable. His oncologist had made it clear that while treatment might extend the quantity of his life, it certainly wouldn't improve the quality.

He was dying; he'd come to terms with that. But damned if he'd spend whatever time he had left hunched over a toilet bowl puking his guts up and looking like an extra on the set of some B-movie disaster flick.

And call it ego, but he also didn't want to be seen on the air or by friends and family while he wasted away to nothing. At least this way, he would look fairly normal and like himself right up until the end.

Unfortunately, his illness apparently wasn't going to let him *feel* normal right up until the end. He groaned, squeezing his eyes shut and covering his face with the back of his arm.

Maybe it was time to ask the doc for that pain medication he'd mentioned. He hadn't wanted to start using it so soon, not until it was absolutely necessary, but if he was going to wake up every morning feeling like this . . . a pill or two might not be out of the question.

"Sean?"

His name echoed in his ears, like someone was calling to him from the end of a very long, very dark tunnel. How was that possible? He'd been alone in his apartment when he'd gone to bed—hadn't he?

"Sean, are you awake?"

That voice again. A woman's voice. Maybe he was imagining it, especially since it sounded eerily like Vivian. Which was impossible. He hadn't seen or spoken to her since he'd dropped her off at her place the night of their . . .

Of their what? Indiscretion? Affair? Surrender to something that had been a long time coming?

A cool hand brushed over his brow and hair, and he lowered his arm, forcing his eyes open.

Okay, so maybe he was drunk. Or dead, if folks were wrong about that whole "no more suffering after death" thing. Because unless he was imagining things or losing his mind—which was a possibility, of course—Vivian *was* whispering his name. She *was* leaning over him, watching him with wide hazel eyes.

"Viv?" His voice cracked, his throat dry and raw, making him cough.

She stroked his arm and patted his shoulder until the fit subsided.

"Are you all right?" she asked. "How are you feeling?"

"Like I've been hit by a bus," he croaked. "Or maybe worked through the digestive system of a *Tyrannosaurus Rex.*" And shit out the other end.

"I'm sorry," she told him. "You'll start feeling better soon, I promise."

He frowned—or thought he did. Why did she

look so guilt ridden? And how did she know how he felt or that he'd feel better soon?

"What—?" He stopped, cleared his throat, and licked his lips. "What happened?"

Had they gotten back together and drunk themselves into comas? Had he passed out and cracked his head on the corner of the sink or something?

"It's . . . complicated," she said, eyes darting everywhere but on his face.

Before he could ask anything more, she jumped to her feet and hurried off, returning only seconds later with a dark brown bottle and a coffee mug that said *And then Buffy staked Edward. The End.* She popped the top off the bottle and poured some kind of thick, goopy liquid into the cup.

"This will make you feel better," she told him, helping to prop him up slightly and bringing the mug to his mouth.

It smelled funny, but also . . . kind of good.

"What is it?" he asked.

Her lips twisted. "Don't ask. Not yet. Just . . . trust me, okay?"

He hesitated a moment, then began to drink. At first, whatever it was nearly made him gag. It was like trying to swallow wet newspaper, heavy and gelatinous. But then the texture grew on him, as did the taste. It was sweet and tangy, oddly metallic, but he liked that.

The more he drank, the more he wanted, grasping the cup with his own hands and tipping it higher even as he tilted his head back to take it all. He finished with a gasp, licking his lips to be sure he didn't miss so much as a drop.

"How do you feel now?" Vivian asked, setting the mug on the low coffee table beside the couch.

He sat still for a second, assessing. Actually, he felt much better. His headache was gone. He no longer felt as though he'd been dragged behind a tractor trailer for twenty or thirty miles, and in fact felt sort of . . . energized.

"Good," he answered. "Really good. What was in that stuff?"

Once again, she averted her gaze. "Oh, you know—vitamins, minerals, all the usual pick-me-ups."

"And why do I need to be picked up?" he asked, suspecting she knew more about his condition than he did.

"You had a bit of an . . . accident," she said slowly.

He raised a brow, pushing himself into a full sitting position now that he had his strength back. His strength and then some. He felt warm, flushed, almost buzzed, like his blood was humming under his skin and he could bench press a Sherman tank without breaking a sweat.

"What kind of accident?"

She studied him a moment. Opened her mouth as though to speak, licked her lips nervously, and closed it again. Then she hopped up and began to pace. Back and forth, back and forth on the other side of the low coffee table, rubbing her hands up and down her arms.

Sean watched her, curious about her sudden case of nerves and what she was hiding from him, but more distracted by her appearance. Her long, auburn hair fell about her face and shoulders in waves. It was obvious she hadn't done anything special with it; no fancy French twist or loose up-sweep the way she often wore it at work. But damned if she wasn't all the sexier for the natural look.

She hadn't bothered to dress, either, still in a sexy silk robe, dotted with tiny rosebuds, the front slit flipping open and closed as she stalked, revealing glimpses of long, shapely calves and the barest hint of pale thighs.

Okay, so now he was not only feeling better, he was horny as hell. A hard-on was working its way due north behind the fly of his jeans, forcing him to shift around on the sofa to find a position that didn't threaten to snap his dick in half.

As he swung around to put his feet on the floor and tried to tug inconspicuously at the crotch of his pants, he realized that the fireplace and pale eggshell walls behind Vivian's pacing form were completely unfamiliar. Come to think of it, so were the sofa and coffee table, and the brightly lit, fully decorated Christmas tree in the corner.

He'd never seen them before. And he sure as hell hadn't bothered setting up a tree at his own apartment.

Brows knit, he broke into her distracted power walk. "This is your place, right?" It was the only logical explanation, especially considering the way she was dressed.

She stopped pacing and turned to face him, arms linked across her chest. The pose did wonderful things for her breasts, pushing them up and forward and causing the silky material of her robe to part.

He swallowed, telling himself to stop ogling her lovely feminine attributes and look her in the eye instead. But damned if his gaze didn't remain right where it was for a good ten seconds, locked on like a heat-seeking missile.

"Yes," she responded.

"How did I get here?" he wanted to know.

"That's . . . kind of a long story," she told him. "And I'm not entirely sure you'll like the answer."

Well, that caught his attention. The reporter in him perked up and stood on point, ready to find out what the devil was going on.

"I'm not going anywhere," he said, his tone letting her know he wasn't going to tolerate anymore beating around the bush. "And like it or not, I think I deserve to know. What the hell's going on here, Vivian?"

TYPE A-POSITIVE

Vivian rubbed her arms, trying to ward off the sudden chill that had her hands shaking and her bare toes curling into the carpet. She knew darn well the apartment itself wasn't cold; nor was she usually bothered much by changing temperatures one way or the other.

But this chill had much more to do with what she was feeling inside—big, fat, Jabba the Hut fear over how Sean was going to react when she told him exactly what the hell was going on, and guilt that he'd been put in this predicament at all. Her own anger at Angelina's rogue behavior was there, too, but taking a distant back seat to the rest of her riotous emotions.

Taking a deep breath to steel her nerves, she linked her fingers at her waist and tried not to fidget while she faced him. Head on, eyes meeting, no running away from this one.

"There are . . . some things you don't know about me," she started slowly.

"Okay," he said, watching and waiting.

"Did you ever wonder why I was more than willing to work with you any time you wanted, for as long as you wanted, provided it was at night? But that if anything needed done during daylight hours, I called in sick?"

His brows knit. "No. We all work late hours. It's part of the job description. And everyone's entitled to a sick day now and then."

Right. Except she was never really sick, and no one else would burst into flames if they agreed to work overtime.

"Fine, you're right, I blend in well. But trust me when I say that I didn't just *agree* to work nights for the network, I accepted the job because I could." And because it was an excuse to be closer to him eight hours out of every day. But he didn't need to know that, at least not yet.

"Here's the thing," she said, deciding another approach was necessary. This time, she was going for the tear-it-off method, just like a Band-Aid. "I'm a vampire. I know you don't care for them, which is part of the reason I never told you, but it's true."

For the longest minute of her life, he simply stared at her, face blank, eyes expressionless. And then he burst out laughing.

"Good one," he told her. "So what really happened? Did I show up at your door after dropping you off the other night and tie one on? Maybe cry on your shoulder until you figured loading me up with alcohol was the only way to shut me up?"

"No." She groaned in frustration. "I'm not kidding. I really am a vampire, and now . . . well, now so are you."

He didn't laugh this time, but he did scoff. "You're a little late for playing trick-or-treat, Viv. Halloween was two months ago. And April Fool's is still a ways off."

"It's not a trick or an April Fool's." Rounding the coffee table, she sat on the sofa beside him, getting close enough that he could look her directly in the eye and *know* she was serious. Then she lifted her lips and showed him her teeth.

"Look," she said, tapping the pointy enamel. "Fangs. And you have them, too."

Reaching over, she pulled back his upper lip and clicked her nail against one of his incisors. "Feel them with your tongue. They're real."

He did just that, and gave a small, startled jerk. With a shake of his head, he said, "Okay, that's a bit far to go for a practical joke. What did you do, glue them in? And how long will the stuff last? I won't have to try to eat with these in, will I?"

Oh, if he only knew. "You never have to eat again, if you don't want to. You can stick to just drinking."

"Drinking what?" he asked, but his voice sounded wary, as though he were finally beginning to believe her, even against his better judgment.

"You know what. Blood. Although you can stick with the synthetic stuff, if you want. It's not quite as good as the real thing, but it's perfectly healthy for you."

"All right, that's enough," he snapped. Jumping to his feet, he rounded the low pinewood table and picked up pacing where she'd left off. "I am not going to start drinking blood. That's just ridiculous. Not to mention disgusting."

She raised a brow at his look of disdain. "I've got news for you, Sean, you already did. And if I remember correctly, after draining the entire glass, you said you were feeling 'much better.'"

His gaze darted to the mug on the coffee table and the empty bottle of NuBlood plasma next to it. He paled slightly, and she saw his Adam's apple bob up and down as he swallowed.

"I had no idea you had such a vivid imagination," he muttered, apparently still in denial. "Or such a cruel streak. But I'm damn well sick of it now, so knock it off. I don't know how I got here or what you've been up to since I arrived, but I think it's about time I went home."

The look of anger, betrayal, and she suspected near-hatred on his face cut her to the bone.

"Wait!" she called out as he headed for the door.

He paused, allowing her to catch up, but didn't turn around. She stopped a few inches from his rigid form, resisting the urge to reach out and touch him.

"I'm sorry you don't believe me," she murmured softly. "I'm even more sorry that you think I'm being cruel or that I would ever lie to you about something like this. We've been together a long time. I'd like to think you'd know me a little better than that by now."

And that was what really hurt; that they'd worked together for more than two years and she'd been half in love with him for every day of them, yet he didn't have it in him to believe her about this, or at least hear her out.

"But here's the truth, whether you choose to take me at my word or not. I'm a vampire. And thanks to a friend who came over to console me after you told me you were dying, you're a vampire now, too. I didn't ask her to turn you. She took that upon herself, wrapping you up in a bow and leaving you on my sofa like some kind of life-size Christmas present."

His head tilted down and he saw the big, red ribbon, which she assumed he hadn't noticed until she pointed it out. And he must not have been amused because he tore it off over his head and pitched it to the floor at his feet.

"The problem is," she continued, ignoring the gesture, "now that you *are* a vampire, there are a few things that are going to take some getting used to."

He didn't turn around, but he wasn't storming out, either, which she took as a semi-decent sign. "The blood, for one thing. You can eat regular food, anything you want. But only blood will fill you up and keep you strong. And for a while, until the transformation has truly taken root, you're going to be hungrier and need more than usual."

She waited a moment to let that sink in, then licked her lips and went on. "I know you want to leave, but it might be a good idea to hang around for a while. I'll fill you in, answer any questions you have, and I've got plenty of plasma on hand to keep you from getting sick. And if you still don't believe me by the time the sun comes up . . ."

She swallowed hard, not wanting to utter the next words, but knowing they were necessary if she was ever going to convince him of his new immortality. "Well, I guess you could always open the blinds and test my theory. Being incinerated is a hell of a lot faster than dying of some slow-moving disease, anyway." Though she wasn't sure it would be any less painful. Thankfully, she hadn't yet had the occasion to find out.

It took another long minute, but he finally, slowly turned around. He met her gaze, but looked none too happy about it.

"You're serious about this, aren't you?" he asked, eyes narrowed. "You really believe you're a vampire."

She nearly laughed at that. Yes, a hundred or so years of living the life had a way of convincing a person.

Her lack of response must have been answer enough for him, because he blew out a breath and let his chin fall to his chest.

"Fine, I'll stay. For a while. But when the sun comes up and I don't burst into flames, I'm going to want to know what I'm *really* doing here."

It probably wasn't the worst night Sean had ever spent, but it was up there.

On the one hand, he was bored out of his skull. Vivian refused to drop her ridiculous assertion that she was a vampire, he was a vampire, everyone, apparently, was a vampire. It made him think of that stupid Dr Pepper jingle from the seventies, and then he couldn't get the song out of his head.

And since all she wanted to talk about was how he'd become a supposed vampire, and all the things he needed to know about being a blood-sucking goon. And he wouldn't *let* her talk about all of her ridiculous undead delusions. . . . Well, it made for a very tense, very quiet evening.

On the other hand, a part of him was enjoying Vivian's company. He'd spent the last two years ogling her from afar. Trying not to be obvious as he watched her slip in and out of his office, stealing glances at her while they worked.

He wouldn't say he'd had a crush on her, exactly, but he was a red-blooded male and she was a very attractive woman. He suspected he'd lusted after her on and off the same as any other man with a flaming-hot secretary would.

Then there'd been the night he'd told her he was dying, when her upset and his efforts to comfort her had transformed into something more.

The "something more" could have been just one of those things. A brief physical encounter that had helped them both blow off steam, but meant nothing and would never be repeated.

Unfortunately, it had gone the other way for him. He hadn't been able to get it out of his head since the moment he'd climaxed inside of her.

It was as though being with her had flipped a switch in his brain and opened a door he'd never considered before. A Pandora's box of thoughts and feelings he had yet to come to terms with or put into any sort of order.

He liked order. He liked things neat and tidy. It was why he had gotten into journalism to begin with, and later joined DNN. Not every story he reported had a pat, happy ending, but his job did. His job had a certain cadence to it; a mix of excitement and adventure, but within a very organized structure.

Which was probably why he was having such a hard time wrapping his mind around the vampire garbage. It wasn't like he didn't believe they existed. Everyone knew that they did, and everyone also knew that they weren't quite the soulless, bloodsucking killers early movies and novels made them out to be.

That was all well and good, but didn't exactly give Sean the warm fuzzies. He couldn't explain it, but the idea that vampires could blend in and walk amongst regular folks without anyone being the wiser . . . it just didn't sit well with him.

Now here Vivian was, telling him that *she*, his trusted assistant, was one of them. And that somewhere along the line, he'd been turned into one of them, too, by her apparently vamped-out friend.

It was too much to comprehend, too much he didn't *want* to comprehend. He was pretty much hoping it was all a bad dream and that any minute, he would wake up. Still sick, maybe. Still moderately horny from spending so many unconscious hours wondering how he could convince Vivian to untie her bathrobe and come sit on his lap, but also still one hundred percent *human*, thankyouverymuch.

The problem was, this didn't *feel* much like a dream. It was weird enough, definitely, but he'd never had a dream that seemed so endless and boring. Usually, they flew by and he found himself waking up before the end, wanting to go back to sleep for just a few more minutes to find out what else might happen.

But this one—if it was, indeed, the dream he was hoping for—was dragging on endlessly. So far, they'd sat in silence for the first two hours, then watched the entire *Matrix* trilogy (and he only really liked the first movie), and played half a dozen hands of gin rummy. He was b-o-r-e-d and starting to think about jabbing a needle or something into his thigh to wake himself the hell up.

Was it possible to be a vampire and still be bored stiff? (No pun intended.) Weren't the undead supposed to have superpowers or something to keep them occupied, even when there was nothing interesting on television?

Deciding to test Vivian's insane claim—because, what the heck, she didn't need to know and it couldn't hurt anything here in la-la land—he concentrated as hard as he could on turning into a bat. *Bat, bat, bat,* he chanted silently, picturing one of the brown, flat-nosed, wide-winged little creatures.

Yeah, nothing. Dream Viv had a few screws loose, that was for sure.

And Dream Sean was experiencing hunger pangs. He called gin and laid out his cards, suddenly realizing that he was starving. But no matter how many food items he imagined biting into—including all of his favorites—not a single one appealed to him. Not pizza. Not lobster bisque. Not even Mister Cho's famous fried rice or sweet and sour pork, which had gotten him through more late nights and bad situations than he could count with his socks off.

Nothing. Instead, he found his mouth watering over the thought of drinking more of that thick red stuff Vivian had poured down his throat when he'd first "woken up."

And how gross was that, if it really had been blood? Or blood substitute, as she'd claimed.

It didn't help, either, that she'd been sipping the stuff throughout their time together, hunkered down in front of the sofa. He could smell it, even from across the full length of the low coffee table.

Sweet and metallic, it tickled his nose, making his stomach rumble and his gums ache. Especially right around the fake fangs she'd somehow adhered to his real teeth.

Another oddity in a night brimming with them. She must have bumped and rubbed his gums a lot while sticking the artificial incisors in.

See, that was a perfectly logical explanation. There were perfectly logical explanations for everything that had happened, and even Vivian's belief that she—and he—were vampires.

On that one, the answer was clear: She was a closet nut case.

His stomach clenched again, his hunger and the scent of whatever the junk was that she was drinking making him feel edgy and weak. Desperate.

And to make matters worse, she'd just taken a drink of the goopy ruby liquid he was *this close* to killing for. A drop remained on her lower lip, taunting him until the tip of her sexy pink tongue darted out to lick it off.

Shit. His dick was a steel pipe in his pants. His blood felt like each individual cell had grown spikes that ripped and tore as they flowed through his veins. And his breathing was choppy, shallow.

He was on the verge of something *not good*, and if he didn't get out of here *now*, five minutes ago, he was seriously worried about what he might do. Violence wasn't like him, but that didn't keep the sensation from thrumming through his brain, pounding in his chest, making his palms sweat.

"All right, that's it," he bit out, his patience finally snapping clean through. Pushing up from the floor, he stood with his hands on his hips and glared down at Vivian.

"You've had your fun," he told her. "Played your little game. You've kept me here all night, for whatever warped reasons you think you had. But I'm done. The sun's coming up, and I need to get me some bacon and eggs."

He pictured a big, hearty breakfast on a plate in front of him, and felt his stomach lurch. Okay, that wasn't good. He liked bacon and eggs. And toast and home fries . . . the whole nine yards of Farmer Brown / Trucker John crack-of-dawn fare. But the thought of chowing down on them had never made him want to vomit before.

Maybe it was the tumor. He'd had bouts of lost appetite before, and aversions to certain food items, so maybe this was just an extension of that. One more sign that he didn't have a lot of time left.

Unaware of the direction his thoughts had taken, Vivian climbed to her feet in a rush. Her robe gaped open, revealing long stretches of pale, shapely legs, and Sean's gut jolted again. Not with nausea this time, but with good old-fashioned lust.

He didn't miss the flash behind his eyes or the sudden throb of his so-called fangs, either.

Christ, this evening was getting stranger by the minute.

"I really wish you wouldn't," she said, voice thready with concern. Her fingers fumbled nervously with the sash at her waist.

"Boy, you're really not going to let this go, are you?" He shook his head, annoyed, frustrated, fed up. "Fine, tell you what. Let's just get this over with. You think you're a vampire. Hell, you think I'm a vampire. You want me to drink blood and hide under the bed until nightfall, but that's not going to happen. I'm going to prove to you once and for all that this is just some crazy fantasy you've cooked up in your mind to convince yourself that I'm not dying."

Wow, that actually made a lot of sense. He hadn't thought of it before, but telling herself he was a vampire was the perfect solution to his announcement that he was dying. If he was a vampire, he could theoretically live forever. And making herself one, too, meant they could live *together* forever.

He never would have suspected that Vivian suffered from mental illness. Nothing in her personnel records had ever hinted at such a thing, but maybe sharing his secret with her the other night—and then giving in to temptation and making love with her—had tipped her over the edge and caused some kind of psychotic break.

There was only one way to prove to her—to them both—that this wasn't a fairy tale, and she couldn't save him by fictitiously turning him into a supernatural creature of the night. With any luck, it would also startle him awake, if this really was a dream, so he figured it was a win-win situation.

Stalking past her—she smelled like cinnamon; how had he never noticed before that she smelled deliciously like cinnamon? he crossed the living room and grabbed hold of the heavy mauve draperies.

"Sean, no!" Vivian shouted. He could hear her bare feet thumping against the carpeted floor as she raced toward him.

She was only a few yards away, but in the split second it took her to reach him, he gave a yank and parted the curtains to the lovely gold-and-pink hues of the coming dawn.

With a gasp, Vivian threw herself to the side, hiding in the shadows behind the unopened section of window.

See, Sean thought triumphantly, *nothing. She's completely delusional.* And then, *I'll have to make sure she gets the best treatment available before I check out.*

Over the scent of cinnamon Vivian was still throwing off—burnt cinnamon now, rank with her fear—he smelled smoke. And not just any smoke, it smelled like . . .

"Sean," came her horrified whisper. "Your hands."

He glanced down, and for a moment couldn't comprehend what he was seeing. The faintest rays of sunlight shone over his entire form, and every bit of exposed skin was beginning to bubble, to burn . . . to send up tiny whorls of smoke.

The smell, he realized as his eyes slowly sent signals to his groggy brain, was his own burning flesh.

TYPE B-POSITIVE

"What the hell?" He jerked back, lifting his hands to examine them more closely . . . only to have his palms sting as they now came in contact with the early morning sunlight and began to scorch.

"Shit," he swore, taking another jerky step back, and then another.

A sound of panic, of urgency, came from Vivian's direction as she lurched forward, dragging the curtains closed without ever stepping into so much as a millimeter of daylight herself, and pushed him forcefully backward to the sofa.

"Sit," she ordered before bustling off down the hall.

Like he had a choice. When his calves hit the edge of the couch, he sank down on the thick cushions, but his knees were so weak, he'd have dropped to the floor if the sofa hadn't been there to catch him.

Holy Jesus. The sun had actually burned him—

and not in the fun, just-got-back-from-a-Jamaican-vaca sort of way.

And it hurt. Shock had kept him from feeling anything for the first couple of minutes, but now the blisters covering his skin stung like a thousand tiny pinpricks.

Not just his hands, either, but his face and neck, as well. He lifted his fingers to his cheeks, but couldn't tell if both were burned or not. It was just a sensation of blisters upon blisters.

So maybe this wasn't a dream, after all. As much as he didn't want to admit that this might be real, he wasn't sure he had a choice. One couldn't feel pain inside a dream, could they?

While he was staring at his hands and trying to come to terms with what was going on, Vivian returned to sit beside him, dumping a handful of items on the coffee table.

"I told you," she said with barely suppressed accusation. "I tried to warn you."

As angry as she sounded, she was completely gentle when she uncapped a tube of ointment and started spreading the greasy stuff in a thin layer across his face. His nose, his cheeks, his forehead, even his lips. Then she took his arms by the wrists and covered his hands, both front and back.

If he hadn't been in a fog of confusion and smarting from second-degree burns, he knew her attentions would have turned him on big-time. As it was, the soft, even strokes of her fingertips had heat pooling in his groin and made him imagine those same fingers caressing him in passion rather than nursing.

"You'll heal completely in a couple of hours," she told him, "but this will help with the pain."

Setting aside the ointment, she opened another bottle of the stuff she'd fed him earlier, stuck a straw straight in, and held it to his lips. He met her gaze for a moment, even though everything in him was screaming for him to drink.

"I know what you think, but I also know how much you want this. Just drink it. I'll pinch your nose for you, if you want me to, but trust me that you'll feel better afterward, and it will help you to heal a lot faster."

He weighed his options for all of half a second before realizing that since this apparently wasn't a dream—damn it to hell—everything she'd told him must be true. From here on out, he vowed, he was listening to her and trusting her with his newly immortal life.

Leaning forward, he wrapped his lips around the straw and sucked. Slowly at first, then faster when the taste of the . . . *It's blood, Spicer. Face it and deal with it.* . . . sent fireworks of satisfaction bursting through his entire system.

Screw bacon and eggs, and even Mister Cho's many Asian delights. He wanted this. He wanted more, and he wanted it forever.

Vivian watched the tendons of Sean's throat convulse as he drank. Putting him in front of an open window at dawn wouldn't have been her first choice for convincing him he was really a vampire, but it certainly seemed to have done the trick. If he kept drinking her synth like this, she'd have to make a blood run sooner rather than later.

"So you believe me now, right?" she asked, just to be safe.

For a minute, he didn't answer. Then his straw made a sucking sound as he emptied the bottle and he released it with a sigh.

"I think I have to," he responded carefully. "I'm not sure I like it, though."

"I know. I'm sorry." She dropped her gaze, studying the familiar rose pattern on the front of her robe and toying with the ends of its sash. "I was so upset about what you'd told me at the office, and when my friend came by and saw me, she thought changing you would be the perfect solution."

She brought her head back up, meeting his eyes and hoping he could read the honesty, the apology in her own. "I said no. I *told* her you wouldn't appreciate the gesture, even if it saved you from your illness. I *did not* ask her to do any of this," she insisted, needing him to believe her. "I swear I didn't."

It took him a moment, but he nodded. "So what does this mean?" he asked. "If I'm a vampire, that means I'm immortal, right? The tumor . . . it's gone? I'm not going to die?"

"You're not going to die," she reassured him, emotion clogging her throat and dampening her eyes. "Not unless you go out in sunlight again. Or get yourself into a situation that puts you between a stake and a hard place."

He inclined his head again, as though absorbing every bit of information she was giving him. "And what about the blood thing? Is that all I can drink from now on? No regular food?"

"No, you can eat anything you want. It won't nourish you the way blood will, so blood is a must, but you'll be able to enjoy food again, too. Right now, you won't tolerate regular food very well because you're still transitioning. Your body needs blood and only blood. Once you get your fill, though, you'll be fine and get on a bit more of a schedule with the stuff."

Licking her lips, she added, "And before you ask, no, you won't have to bite or kill anyone to feed. There are lots of ways now to get real blood, and plenty of synthetics on the market."

He was silent for so long, she wondered if he was even listening. Then he raised his head, his green eyes snapping as they bored into hers.

"I guess I have a lot to learn," he said quietly. "And a lot to get used to. But you were right about one thing—I wouldn't have chosen this, not even to escape a fatal disease."

The accusation—and that's exactly what it was, an accusation, placing the blame for his current, unwanted condition squarely at her feet—went straight to her heart, squeezing like a vise. Tears stung her eyes and she blinked to hold them at bay.

She deserved his condemnation, she knew that. And not for the first time, she cursed Angelina for her stubbornness, and for taking matters into her own hands when Vivian had clearly asked her not to.

Because the only thing that could possibly hurt more than the pain of losing him to a natural human death was losing him to the hatred and dis-

dain he felt toward her now—and knowing that
thanks to his new immortality, that hatred was
going to last forever.

Vivian did the best she could to mend Sean's
wounds and fill in the gaps for him as far as his
healing went and what he should expect during
his first few hours and days as a vampire. It was
Bloodsucking for Beginners—which would have been
moderately amusing, if the circumstances hadn't
been so serious.

Most mortals who decided to cross over the line
into immortality did it with a clear knowledge of
what they were getting into. The days of turning
someone without their consent were, for the most
part, long gone.

Thanks to Angelina, however, Vivian had been
dropped smack in the middle of a tension-filled,
turned-against-his-will situation. And even though
she'd had absolutely nothing to do with it, she was
the lone target of Sean's blame . . . and her own
self-flagellation.

"You should get some rest," she told him when
the silence between them dragged on longer than
her already frayed nerves could handle and she
noticed his eyelids beginning to droop.

"So, what? Now I'm going to slip into some sort
of coma until it gets dark again? Do I have to sleep
in a coffin, too?"

Despite the sarcasm in his tone, she almost
smiled. "You can stay awake around the clock, if
you like. Just because we can't go out in daylight

without turning into crispy critters doesn't mean we can't stay awake through the day, the same as humans can pull all-nighters. Eventually you'll need to catch up on lost sleep, but there's no forced loss of consciousness, going stiff and un-wakeable," she told him. "Because your transformation is so new, though, the higher the sun gets in the sky, the more tired you'll become. For the first week or so, anyway. The same as your thirst for blood will be stronger for a while. Then you'll acclimate and start to feel much more normal."

"Normal," he scoffed. "Right."

What more could she say? she wondered as guilt twisted inside her for the six- or eight-thousandth time.

"I'm sorry this is happening to you. I'm sorry you didn't get a choice in the matter," she told him. "But I'll do my best to help you adjust, and I think that once you get used to your new reality, you won't mind it so much."

He didn't respond, which was fine with her. Chilly silence was better than something that would only dump more guilt on a pile that was already so high, weighing down her heart so much, she didn't think it could take even a salt grain more.

"You can sleep in my room," she said, rising from the couch and leading him down the hall. He followed without a word, standing in the doorway while she turned down the covers.

"The sheets are clean," she told him, explaining where everything else was that he might need. Extra towels in case he wanted to shower, an extra toothbrush in case he wanted to brush his teeth. Then she quietly left the room, closing the door behind her.

She'd always thought spending two years loving Sean from afar was a lesson in self-torture. Then he'd told her he was dying, and she'd experienced a pain unlike any she'd ever felt before. And somewhere in-between was her current emotional roller coaster.

One minute up because Sean was alive. He was no longer suffering from a fatal disease, no longer had one foot in the grave, and he was *here* in her apartment, with her.

The next minute, it was as though the ground dropped out from under her and she was headed straight down at a rapid pace because she knew this wasn't what he wanted and that he blamed her for it.

Well, she blamed Angelina, she thought with a sudden flare of anger.

Grabbing up the cordless phone as she passed, she carried it with her while she cleared the coffee table. It took all her patience and five very white knuckles clutched around the phone to wait until she thought Sean would be asleep so he wouldn't overhear when she ripped Angelina a new one in a very loud whisper.

After ten long minutes without a sound from the back bedroom, she moved to a corner of the apartment as far from Sean's location as she could get and furiously punched in Angelina's phone number. Of course, since the sun had already been up for quite some time, and her friend was likely already in bed, it rang. And rang. And rang.

Voice mail picked up, but before the electronic voice could inform her that no one was home to answer her call, she hung up and dialed again. Let it ring. And ring. And ring.

It took three hang-ups and redials before a deep, annoyed voice, groggy with sleep, came on the line. *"What?"*

"This is Vivian Harrison," she told Ian, Angelina's live-in lover and partner for as long as she and Vivian had known each other. Normally, the rough-and-tumble cop intimidated the heck out of her, but she was too annoyed at the moment to remember that. "I need to talk to Angelina. Now."

A second later, Angelina's equally drowsy voice came on. "Viv?"

"How could you do this, Angie? I told you not to. I told you he would hate this. How could you do something so monumental, so *irreversible* against both our wishes?"

To her chagrin, her voice began to wobble at the end, and despite her intentions to whisper so Sean wouldn't overhear, her riotous emotions had her growing increasingly louder.

In complete contrast to Vivian's upset, Angelina remained completely calm. "Sweetie, he was dying. And he wasn't going to go peacefully. He was going to get sicker and sicker, weaker and weaker, suffering untold pain before his final end. He may not be happy right now, but give him a little time and he'll realize it was for the best."

"How can you say that? He hates me now. He may not have thought of me as anything but his assistant before, but at least he didn't *hate* me, and it's all your fault!"

"He doesn't hate you," Angelina replied coolly, "he's just mad about being put in a situation he's unsure of and afraid of how it's going to change his life. Give him some time to get used to his new condition and he'll be fine."

"You really think it's that simple?" Vivian asked. The question came out half angry, half curious. She so wanted her friend to be right, but couldn't seem to wrap her mind around the notion that Sean would ever forgive her.

"I wouldn't say it's going to be simple, but if he hates being a vampire so much, he can still end it. Tell him to go stand on the roof at sunrise or fall heart-first onto a chair leg or something. If he wanted to die so badly as a mortal, he can die just as easily as an immortal, just in another fashion."

For a moment, Vivian couldn't respond. She still wasn't happy, but Angelina made a good point. Sean had come to terms with his illness and been ready to die. He was unhappy knowing he'd been given a second chance in a manner he considered to be unnatural. So if he hated being a vampire so much, being *like her*, he certainly didn't have to stay one for long.

Lord knew dying as a vampire was a heck of a lot faster and less painful than dying of a slow-moving human disease like brain cancer. Sunlight or a stake to the heart . . . either would be over fairly quickly, and the vamp in question would barely know what hit him.

It wasn't ideal, and Vivian knew that if that was the option Sean chose, it would break her heart all over again. But if he was going to be this unhappy with the idea of living forever in a body and a way he didn't like . . . well, she didn't want him to be that unhappy, especially if he continued to lay the fault at her feet.

When the silence continued to stretch between them, Angelina's tone softened and she said, "I gave you a second chance, honey. You spent two years working for this man, wanting him, but never making a move to let him know. Then when something finally happened between you, it was with the prospect of a very short, very painful future."

Vivian heard a low grumbling in the background on the other end of the line, followed by Angelina's soft, placating voice telling Ian she would only be another minute or two. Then she was back.

"He may not be thrilled right now. He may hold this new turn of events against you. But if you still want him, then fight for him. Fight *him*, if you have to, to let him know how you feel and how things can be between you, if he accepts and embraces his new existence. And if he's still being an asshole, stake him yourself. Or send him to me and I'll undo what I did to him for you."

TYPE O-POSITIVE

After hanging up with Angelina—feeling less angry, but just as confused—Vivian spent as much time as she could rummaging around her apartment, trying to find things to keep herself occupied.

She shouldn't be tired, given how long she'd spent in bed the past couple of days, crying herself to sleep in a fit of massive depression, but she was. Her eyes were dry and scratchy, and she had to keep stifling yawns.

Tiptoeing her way down the hall to the bedroom, she told herself she would just peek in to check on Sean, make sure he was safe and comfortable, then she would come back out and curl up on the couch. The door opened soundlessly and she padded barefoot across the plush carpeting.

The room was dark, but her night vision was even better than during the day, so rather than simply a lump on the right side of the bed, she could clearly see the outline of Sean's long, lean body beneath the blankets. His crop of blond hair rested on one of her pale peach pillow cases, his shoulders and one arm bare above the covers.

A trickle of longing slid through her, the same as it always did whenever she was within a hundred-yard radius of this man. Even knowing he hated her right now, her desire for him couldn't—*wouldn't*—be diminished. And knowing that he was a vampire now, like she was, and would live forever . . . or could, if he chose . . . only seemed to increase her attraction to him.

Oh, the life they could have together. Hot, sweaty, sharp-fanged sex all night long; sleeping in each other's arms all day. They could go anywhere, do anything they wanted. Spend centuries wandering the globe, or settle down right here in Boston like an undead version of Ward and June Cleaver.

With a sigh, she tamped down dreams of all the things that were never going to come true and moved closer. His breathing was deep and even, completely normal. No twitching, no panting, no signs of nightmares.

Sometimes, if a person's turning was rough or traumatic, their first few nights of rest and recovery could be filled with them. And from what she'd heard, they were nasty. Not run-of-the-mill nightmares, but truly horrific, inescapable visions and hallucinations.

Angelina may have done something she shouldn't have, but at least she'd apparently been gentle about it. Vivian found herself feeling both relieved and grateful.

And if she only had a handful of hours more with Sean before he decided to either walk out of her life forever . . . or walk into the sunrise and end it all, then she wanted them. She wanted to be as close to him as she could be, for as long as he would allow—even if he wasn't awake to know about it.

Readjusting the folds of her robe to make sure they were snug, she carefully pulled back the covers and slipped in beside him. Not touching, leaving an inch or two of bare mattress between them, but still *near* him.

It wasn't her first choice. She would have preferred to snuggle up to him, wrapping her arm around his waist, and spooning against his back. But unless he had a change of heart about being turned into a vampire and the role she'd played in his transformation, this was as good as it was ever going to get.

Sean slowly drifted closer to consciousness. He wasn't sure where he was or how long he'd been asleep, but he could hear noises from the street below: tires rolling over wet, slushy asphalt, brake pads squeaking, the occasional honk of a horn . . . and smell cinnamon.

His brows crossed in annoyance as he blocked out the sounds of traffic and concentrated instead on that spicy scent. He rolled over under the covers, to his other side, and the scent grew stronger. Deliciously strong, making his stomach growl and his blood heat.

Letting his eyes flutter open, he found himself staring at the most beautiful thing he'd ever seen.

was lying beside him, her red hair spread
around her head like a halo, her features relaxed and angelic in sleep.

He took a deep breath, letting that cinnamon
fragrance fill his lungs and seep into his very
pores. It was coming from her. *She* smelled like
sugar and spice and everything nice.

Previous events flashed through his mind in
short order, a fast-forward slide show of the good,
the bad, and the ugly. He tried to work up his old
mad at what she was, what she'd done, what she'd
turned him into . . . but damned if he could manage it while she was lying so close and smelling so
good, and while arousal was beating in his heart
and brain and groin.

Reaching out, he touched one of her long curls,
rubbing the silky strands between his thumb and
forefinger. She didn't move, didn't so much as
change the soft, even pattern of her breathing.

He tucked the hair behind her ear, letting his
hand drift over the side of her face. Her lashes
fluttered, but still she slept.

Moving lower, he traced the line of her jaw, her
slim throat, the bit of pale skin peeking out from
the low vee at the top of her robe. With light,
quick fingers, he undid the tie at her waist, letting
the rose-stamped satin fall open to reveal even
more soft, fragrant flesh. A long strip from neck to
waist and the curve of one heavy, pink-tipped
breast.

Sean's mouth watered. His teeth—those front
two that were now chiseled into sharp pinpoints—
throbbed, and he wanted to both lick and bite all
of that lovely smooth skin.

Dammit, what was wrong with him? He'd never wanted to bite a woman before.

He'd also never gotten this hard this fast without a bit of heavy petting and stroking first. Or been able to smell a person's scent. Not just her perfume or the lingering hint of her shampoo, but her very essence.

Vivian had always been attractive, and he'd always been attracted to her, in that way men had of being attracted to just about anything with cleavage and a tight skirt. But now she was almost achingly beautiful.

Her hair seemed redder and glossier, her skin practically glowing. Her curves called to him like an oasis in the desert, and her lips looked as soft as rose petals—so much so that he had to touch them and find out for sure.

They were—soft and silky and soon to be ravished.

At the first brush of his lips across hers, her eyes popped open, bright and flecked with bits of green and brown. His hands were on her hip and cupping her bare breast, but he didn't move them, and she didn't ask him to.

"What are you doing?" she whispered, voice wary and raspy with sleep.

"Making love to you," he said just as softly.

"But—"

"Shhhh." He pressed a quick kiss to her mouth to keep her from finishing what he knew she'd been about to say. "Let's not talk about that right now."

There were issues to be dealt with, no doubt about it, but he didn't want to think about them at the moment. Not with Vivian in bed next to him, naked under her robe, her body heat warming him in all the right places.

He almost expected her to argue, but she didn't. Instead, her arms came up to wind around the back of his neck and she lifted her head to meet him halfway.

She tasted of cherries and mint, which surprised him, given the strong scent of pumpkin pie spices filling his nostrils. He wouldn't have thought the mix of flavors and fragrances could be an appealing one, but he'd have been wrong. They were mouthwateringly appetizing, like waving a slice of piping hot pizza under the nose of a man who hadn't eaten in weeks or even months. It made him dizzy and horny and stole his breath.

He'd kissed his share of women over the years . . . hell, he'd kissed this woman just a few days earlier . . . but even without the heady cocktail assaulting his senses of taste and smell, this kiss would have registered as The Best Ever. Not just on his scale, but in the history of lip-on-lip, tongue-on-tongue action.

Without taking his mouth from hers, he parted the sides of her robe and pressed until she helped him slip the material off her shoulders and down over her arms. He stroked her bare skin, up and down from hip to breast. Her waist, her thighs, the curve of her belly.

His fingertips tingled as though in contact with a low-level electrical charge. Everywhere he touched, he felt the spark. It ran through his fingers, up his arms, and straight to his solar plexus, radiating out to his chest and stomach, and his aching cock and balls.

Like his ability to hear the flow of traffic several stories below, even though the windows were closed and the drapes were drawn, everything was suddenly *more*. Brighter, sharper, louder. Deeper and more potent.

He felt as though he'd never breathed air before, never used his eyes, never touched a woman's supple flesh. If this was one—or several, rather—of the side effects of being turned into a bloodsucker . . . provided he even believed Vivian's story of how he'd gotten to her apartment in the first place and what he'd supposedly become . . . then he was all for it. At least in theory.

She opened her legs, bringing him more snugly into the cradle of her thighs. The heat and dampness of her sex pressed against his abdomen while she rubbed her feet along the back of his calves, her hands along the flat of his back. He growled and pressed his erection tighter against her inner thigh, rubbing, wanting to feel that warmth and wetness surrounding him, squeezing him, bringing him to his knees.

They were both panting, gasping for breath as their lips pulled apart with a little suction-cup *pop*. But lack of oxygen didn't slow them down, especially considering neither of them needed it; it simply added to the sounds of passion filling the room, the muted chorus of "Baby, It's Cold Outside" coming from another apartment somewhere down the hall.

"Sean," Vivian breathed in his ear as he kissed

her throat, suckling the taut cord of muscle running from jaw to collarbone. "More, Sean, more."

"Oh, there's more," he promised, voice ragged with his own need.

Slipping his arms behind her back, he raised her up into a near-sitting position, leaning back on his own heels while he licked and nipped and fed at her beautiful breasts. He tongued the raspberry tips, her moan of pleasure the most powerful of aphrodisiacs, making his cock burn and grow and leap with hunger.

Her sharp nails scored his back, urging him on, and he could smell her arousal, thick and earthy like bright green moss. It wouldn't take much to push her over the edge. Thank God, because he didn't know how long he could hold back himself.

Tangling his fingers in her silky red hair, he tugged her head back, forcing her to meet his gaze. Her lashes fluttered over glazed hazel eyes.

"I want to take you, fuck you, hard and fast," he told her. "Are you game?"

Her head moved on her neck like she was trying to nod, but her muscles wouldn't work properly. Her mouth opened, the tip of her tongue darting out to lick her delectable pink lips.

"Please," she said, and it was all the encouragement he needed.

Lifting her like a rag doll, he draped her against his chest. "This whole vampire thing . . . I means no diseases, right? No need for safe sex?" Though why he felt the need to ask now, when it hadn't occurred to him the first time they'd made love, he had no idea.

Still resting limply against him, she managed a short nod. "The only danger is in the biting . . . or taking too much blood. Especially if you're with a human."

His penis gave a jerk of agreement as he pictured doing just that—burying his fangs in her throat, tasting the sweet metallic tang of her blood.

Christ. He hadn't wanted to believe all of her crazy creatures-of-the-night mumbo jumbo, but his sexual fantasies had never before included the idea of bloodletting; he was pretty sure the thought would have made him almost physically ill.

Now, though, he couldn't stop the projector reel of images playing through his head or the white-hot arousal sizzling through every cell of his body, collecting in his testicles and the tip of his stick.

"You wouldn't mind that?" he asked, trying to keep the desperation out of his voice and his sweating to a minimum. "If I bit you?"

He felt the shiver run through her, and he didn't think it was from apprehension.

Her hair bounced as she shook her head. "It's better if you do. And if I bite you back."

It was a miracle, a certified, verified, Pope's seal of approval miracle he didn't come right then and there. A sound worked its way up his throat . . . he feared it might have been a whimper and he quickly swallowed, turning it into a feral growl.

Pulling her up, he gripped the thick root of his cock and aimed the tip at her slick, swollen core. He could feel her wet heat even before they touched, and once they did, it overwhelmed him.

Sensation swamped him, making his lungs hitch and his ears ring as he sank in inch by slow inch.

"Yes," Vivian gasped, clutching at him with both her hands and the tight walls of her sheath. "God, that's so good. More, please, fill me."

Good didn't quite cover it. Not in his book. There wasn't a word in the English language—or any other, he'd be willing to bet—that could accurately describe how it felt to have her in his arms and in his lap, to be drowning in ecstasy.

With one final thrust, he did as she'd asked—he filled her. She gave a startled gasp before wiggling slightly and seating herself just right on his raging erection. Wrapping her arms around his shoulders and her legs at the small of his back, she offered him a small, contented smile.

"Remember, hard and fast. You promised."

It couldn't get much harder. And as for fast . . . well, he was about to go off like a rocket just from being buried to the hilt inside her, so he wasn't sure he had much choice there, either.

Gripping her waist, he held her in place and shifted so that he was lying flat on the mattress, stretched out beneath her. This way, she could control the speed and friction—or have a bit more say in it, anyway—and he stood a chance of holding on for more than five short seconds.

"Ride me," he ordered through gritted teeth.

And she did. Bracing her hands on his chest, and her knees along his hips, she slowly brought herself up . . . then down. Up . . . then down.

His vision blurred, and he honest to God thought he might pass out. But . . .

"What happened to fast?" he wanted to know, the words coming out in short, puffing breaths while his fingers dug into the plump flesh of her hips.

"I like this better," she said, still performing that excruciatingly slow up-and-down slide that made his vertebrae quiver like dice in a cup. Her eyes were closed.

Her teeth—fangs included—bit down on her bottom lip. And her breasts . . . Oh, man, her breasts were like cherry-topped sundaes, begging him to dive in and devour them in one delicious bite.

Leaning up, he closed his mouth over one straining nipple and puckered areola, suckling gently before letting his fangs . . . Christ, did he really have *fangs?* . . . score the pillowy mound. She gasped and her inner muscles flexed around him. He groaned in response.

So maybe she really did like biting. God knew it was a gigantic freaking turn-on for him.

Suddenly, though, the long, slow slide thing wasn't doing it for him. Too much more of that—and the rhythmic squeeze of her silken folds around his over-sensitized dick—and he wouldn't get the chance to blink, let alone break in his fancy new razor-sharp incisors.

Sucking in a breath, he let her rise up off his cock again (disco ball lights flashing behind his eyes), but held her there before she could drop back down.

"Turn around," he ordered.

Her lashes fluttered open and she stared at him, confusion in her glossy hazel eyes. "What?"

As loathe as he was to lose the hot clasp of her embrace, he moved her back a few inches, pulling out completely. She whimpered in disappointment, and he clenched his teeth to keep from groaning aloud. But the separation wouldn't last long, if he had anything to say about it.

Kissing her briefly, hard on the lips, he told her again, "Turn around."

This time, she did as he asked, twisting around on her knees to face the other direction. He moved up behind her, pressing her back to his chest, his rigid cock against the curve of her buttocks, wrapping his arms around her to crisscross at her waist and cup her generous breasts.

He nuzzled her hair away from her throat, inhaling its bottled ginger-grapefruit scent. Kissing the pulse point just beneath her ear, he whispered, "Lean forward. Hold on to the headboard."

It took her a moment to comply—whether from apprehension or the thick fog of arousal, he didn't know—but then she did as he asked. The beautiful slope of her back bowed forward, her hair spilling around her face like a thick copper curtain.

Her long, manicured fingers reached out to wrap around the upper curve of the wooden headboard. And her ass . . . God, her ass made everything in him ache—fangs, cock, and heart. He pressed into her, just slightly, just to feel those soft globes against his penis, and lower, against his scrotum.

Running the flat of his hand down the long line

of her spine, he felt her shiver . . . and felt that shiver leap under his own skin.

"You wanted hard and fast," he murmured, bending over her, continuing to lick and suck at her throat and the taut muscle running from neck to shoulder. "And I'm going to give it to you."

TYPE A-NEGATIVE

He was as good as his word.

Parting her cheeks and folds with his hard, hot penis, he drove back into her, filling her all at once and knocking her forward with a gasp. She screwed her eyes shut, nails digging into the smooth wood of the headboard while she tried to school her breathing and keep her body from flying apart in complete and total ecstasy.

There was no tender stroking this time, no sweet foreplay or easing into motion. Instead, he covered her hands with his own, his warm, sweat-slick skin pressing against her arms, her back, her buttocks. Everywhere she was yielding, he was firm, his flat planes molding to her feminine curves.

Without warning, he pulled his hips back and pumped forward, hard and fast, just as he'd promised. Her mouth dropped open in surprise, but no sound came out; she wasn't sure there was a drop of air left in her lungs.

Again and again, he drove into her. Harder,

faster. Harder, faster. The room filled with the musky scent of wild, amazing sex; the sound of skin slapping against skin and their low, desperate moans and pants.

She threw her head back, moving with him, meeting his quick, powerful thrusts because she couldn't *not* move. Her teeth—regular and pointy—cut into her bottom lip as she tried to hold back her cries.

Not missing a beat in the pounding rhythm of his hips, Sean slid his hands down her arms, over her shoulders, and around to her breasts. Squeezing them, plumping them, tweaking the already puckered, sensitive nipples. She whimpered and felt a spasm of pleasure rip through her.

Oh, she was close. So close. Just a little more. *Please.*

"Please." The word tumbled past her lips without conscious thought. But once it was out, she couldn't seem to stop herself from begging, pleading. "Please, Sean. I'm so close. Finish me off, *please.*"

"God, baby. Me, too."

One big, rough palm left her breast and trailed its way past her ribs, her stomach, into the thin nest of tight curls at the center of her thighs. His fingers slid unerringly between her slick folds, finding her swollen bud of desire.

He flicked it, and shockwaves rolled through her. She yipped, actually yipped like a puppy with its tail caught in a door.

Sean's warm, staccato breaths dusted her face as he whispered in her ear. "Now, Viv. Come now."

And then his teeth sank into her neck, piercing her jugular in a sharp, sweet tear of flesh. Her blood raced, pouring from her throat and into his mouth. But rather than hurting, it was the most exquisite pleasure she'd ever experienced.

Sensations rocked her, bringing her to orgasm in the blink of an eye. An incredible, wonderful, coma-inducing orgasm that blew the top off her head and had her screaming in delight.

Sean continued rubbing her clit, banging into her from behind again and again. And then, with a loud shout of completion, he stiffened, spilling inside her as he came.

"Is it always like that?" Sean asked sometime later, his voice a raw, scratchy whisper.

Her head was on his shoulder, her hair fashioned in the style of banshee-chic, she was sure. The covers were twisted and scattered around them, one corner of a pale peach sheet pulled up to cover . . . well, most of their sweet spots, anyway, leaving a lot of flesh bare to the cool night air.

Another resident of her apartment complex was apparently in the holiday spirit, playing Christmas music nonstop. At the moment, it was one of her personal favorites, Eartha Kitt's "Santa Baby."

Stretching slightly, she rubbed the arch of her foot up and down the rough length of his calf. "Like what?" she asked.

"Just . . . incredible," he admitted after a second. "Everything was brighter, sharper, more intense. I've never had sex like that in my life. Is that you, or this . . . vampire thing, or is it just some crazy fluke?"

"I don't know," she answered honestly.

She would have liked to lay claim to whatever "incredible" experience he'd had, to tell him she was the sole reason his eyes had rolled back in his head and his toes had curled when he'd climaxed. It was all her, and he would never feel that way again, *ever*, with any other woman.

Oh, yes, she would have loved to tell him as much. But she couldn't, because she didn't know if it was true or not.

"And the biting," he continued when she couldn't offer more.

His fingers came up to brush her throat. She barely felt the injury anymore, but was sure the puncture marks were still there, probably a bit ragged around the edges and beginning to bruise.

He'd really gone at her, biting harder and drinking longer than most partners would have. But then, he was newly changed, so it was going to take him a while to learn his new strengths and limitations.

"A month ago . . . hell, a week ago, if you had told me I'd enjoy something like that, I'd have thought you had a screw loose. But God, you were right—it was amazing."

His fingers continued to stroke lightly along her skin. "I didn't hurt you, did I?"

She rolled her head back and forth on his shoulder. "You can't hurt me, remember? I'm a vampire."

"Yeah," he murmured softly. "And I guess so am I."

"You believe me now?" she asked, and found herself holding her breath, awaiting his answer.

"I'm not sure I have a choice," he answered a second later, his tone only marginally hesitant. "Unless this is the longest, most whacked-out dream I've ever had, it's time to face facts."

She let that sink in for a minute, wondering exactly what he was thinking and what his idea of "facing facts" was. Was there any chance they might include her?

Her stomach dipped and the heart in her chest kicked up a nervous beat. Licking her lips, she pushed away from him into a sitting position, taking the corner of the sheet with her to cover her breasts.

Amazing that she had an ounce of modesty left after everything they'd done together. But now that the burst of mindless lust had past, rational thought and doubts were creeping in.

"I'm hungry," she said, sliding out of bed and pulling on her robe. He'd fed from her, but she hadn't eaten in hours. "Do you want anything?" she asked all the same.

He shook his head, staying where he was, stretched out across the wide bed, staring at her through dark, hooded eyes. Ignoring the goose bumps that popped up along her arms at the sight of his wide chest and well-muscled abdomen, she padded barefoot into the hall and toward the kitchen.

She drank her first bottle of NuBlood standing in front of the refrigerator, like a football player swigging Gatorade between quarters. For the second, she used a glass and sipped it more slowly.

She heard Sean before she saw him. He came

out of the bedroom to use the bathroom and a moment later appeared on the other side of the kitchen counter.

He was once again fully dressed, his jeans and shirt as rumpled as his sandy blond hair after nearly two days of wear while he'd been trapped in her apartment. Stuffing his hands in the front pockets of his pants, he rolled back on his heels and refused to meet her gaze.

The words, when they came, weren't a surprise. She'd known what he was going to say from the moment she heard him get out of bed.

"I'm going to go," he said simply, quietly.

She nodded. Partly because she understood his desire to leave, to get out, to get some fresh air, so to speak, and clear his head. And partly because her throat was dry, tightening by increments to keep any sound from escaping.

Having him here with her, as a free-of-disease, live-forever immortal was supposed to bring them closer together, not drive him away. That had been Angelina's theory, anyway, but it looked like her plan was backfiring.

"I'm still not sure how I feel about all of this," he went on, "but I appreciate everything you've done. Helping me to understand, nursing my wounds."

He held his hands out in front of him, turning them over to show that there were no more burns, no sign of his earlier run-in with direct sunlight. Her eyes nearly watered at the sight. Not because he was healed or even because he'd been injured in the first place, but because it was yet another reminder that even though he was one of her kind now, there was a really good chance she would never see him again.

"I think I just need to . . . get back to my own place, give it some thought. Decide what I'm going to do from here on out."

She gave another short, half-nod while the pain in her chest grew and she wondered if a stake through the heart was the only thing that could kill a vampire. Maybe a plain old broken heart would do the trick just as well.

"Okay, then." He stuck his hands back in his pockets, then pulled them out again. Shifted from one foot to the other.

It was wrong, she knew, but a tiny sliver of satisfaction took up residence just under her rib cage. At least he was having trouble walking away. At least his conscience was nudging him just a millimeter or two toward guilt at leaving her when they really were spectacular together.

It wasn't a marriage proposal offered on bended knee, but it was something.

Finally, he managed to break through the tension sucking all of the oxygen out of the room and stride stiffly, sideways, toward the door. One step, followed by another, and then another.

With his hand on the knob, he cocked his head to look at her once more. His green eyes met hers for the briefest of moments and then he quickly muttered, "I'll see you around."

A second later, he was gone, the door closed firmly behind him as though he'd never been there at all.

*   *   *

"'*I'll see you around*'? *I'LL SEE YOU AROUND?!*'"

Vivian leaned back, very afraid Angelina's head was about to explode. She'd never seen her friend so aggravated. Her face was flushed, her eyes round as golf balls, and her long, red nails were actually leaving score marks in the top of the table where they were sitting.

After Sean had walked out of her apartment, she'd wandered around for a while, feeling numb and alone. When she'd started to feel antsy and guilty-slash-betrayed, the only thing she could think to do was call Angelina. The meddlesome woman may have been the cause of all her angst, but at least she knew what was going on and would hopefully understand.

Angelina had immediately suggested they meet, so here they were at Hallowed Grounds, a twenty-four-hour coffee shop that catered to night-dwellers like themselves—at least after sundown—for a cup of joe . . . or maybe a cup of O. Vivian had opted for both; one for the plasma, the other for the caffeine. Angelina was sticking with straight cappuccino.

"What kind of jerk-off says 'I'll see you around' after two bouts of hot sex and untold hours of coaching about *How to Be a Blood Drinker in Three Easy Steps?*" Angelina griped. And then she answered her own question. "A former sun-walker, that's who. *Humans*," she spat, as though it was a dirty word.

Unsure of whether she agreed with her friend's outrage or not, Vivian sipped her low-fat caramel frappuccino, saving the O-pos for later. Oh, she was sad and hurt, and those emotions tended to blend into anger, but she also understood how Sean must be feeling.

One minute, he'd been mortal; worse, a mortal facing his imminent mortality. The next, he'd woken up in a strange apartment with his ex-secretary hovering over him, telling him he was a vampire. Put that way, she was a little surprised he hadn't screamed in terror and exited stage left.

"He was overwhelmed," she told Angelina, leaping to his defense. "He barely had twenty-four hours to come to terms with his new reality. That can't be easy."

Angelina scoffed. "But he had enough time to bang you like a tambourine, right? And he certainly took to the whole bloodsucking thing quickly enough."

Vivian's hand flew up to cover the faint bite marks on her neck like a human would try to hide a hickey. She knew the holes were nearly invisible by now, but vampires could smell fresh wounds—even recently closed ones—from a mile away.

"Was he still trying to pull a guilt trip on you, or did you tell him he could end it any time he wants?"

She shook her head. "It never came up," she said quietly.

"Well, he'll figure it out soon enough. Everybody and their offspring knows how to do in a vamp, thanks to Bram Stoker and his ilk."

"I hope he doesn't, though," Vivian whispered. She couldn't imagine a world without Sean Spicer in it. Didn't want to live in that world. Even if she couldn't be with him, at least she could know he was out there somewhere, safe and happy and making a life for himself.

"I know," Angelina whispered comfortingly, changing her tune and reaching out to pat her hand. "Believe me, I know. You love him, and no matter what, you want him to be safe and happy."

Tears sprang to Vivian's eyes, and she swallowed hard to hold them back. She gave a jerky nod, unable to force words past her tight throat.

"You know what you need?" Angelina asked, leaning back and using both hands to take a drink from her bright orange, oversize coffee cup.

The split-second change in tone and demeanor—not to mention the question—was so typical of Angelina, Vivian smiled. It was a crooked, watery smile, but a smile all the same.

"What do I need, Angelina?"

"You need to shake off the doldrums, forget about that brainless beefcake for a while, and have some fun." Her giant cup clinked against the matching orange saucer as she set it down.

"Come with Ian and me to Connor Drake's Christmas party next week. It's the first he's ever thrown, thanks to a new love interest. She's mortal, but since I'm the one who set them up, we won't hold it against her," she added with a wink. "She actually seems to be quite good for him, and I'd venture to say he's nearly ecstatic about inviting everyone to Drake Manor for a good, old-fashioned holiday get-together."

Vivian opened her mouth to refuse, then paused. She wasn't sure she was up for a party just yet . . . but then again, maybe getting out of her apartment and mingling with a few fanged friends for a while was exactly what she needed.

"I'll think about it," she said instead.

"Good enough," Angelina replied, letting her off the hook more easily than she would have expected for the headstrong matchmaker and consummate buttinski.

Grabbing her purse, Angelina dug around for enough loose bills to cover both their orders and tossed them on the table. "Now let's blow this pastry stand and go do something more interesting than talking about the fickleness of men."

"Like what?" Vivian asked, standing to shrug into her long woolen coat.

Angelina grinned, a devilish spark glinting in her sapphire eyes. "Shoe shopping!"

TYPE B-NEGATIVE

Sean sat at a table at the very back of the club. Of all the names its owners could have come up with to call the place, they had picked Club Dead.

He nearly rolled his eyes. Real original. And if they were hoping to fly under the radar, they'd failed miserably. But then, judging by the patrons of Club Dead, they weren't looking to blend in.

It had taken him all of five minutes to Google local vampire hangouts, and if that hadn't pointed him in the right direction, all the black leather, excessive piercings, and bulging bad-assery would have.

Every stereotype imaginable surrounded him. Long black capes and pale skin. *Matrix*-like getups mixed with outfits that looked as though they'd stepped straight out of the 1800s. The women, especially, seemed enamored of white blouses and black bustiers that turned them into modern-day, top-heavy pirate wenches.

Maybe he'd chosen the wrong bar for his first foray into vampire society, he thought, swirling the dark liquid in the highball glass in front of him as the loudest techno-punk he'd ever had the displeasure of hearing burst his eardrums over and over again. The learning curve was steep, to say the least.

After leaving Vivian's penthouse, he'd hopped a cab back to his own apartment and holed up for a while in the dark, trying to make sense of everything that had happened. He was past denying that he'd been changed, physically, in a fundamental way. Now he was simply trying to figure out how he felt about it . . . and how he was going to move forward from here.

Could he go back to work, or would he have to find something else to do? How was he going to tell his family and friends who'd known about his illness and were bracing for his imminent demise that he was both cured *and* going to live forever? (Surprise!)

What bothered him most, though, and seemed to plague him both day and night . . . yes, during both his waking and sleeping hours, even though the two were now flipped . . . was Vivian.

As furious as he'd been with her in the beginning, sex hot enough to scorch his bone marrow had a way of dampening it a bit. And a part of him—a really deep, dark, intense part of him— wanted to stay with her, be with her, maybe even . . . Well, the L-word came to mind.

He wasn't sure he could trust his feelings right now, though. If his transformation from *homo sapiens* to *blood-o suckiens* was powerful enough to change his love of sun and sand to an inherent fear of it, and his disgust at the idea of drinking blood to a craving for it, how could he know his heart and head hadn't been changed, as well?

Vivian had worked for him for over two years, and though he'd stolen glances at her tommy-knockers or admired her rear end in a tight skirt from time to time, he'd never once considered having an affair with her.

Okay, so that wasn't entirely true. The thought had crossed his mind once or twice, he was sure, but only in the most superficial, "Dear Penthouse . . ." sort of way. But not in terms of asking her out to dinner, getting to know her on a more personal level, and possibly building a relationship.

The encounter in his office the night he'd told her he was leaving-slash-dying had been—he'd thought—a fluke. A very passionate, very enjoyable fluke, but still just a one-night stand.

He was never supposed to see her again, let alone wake up in her apartment with a freaking giant red ribbon strung across his chest and someone else's blood pumping through his newly immortal veins.

But no matter how hard he tried, he *could not* get her out of his head. He wanted to go back to her apartment and kiss her, stroke her, bury himself inside her as far as he could go, and drive them both over the edge. He wanted to talk with her and let her teach him more about this undead thing. There were things she could tell him that he wouldn't hear anywhere else, and the idea of spending the next twenty, fifty, *three hundred* years with her, learning them all wasn't a terrible one.

Which is what had him feeling a little shaky. Before he went back to her on the basis of simply the best sex *ever*, he needed to know if that's all it was—terrific sex—or if it was more. If it was *Vivian* who called to him and made him think that maybe drinking blood and living forever wouldn't be so bad as long as he could do them with her.

He tossed back the rest of his drink. After a bit of taste testing, he'd discovered he liked a nice lukewarm human (*gack!* the concept still made him squirm, even though he knew it came from entirely willing donors) AB-negative best, but could tolerate or even enjoy other blood types, as well as several of the synthetics that were more readily available. Standing, he made his way onto the dance floor. The music throbbed through the room, rattling his molars, and the crush of bodies filling the high-ceilinged bar raised the temperature of the room by at least twenty degrees.

Though he hadn't gone full Goth—it would take a lot more than suddenly discovering he was a vampire to send him that far onto the dark side—he'd been smart enough to dress the part of both a club goer and a vamp. Slicked-back hair, leather jacket over a dark blue silk shirt, and a pair of Ferragamos he hardly ever wore.

He looked smooth, if he did say so himself. And judging by the looks he was getting from some of the women crowded around him, they agreed.

Good. It would make this little experiment easier.

Sauntering up to a tall, supermodel-sexy blonde, he started to sway with her in time to the throbbing, thumping music. Her makeup was heavy, her eyebrow pierced, and he'd bet a year's salary her breasts were Play-doh.

How did that work? he wondered briefly. If vampires healed almost immediately, how did their bodies react to foreign objects implanted under the skin? Or had she done the op before her transformation, so they stuck?

Whatever. He had more important things to worry about at the moment, and it wasn't like he was in the market for a boob job himself. Not today, at any rate.

The woman smiled, letting him know she was interested. It had been a long time since he'd played this game, but he still knew when he was getting the green light from a willing female.

Shifting closer, he let her breasts bump his chest and slid a hand behind the curtain of her long hair to tug her forward. Still moving with the beat of the current song—if migraine-inducing noise could even be called such a thing—he covered her mouth with his own, letting his tongue slide past her lips. Tasting, tangling, waiting for sparks and flares and the rocket's red glare.

Nothing.

He pulled back, straightened, and waited for attraction or arousal to strike. The blonde was still grinning like a hungry crocodile.

"Sorry," he shouted over the music as he shook his head. "I have to go."

Without waiting for her reaction, he waded deeper into the crowd, trying again. He went for a brunette this time. Short, gel-spiked hair, a row of silver studs dotting the entire curve of one ear, a silver dangle brushing her bare shoulder from the single hole in the other. A nose ring, and a surprisingly feminine rose tattoo showed over the top of her stiff, form-fitting black-and-red bustier.

Normally, he would have steered clear of someone like her, since he was pretty sure she was tougher than he was and maybe even had bigger balls hidden in those skin-tight leather pants. But now that he was packing some of that super strength that came with being an otherworldly being, he figured that even if he couldn't take her, he could at least hold his own. That was, if she took exception to his advances and decided to coldcock him.

When she grabbed him first, however, rubbing and gyrating against him, he knew the chances of that were slim. Her eyes were dark and flat, her mouth a thin, emotionless line. But that didn't stop her from closing in and sticking her tongue down his throat.

Maybe it was her overly aggressive demeanor. Maybe it was the fact that he wasn't normally attracted to her type. Whatever the case, he felt nothing. No zip, no flash of excitement, and definitely nothing below the equator.

She didn't seem to mind at all when he backed away, simply turned to dance—and possibly make out—with the next available guy.

He scanned the crowd, looking for someone, *anyone* who could get his motor running. One song ended and another began. Not that Sean noticed a discernable difference.

A redhead. That's what he needed. He'd always had a penchant for redheads, and Vivian had gorgeous copper curls that made him hard just thinking about them. So it stood to reason that if any of the lady vamps milling about Club Dead tonight were going to flip his switch, it would be someone with similar hair, a similar build. . . .

It took him twice around the dance floor before he found someone who fit the bill. She was sitting at the bar, swirling the last half inch of a bright green martini instead of the blood or blood-related cocktail he would have expected.

Okay, good sign. She also smiled at him. Not a predatory or mocking smile, but one that seemed welcoming and sincere.

She was pretty, but nowhere near as beautiful as Viv. That was either an indisputable fact . . . or another sign that his feelings for Vivian might be genuine.

"Mind if I sit here?" he asked in a raised voice, gesturing to the empty, extra-tall stool to her left.

She shook her head and waved a hand, gesturing for him to help himself. He slid onto the cushioned seat, signaling for the bartender—a Chyna-like Amazon of a woman who looked as though she'd be more at home in a wrestling ring than serving drinks to the masses.

"NuBlood A for me, and another . . ." He paused, unsure of exactly what the green stuff was in her glass.

"Appletini," she provided helpfully.

Vivian would enjoy an appletini, he thought, digging cash from his wallet and sliding it across the bar. She didn't need it, and according to his research, it took *a lot* of alcohol to affect vampires the way it did humans. But he imagined she would enjoy the bright color and the mix of sweet and tart.

Stick another checkmark in the "Feelings for Vivian Might Be Real" column. Otherwise, he wouldn't know what kind of cocktail she'd like, and wouldn't give a flying fig either way.

Rather than go in for the kiss right off the bat, he sat with this woman—she introduced herself as Naomi—and chatted. It wasn't easy, given the decibel levels surrounding them, but they tried. And after a few minutes, when he realized he actually liked her, he simply asked for what he needed rather than forcing himself on her or trying to coerce her.

"Would you mind if I kissed you?" he said, moving closer so he wouldn't have to yell. "I need to know something about myself, so I'm conducting a bit of an experiment, and I . . . I just need to kiss you, if that's all right."

Her eyes widened a fraction. He didn't blame her; that couldn't be something a woman heard every day, and he was aware of how bizarre it sounded. Instead of making a break for it, though, she slowly nodded and let her lips go slack, waiting.

Leaning in, he pressed his mouth to hers. Soft at first, then more firmly. Her lips parted on a breathy sigh and he accepted the invitation, sliding his tongue along her teeth, then inside to taste and explore.

This kiss lasted longer than the others. He took his time, learning her texture and letting his fingers trail up and down her arm while their mouths continued to mesh.

Long minutes later, he pulled away.

"Thank you," he said gently. "I think I have my answer now."

And then he slid off the stool, downed the last of his drink, and walked out of Club Dead.

Type O-Negative

Vivian smiled until she thought her face would crack. She didn't want to be here, but Angelina had insisted.

Insisted? Ha! She'd all but dragged Vivian out of her apartment by the hair.

Calling until Vivian had wanted to scream and stopped answering the phone altogether. Showing up at her door three days before the party at Drake Manor to make sure Vivian had something appropriate in her closet, and when she didn't, forcing her practically at gunpoint to go shopping.

She had been informed, in no uncertain terms, that Angelina and Ian would pick her up in front of her building at precisely eight o'clock, and if she wasn't there, the couple would come after her. Words like *stake* and *dawn* and *holy water* had been tossed around. And though only two of the three could hurt her, she'd decided not to risk Angelina's apparently homicidal wrath.

Besides, it was just one night. She could grin and bear being out in public, out with happy, laughing people celebrating the holidays for one night. Her apartment would still be there when she got back. As would her unmade bed, her on-the-way-to-ratty robe, and the stash of synth, junk food, and sappy DVDs she'd been wallowing in for the past two weeks.

That's how long it had been since Sean had walked out and once again left her a lonely, pining mess.

Two weeks.

Fourteen days.

Well, thirteen days, eight hours, and . . . she tipped her arm—the one not holding a glass of thick, generously spiked eggnog—and checked her watch . . . twenty-seven minutes. Not that she was counting.

Christmas music played softly through the entire first floor of Connor Drake's expansive home. Vivian had never visited the mansion before; there was no reason she would have, since she knew only as much about the wealthy (vampire) restaurateur as she read in the paper or saw on the news.

She hoped the man wouldn't mind her crashing the party . . . and if he did, she was totally going to blame it on Angelina. Let her absorb the brunt of the man's displeasure while Vivian made a run for it.

"You're not going to meet anyone standing in the corner by yourself," Angelina chastised, coming up beside her with her own flute of champagne.

As usual, Angelina was more gorgeous than just about any other woman in the room. She had a very glamorous, Catherine Zeta-Jones look about her, her makeup always movie star perfect, never a hair out of place.

Vivian was no slouch in the looks department herself, but where she got home from work and traded her nicer clothes for a comfortable shorts and cami set, she couldn't imagine Angelina crawling into bed in anything less than the sexiest, most luxurious lingerie like some twenty-four/seven Victoria's Secret model.

Still, Angelina's keen fashion sense was the only reason she wasn't fidgeting with her own dress and accessories right now. While she'd stood there pretty much like a department store mannequin, her friend had held gown after gown up to her, quickly accepting or dismissing colors and styles.

After trying on a handful of the acceptable choices, Angelina had given an enthusiastic thumbs-up to a red strapless number that even Vivian had to admit was spectacular. It was simple but sexy, and a few well-chosen pieces of gold-and-diamond jewelry—well, cubic zirconia, she could afford the real stuff if she wanted, but didn't see the point in wasting money on a necklace and earrings she would probably never wear again—pushed it over the line into va-va-va-voom.

Rather than making her feel empowered and desirable, however, the outfit threatened to depress her even further. The only person she wanted to wear something like this for was Sean, and he was nowhere around to see it.

"I'm not here to meet someone," she informed Angelina. Not that she hadn't told the woman roughly the same thing nine hundred and fifty-seven times before. In the past two days alone.

"Sweetie, if that man were going to come back to you, he'd have done it by now. I have to say, I'm regretting ever changing him, given how ungrateful he's turned out to be." Her fuck-me red lips—nearly the same shade as Vivian's dress—twisted into a pouting moue. "You would think a man who'd been given a second chance at life *and* at a beautiful woman who loves him would be a bit more appreciative."

Vivian's stomach tightened at her friend's flippant remark. Yes, Sean was gone. And in time, she would come to accept that. It shouldn't take more than two, maybe three hundred years, tops.

But even so, even if her broken heart never mended, she truly did take comfort in the knowledge that he was out there somewhere, healthy and alive and—she hoped—happy.

"But since your Sean seems incapable of showing a bit of simple gratitude, you need to get over him and move on."

At that, Vivian's stomach didn't just tighten, it threatened to revolt. Angelina meant well, she knew that, but it didn't make her unsympathetic remarks hurt any less. And she was *sooooo* not ready to move on.

If Sean had walked out of her apartment and her life centuries rather than only weeks ago, she *still* wouldn't be ready. Not while her chest felt as though it were filled with rusty nails and the image of his handsome face still came to her so clearly when she closed her eyes.

Before she could voice as much, however, Angelina wrapped a manicured hand around her elbow and steered her through the crowded ballroom. She was introduced first to the party's hosts, Connor Drake and Jillian Parker.

Though Angelina mentioned that Jillian was an events planner, and almost solely responsible for the evening's gathering, it was clear the petite brunette was more than that to Mr. Drake. They were standing too close, and his hand at her waist was too proprietary for them to be simply business acquaintances. Add to that the fact that she was literally the only human in a roomful of openly vampish vamps—without being hog-tied in the middle of a dinner table with an apple in her mouth—and the nature of their relationship was obvious.

Connor's younger siblings, Liam and Maeve, were also in attendance. While everyone else was dressed in their holiday finery—classic suits and elegant cocktail dresses—they'd opted for T-shirts and leather. Although the girl's tights were red and green, and her top did have a sprig of mistletoe embroidered on the front with a sad-looking black cat sitting beneath.

From there, Angelina dragged her from unattached male to unattached male, whispering, "Trust me, darling, this is what I *do*" more than once.

Vivian didn't care that Angelina was a professional matchmaker. She didn't care that she was good at her job, or that hundreds of vampire couples were now living their *Dark Shadows*-meets-*The Brady Bunch* happily ever after because of her.

If she were in the market for a romantic setup, Angelina would have been her first phone call, without a doubt. But since she wasn't, her friend's interference—as well-intentioned as she knew it was meant to be—was simply annoying.

Once Angelina got something into her head, though, there was no shaking her off . . . or so Vivian realized after her introduction to Undead Bachelor Number Five.

A booming, Dr. Phil–like Texas drawl sounded in her head, *How's that working' for ya?*

Definitely not well. So if balking at Angelina's demands that she climb back up on the dating horse weren't working, she needed to change her strategy. Either that or risk being paraded around the rest of the night like a high-priced call girl up on the auction block.

And so, when her friend trotted her over to stand in front of Undead Bachelor Number Six— also known as Ben—Vivian pasted a bright smile on her face and acted delighted to meet him.

"Hi, Ben," she greeted him. "I'm Vivian."

They shook, and his grip was firm, his skin warm . . . undoubtedly from the fresh B-neg cradled in his other hand. She asked what he did for a living. Contrary to popular belief, vampires did not all reside in dank caves and spend their waking hours terrorizing humans; very few of them did, in fact. Instead, most of them held down normal—albeit nocturnal—jobs, the same as anyone else.

Most of them also tended to be fairly well off, since they were able to squirrel away money year after year, decade after decade. She imagined banks weren't too keen on having an overabundance of immortal customers, given the interest that could build up on such hefty accounts after that amount of time, but that didn't keep them from accepting her kind's business.

Ben was in real estate, and quickly launched into a lengthy discourse about the state of the market and some of the properties he currently represented. Vivian couldn't have been less interested, but pretended to hang on every word while humming along with "Holly Jolly Christmas," the carol currently playing over the sound system in her head and randomly reciting lines of poetry by Keats and Poe.

It was ironic, really, that mortals had such a dark, mysterious, larger-than-life impression of vampires. Little did they realize that blood drinkers could be just as boring and self-absorbed as humans . . . more so, even, because they'd been around longer and had so many more lame-ass stories to tell. She was sure that if she asked, Ben would be able to tell her *ad nauseum* about the housing market back in 1842, as well.

Taking a sip of her eggnog, she slanted a glance at Angelina. Her friend was watching her, carefully monitoring her body language and facial expressions. Still smiling, Vivian gave a small nod, relieved when Angelina beamed and slowly started to back away, leaving her alone with Ben.

An hour later, she was caroled out, and there wasn't one more line of poetry on the planet for her to run through. If Jolly Old Saint Nicholas himself had burst through the ceiling to run over her with his sleigh and all eight reindeer, she would have welcomed the distraction.

Yet when Ben kindly asked her if she'd like a

ride home, she accepted. Not so much because she wanted to spend more time in his company, but because she didn't think she could stand another second stuck inside Drake Manor with all these shiny, happy people.

It was a lovely home and a lovely party; very traditional and Christmasy, which she gathered had been Connor's purpose in hiring his new party-planner-turned-love-interest in the first place. And if she'd been in a different frame of mind, she was quite sure she'd have enjoyed herself.

But at the moment, she just wanted to go home—without Angelina snapping at her heels and hounding her to "move on" every step of the way.

So she let Ben collect her wrap and lied through her teeth when she whispered to Angelina that she and Ben had really hit it off and were going back to her place. Judging by the vamp-who-ate-the-housekeeper grin spreading across Angelina's face, the fib had just bought her at least forty-eight hours of being left the hell alone. After the holidays, she would confess to her friend that she'd made it all up and ditched Benny Boy at the curb.

Twenty minutes later, Ben's sporty little car purred like a kitten as he pulled up to said curb. Before he could cut the engine and offer to see her safely inside—no doubt for a nightcap that he fully expected to lead to more . . . yeah, fat chance, buddy—she had her door open and was stepping onto the sidewalk.

"Thanks for the ride," she told him, ignoring his dropping jaw and whatever he might have tried to say if she hadn't slammed the door in his face.

Her heels clicked on snow-dampened cement as she hurried up the walk, silently cursing Angelina for making her go out on the coldest night of the year in a dress that barely covered her ass, and a wrap that did next to nothing to protect her bare shoulders and chest. Maybe she should rethink this whole "Angelina is my friend" business.

She yanked open the front double doors and stomped inside, ready to get upstairs to her apartment where she could be warm and dry and out of the three-inch heels that were beginning to give her both blisters and bone spurs. Letting herself into the penthouse, she relied on her excellent night vision rather than turning on the lights as she kicked off her shoes and crossed the sprawling living room area.

Stars sparkled in the clear black sky outside the floor-to-ceiling windows, and here and there across the wide expanse were red and green Christmas lights dotting the blanket of black.

She dropped her wrap over the back of the sofa, then padded to the windows, admiring the view while she reached beneath her skirt to remove the annoyance of her pantyhose, then behind her back to unzip her dress.

"Nice," came a low voice from the other side of the room, scaring her half out of her panties. "If I'd known you were going to strip, I'd have brought more one dollar bills with me."

TYPE AB

Vivian yipped ... actually yipped like some frou-frou pocket Chihuahua ... and spun around to find Sean standing in front of the fireplace.

Even though the room was dark, her exceptional night vision let her see him clear as day. He looked as if he'd just come from a party, too. He was wearing dress slacks and an expensive blue silk shirt, hair slicked back in a style she'd rarely seen.

The lights from the Christmas tree in the corner were reflected on the shiny surface of his leather jacket and on either side of his tall frame, old-fashioned red-and-white stockings hung from the mantel. She wasn't exactly Suzy Snowflake, but she'd thrown up a few decorations to make it feel more like the holidays inside her private, lonely space.

"Geez," she swore, pressing a hand to her chest where her heart was still pounding. "You scared me half to death."

His brows lifted at her turn of phrase, and she

rolled her eyes. "You know what I mean. What are you doing here?"

"Hoping you'll keep going with your little striptease," he murmured with a crooked, suggestive half-smile.

Normally, that grin would have shot straight to her core, warming her and making her want to climb him like a monkey in a mango tree. But not now. Not with a million questions swirling through her brain and her emotions so rattled, she felt like Sybil on a bad day.

"What are you *doing* here?" she asked again without a trace of humor.

After the way he'd left, she hadn't expected to ever see him again. Hadn't let herself *hope* to ever see him again. Yet here he was, in her apartment, standing no more than ten feet from her.

She licked her dry lips, waiting for him to respond. Maybe he was here to kill her. You know, to exact revenge for her part in turning him against his will.

Or maybe he was here for more vampire lessons. As far as she was aware, he didn't know any other immortals, at least not personally. He might be planning to use her as a real-life *Encyclopedia of the Undead, A to Z.*

She wasn't sure how she would feel about that. About seeing him and talking to him on a regular basis, but not being able to *be* with him. It would be just like before, when he'd been her boss and she'd been his personal secretary, so it would certainly be something she was familiar with . . . but she didn't know if she could go back to something platonic, something meaningless after what they'd shared.

"I came to see you," he replied after a moment of tense silence.

Yeah, she'd gotten that much. If he'd wanted to see the Dalai Lama, he'd be in a completely different apartment.

"Bet you didn't know I could pick locks, huh?" he said, flashing her another amused glance. "Chalk it up to a misspent youth."

When she didn't respond, he cleared his throat and stepped forward. Moonlight spilled over his face, illuminating his green eyes and strong, slightly stubbled jaw.

"You were out," he murmured. "At a party?"

He wanted to talk about the party. Her ears were ringing, and she felt as though she'd stepped through the looking glass, but he wanted to talk about where she'd been.

She nodded stiffly. "Christmas party. Angelina made me go. Said I needed to get back on the horse."

He raised a brow at that. "Horse?"

"You left. I was upset. She thought meeting someone new might help."

"A man, you mean. She was trying to set you up with another man."

She couldn't tell if he sounded jealous or amused, so she simply shrugged. "She is a professional matchmaker. It's kind of what she does."

"That, and turning people into vampires," came his flat reply.

Vivian sighed. Her eyes fluttered closed. Her

hold on the bodice of her dress loosened until the material began to slip and she quickly grabbed it tight again.

So that's why he was here. Not to declare his undying love for her, or even to tell her he'd come to terms with his new immortal existence and wanted to remain friends.

Friends, *blech*. She didn't want to be friends with him. She wanted to be his love toy . . . or have him be hers. Not that she wouldn't take plain old friendship if that was all he was willing to offer, but "friends with benefits" definitely wasn't at the top of her Wish List when it came to being with Sean.

No, he was still pissed about being turned to begin with. And apparently he felt the need to come back and rub her nose in it a bit more. Like her guilt wasn't already the size of Godzilla destroying the city.

"Look, Sean," she finally said, opening her eyes and pulling her shoulders back. She was so tired of this, she literally could not take any more. "I'm sorry for what Angelina did. I'm sorry that I confided my feelings for you to a friend and that she took it upon herself to turn you into something you don't want to be. I didn't ask her to do it and would have tried to stop her if I'd known what she was planning, but there's nothing I can do now."

Taking a deep breath, she barreled on with words she really didn't want to utter, but knew needed to be said. "If you hate it so much, you'll just have to do something about it. Walk into the sunrise, throw yourself on a chair leg, whatever. It will be quicker than the tumor was going to take you, that's for damn sure."

Her chest was tight as she stood there, barely breathing, her stomach sinking by degrees like an elevator car in slow motion. With every second of heavy, awkward silence that passed, the elevator dropped another floor.

Finally, Sean shifted, his leather jacket squeaking as he crossed his arms over his wide chest. "Are you finished?"

Not quite the response she'd expected, but . . . "Yes."

"Good," was his firm response. Then he dropped his arms and crossed the carpeted floor to stand only inches in front of her.

She could feel the heat of his body . . . a nice, sizzling warmth that told her he must have fed—or drunk—recently. His hand came up, his fingers brushing through the hair at her temple, and her eyes drifted closed again.

Oh, lord, he smelled good. And felt good. And looked good. He even sounded good, his heart beating strongly in his chest.

"I've done a lot of thinking these past two weeks," he said softly, still stroking her hair and the side of her face. "I can't say I was thrilled when I woke up here and you started telling me about how I'd been changed, what my life would be like from that point on. But I'm kind of used to it now. I've still got a lot to learn, I'm sure, but sunbathing or committing hari-kari isn't something I'll be contemplating anytime soon, believe me."

With his other hand, he lifted her chin and waited for her to open her eyes. When she did, his own beautiful, sea-green eyes were staring down at her, and she had to bite her lip to keep from sobbing.

"What we have is amazing. The way I feel when I'm around you is something I've never felt with anyone else. You make me feel stronger, better, more alive than ever before. And I mean *ever*. Before your friend bit me or after."

He chuckled at that, and the elevator stopped. Stopped drifting down to the soles of her feet and started slowly moving upward instead.

"I was worried that was the newly formed vampire side of me talking, though. When I woke up—after the transformation—everything was louder and brighter and sharper. How could I know that what we shared wasn't just another aspect of that? How could I be sure that hot human sex didn't simply translate into even hotter vampire sex?"

Well, that wasn't very flattering, she thought. But he was touching her and whispering softly, and whatever he had to say, she wanted to hear.

"So after I left your apartment, I decided to find out."

Oh, that was nice of him.

Wait.

What?

She took a step back, pulling away from his warmth and the stroke of his hand. *Whimper.*

"What do you mean you 'decided to find out'?" she demanded. "You went out and *slept with other women?*"

She shouldn't be upset. She had no right to be, even if the thought of him with other women—in bed or out—made her want to bite their necks and *not* bring them back from the brink of death. Rip out their intestines and use them to make macramé plant holders. File some pieces of driftwood into nice, sharp points and play a round of pin-the-stake-on-the-bimbo.

She knew her gaze was blazing, could feel the blood boiling behind her eyeballs, turning them an unhealthy shade of pink—even for a vampire. But Sean didn't seem to notice. Instead of being intimidated, he simply stepped forward to once again close the distance between them, and re-sumed caressing her cheek and the side of her throat.

"I didn't sleep with them, no. But I needed to know if I would respond the same way to any fe-male vamp . . . or if it was you."

Licking her lips, she swallowed. "And . . . ?"

"I went to a club. A vampire club. And I met some women."

She raised a brow, half in curiosity, half in an-noyance. He couldn't just come and tell her, could he? Oh, no, he had to draw it out, share the whole sordid story from start to finish.

"You know that saying 'You have to kiss a lot of frogs to find your prince'? Or in this case, *princess.* Well, I did. Kiss a lot of frogs, that is."

She pictured a row of women lined up, waiting for a kiss from Sean. And then—*poof*—every single one of them sprouted a slimy green, wart-covered frog face. It was rather appealing, actually.

"*And . . . ?*" she prompted again, getting really antsy now. The pressure behind her eyes was build-ing and the blood in her veins was beginning to boil, prickling beneath her skin.

He tipped his head, his lips curving slightly as

he stared down at her. "Frogs, every one of them. I even tried one with curly red hair and pouty pink lips who reminded me of you."

His smile widened, and he traced the outer edge of her lower lip with his thumb. "Nothing. Looks like you're my princess, vampire or no vampire."

Stakes be damned. Her heart melted at his words, right there on the spot. Any signs of anger or jealousy receded, replaced by a feeling so big, so wonderful, she wasn't sure her body could contain it all.

"That's why I'm here," he continued. Reaching into his jacket pocket, he pulled out a wad of something red and wrinkled. "I thought you might be willing to let me stay with you again, maybe even move in. Keep teaching me all the in*s* and out*s* of this immortality gig."

He shook his arm and the red, wrinkled thing expanded, falling halfway to the floor. It was the ribbon. The big, red ribbon, complete with sadly flattened and wrinkled bow, that he'd been wearing when she'd found him on her sofa. Dipping his head, he draped it over one shoulder and across his chest, Mr. America–style.

"Merry Christmas," he said. "If you'll have me."

If she'd have him? She'd only spent the last two years lusting after him until she thought she'd go insane.

She didn't bother with words. Couldn't, because her throat was so thick with emotion.

Instead, she threw her arms *and* her legs around him, hugging him tight as she kissed him and kissed him and kissed him. Light pecks along his jaw and cheekbones, harder presses of her lips to his.

"I'll take that as a yes," he chuckled when she let him up for air.

"Yes. Oh, yes," she told him, hanging onto his neck, held up by his hands on her bottom and her ankles locked behind his back. "Do you have any idea how long I've been in love with you? How long I've waited for you to be here with me like this?"

"Yeah," he murmured quietly, "I think I do. It just took a pesky little brain tumor and a meddlesome vampire matchmaker to help me see it."

He kissed *her* this time, for a long time. A long, drawn-out kiss that melted her bones and scrambled her senses.

When he released her, his breathing was ragged and his mouth was twisted in a lopsided, self-deprecating grin. "I get it now, though. And the good news is that we've got forever—literally *forever*—to make up for lost time."

She smiled back. Beamed was more like it. "That is one of the up sides of being immortal."

Walking her backward toward the bedroom, he said, "I'm starting to notice a lot of up sides to being immortal. We may have to send that friend of yours a fruit basket to thank her for turning me."

Vivian laughed. "Angelina would probably prefer something a bit fresher. And breathing."

"A dozen ripe young co-eds it is, then," he teased, and they both laughed as he dropped her into the center of her wide bed, then followed her down.

"I'm so glad you came back," she said, running her fingers through his blond hair, reveling at his weight covering her like a warm, soft blanket and pressing her into the mattress. "You're the best Christmas present I've ever gotten."

"Ditto, sweetheart. And there's so much more to come."

Oh, she was counting on it.

IT'S A WONDERFUL BITE

SIP ONE

Christmas Eve

The soft, instrumental strains of "O Holy Night" filled the large dining room, mingling with the sounds of voices and laughter from the guests seated at the great mahogany table. In one far corner, a giant Douglas fir just missed brushing the high ceiling with its snow-dotted angel topper, twinkling clear lights, and sparkling blue and white glass ornaments.

In the fireplace, a stack of fresh logs blazed, and pine boughs dotted with red velvet bows framed the eggshell-white mantel. A line of tall, white candles flickered softly in a straight line down the center of the long dining table, and there was even a healthy sprig of mistletoe hanging above both entryways to the room.

It was a perfect holiday gathering.

Angelina Ricci took a sip of claret, using the maroon-tinted crystal, almost as dark as the wine it held, to hide her smile. She'd done it again, and if it wouldn't have ruined the lines of her brand-new Dolce and Gabbana gown, she would have reached around and patted herself on the back.

Granted, Connor—their host for the evening—had come to her looking for someone to help plan and execute the perfect Christmas holiday, but *she* had been the one to send the lovely Jillian Parker his way.

Connor might be a vampire, and Jillian might be exceedingly human—at least at the moment—but it hadn't taken long for sparks to fly from more than a faulty string of lights. Literally. They had known each other only a matter of weeks before Jillian had moved into Drake Manor in more than just a party-planning capacity. Connor had even allowed her to bring her cat, which was a sure sign he was feet over fangs in love.

And the fact that Connor's two younger siblings were sitting at the table with them this evening was another testament to how well Jillian fit into the Drake family. Not only did she accept their undead qualities, but she'd managed to win over Liam and Maeve, who until recently had seemed to make it their eternities' work to drive Connor into an early coffin.

Since Jillian's arrival, however, they'd come to get along with their older brother better, as well as moving out of the family mansion to pursue interests of their own. Interests other than partying and causing trouble, that was.

Liam, it turned out, was an excellent cook. Ironic, given he didn't need food to survive, *and* because he'd so often mocked others' need or enjoyment of the stuff. But it had been Connor's success at running a string of five-star restaurants of his own, both nationally and internationally, that had caused the young man to hide his talents in the first place. Liam hadn't wanted to be compared to his older brother, especially if he set out on his own.

But while Connor hadn't handed anything to Liam on a silver platter, he'd made it clear he would support his brother in every way possible— starting with a job at one of his own downtown Boston eateries. At the moment, Liam was merely a sous chef, working under and taking orders from others. But from what she'd heard, he was well on his way to becoming an executive chef, and one day possibly even opening his own restaurant.

Maeve had gone in a completely different direction. She'd moved into an oversized apartment in a renovated warehouse in the harbor area and turned it into a home/art studio, where she created paintings and sculptures that were already getting a bit of buzz in the art world. Her first gallery showing was scheduled for the new year, and word had it her pieces were being marked in the high thousands.

And at least for tonight, both siblings had foregone their obsessions with leather and torn clothes, piercings and tattoos.

Maeve wore a short black skirt and ankle boots with a youthful red shell and sweater set. She looked for all the world like a bank teller or school teacher—except for a few bits of large, unique jewelry Angelina suspected she might have designed herself, and the random streaks of pink in her black, upswept hair.

Liam wore a casual black suit, his dark hair only moderately (much less than usual!) gelled and spiked. In addition to wicked cooking skills and a great head of hair, the young man also had a great sense of humor, as evidenced by his wide blue tie with a giant image of Rudolph the Red-nosed Reindeer on it—complete with a tiny lighted bulb to showcase the cartoon character's glowing sniffer.

And the meal, everything a traditional Christmas Eve dinner should be, had also been generously prepared and provided by Liam. Angelina got the distinct impression he was showing off a bit, but Jillian hadn't stopped singing his praises since they'd sat down. Not only had his willing participation been part of the "perfect Christmas" Connor so desired—and that Jillian had promised to do her best to provide, both as a professional events planner and his shiny new girlfriend—but having a close family member take responsibility for tonight's dinner had freed her up to focus on other things, like decorations, invitations, and seating arrangements.

Yes, indeed, Angelina was the Queen of Matchmaking. True, her *official* dating agency, Love Bites, mostly worked to pair up vampires with other vampires, but she wasn't above putting her skills to use when she saw human/vamp match potential.

Connor and Jillian and Vivian and Sean hadn't even been clients of Love Bites. They were simply friends in need of a little romance, and she'd managed to work her magic yet again. Just in time for Christmas.

The last strains of "O Holy Night" trailed off and the first notes of "Silver Bells" began just as the Drake Manor staff cleared away everyone's dinner plates, serving decadent slices of chocolate sformato for dessert. *Ooh*s and *ahh*s went around the table at the sight of the baked pudding disk with almonds and Amaretto whipped cream. Liam's cheeks brightened at the bevy of praise directed his way, but Angelina suspected he was secretly delighted with the shower of compliments.

Digging into her dessert more slowly than the others, she considered her fellow dinner companions. They all looked so happy. And that was good. The love matches she'd made were solid ones. Many of the plans she'd put in motion (some more stealthily than others) seemed to be moving along at just the right romantic pace.

But while she was exceptionally proud of *all* her work and loved her job, she couldn't claim to be truly content. Not that she would ever admit such a thing to anyone . . . not even under threat of direct sunlight or a pointy stick.

How could she be happy or claim to be an expert on romance, though, when her own lover of more years than she'd been alive was *only* that— her lover? Ian Hart might be brave and strong and ruggedly—yes, ruggedly—handsome. He might even be better than chocolate and a jackrabbit vibrator in bed.

But he wasn't her husband.

And was it so wrong that she wanted to be married? That she didn't want to go the rest of her undead life being merely boyfriend and girlfriend?

It sounded pathetic. And for them, the rest of her life could be ten millennia.

Vampire or no vampire, she was still a woman. She still wanted the man she loved—and whom she was certain loved her—to declare his undying (ha!) love and make a commitment to her. More than simply living together. More than simply agreeing to a devoted, monogamous relationship.

She wanted more, dammit. The kind of more that came with a sparkling diamond ring and the exchange of heartfelt vows . . . maybe even a full-blown, old-fashioned wedding ceremony, if she could talk Ian into it.

Not that she had ever so much as broached the subject with him. It had seemed silly, given their current living arrangements, and she sort of wanted *him* to be the one to think of it, to ask her, to make a Grand Romantic Gesture.

But now, looking around the long dining table at some of her closest friends, who were paired off and beginning their own personal happily-ever-afters, she thought a memo or two might not be such a bad idea. Especially since Ian, who was extremely smart about some things, wasn't exactly Employee of the Month in the romance department. She loved him dearly, but in all the time she'd known him—and he had turned her, so they were talking a considerable number of years—he had never brought her flowers or planned a surprise party or gifted her with a piece of jewelry just because.

Another hour passed while dessert plates were cleared away and coffee was served. While guests carried their delicate china cups and saucers into

the library to gather around yet another beautifully decorated Christmas tree.

This burgeoning Douglas fir was twelve-to-
fifteen feet tall if it was an inch, with a brilliant
gold star at the top. Strands of blinking, multi-
colored lights sparkled amongst the dark green
needles and small red and gold glass bulbs.

It took some wheedling, but Jillian was finally
able to convince everyone to sing carols until the
clock chimed three, when the party started to
break up because all of the guests needed to get
home before sunrise or risk having a very *un*Merry
Christmas and zero chance at a Happy New Year.

They said their good-byes and thanked their
hosts for a lovely evening while Ian helped her
into her long, cream-colored woolen coat and
shrugged into his own short leather jacket. A second later, cold air slapped them in the face and
Angelina shivered as they stepped from the cozy
warmth of Drake Manor into the dark December
night.

Since the weather had been questionable even
before they'd left for the dinner party, they'd
opted to take Ian's black Chevy Suburban over her
sleek silver Mercedes. Always the gentleman, Ian
opened the passenger-side door and lifted her in,
then went around to climb in on the driver's side.

Angelina didn't speak until they'd gone a few
miles down the road and the heat blowing from
the vents on the dash had the inside of the SUV
toasty warm. Sliding off her gloves, she laid them
carefully on her lap.

"Well," she said quietly. "That was fun."

"Yeah."

A man of few words, that was her Ian. Reaching inside his jacket, he pulled out a pack of cigarettes, stuck one between his lips, and lit the tip. It wasn't a habit she encouraged, but since it wasn't going to hurt either one of them, she didn't bother pestering him to quit.

"Dinner certainly was delicious."

Another short, one-syllable reply. "Yep."

She slanted a glance in his direction. "You just want to get home so you can get out of that suit and tie, don't you?"

He cocked his head, taking his eyes off the road for only the fraction of a second it took to shoot her a cocky grin. "Yep."

She chuckled. Oh, yes, she knew him so well. And still she loved him. Still she wanted to be with him for their version of forever.

Only a handful of minutes later, he pulled into the driveway of the large, three-story Victorian they'd been sharing for the past decade. They'd refurbished it themselves—or most of it, anyway—and had a grand time doing it.

Given her taste in designer clothes and shoes, and her love of all things high style, from regular mani/pedis to biweekly visits to the salon, she knew the simplicity of her home would surprise many of her acquaintances. They probably thought she would settle for nothing less than a penthouse apartment overlooking Boston proper, or a large, affluent home on Beacon Hill with state-of-the-art everything.

But though it was old and creaky, and parts of it were still in disrepair, this house suited her. Partly because it was so much like Ian—rough around the edges, but solid and reliable and attractive in its own unique way.

Not waiting for Ian to come around, she opened her door on her own and met him at the front of the Suburban, where he waited and offered his arm to see her safely up the slick brick walk.

"Connor and Jillian and Sean and Vivian seem happy together, don't they?" she murmured as he unlocked the front door and let her pass inside before him.

"Uh-huh." He shrugged out of his jacket and draped it over one of the hooks on the coat tree in the corner of the small entryway. She handed him her coat and he hung it next to his own.

Sigh. Had she mentioned thickheaded? He could be extremely dense—sometimes intentionally, sometimes not.

She wasn't sure which was the case at the moment, but suspected she was going to have to drop much larger hints before Ian caught on to what she wanted from him in the very near future.

Typical of his evening routine, Ian trailed through the house, double-checking all the door and window locks. Angelina had never seen the need to be so security conscious, given that very little could harm them and the chances that they would hear a burglar trying to break in before he ever actually *got* in were extremely high. Heck, on a quiet night, they could hear silverware clacking as their nearest neighbors ate dinner half a mile away. But the cop in him couldn't go to sleep in the morning until he'd made his rounds and made sure everything was safe and sound.

When he was finished, they walked upstairs together and started getting ready for bed. As usual,
he flipped on the TV and started surfing channels
while he loosened the tie at his neck. A second
later, he set aside the remote control and some
very distinct Jimmy Stewart dialogue filled the
room.

"*It's a Wonderful Life?*" she asked from half inside
her walk-in closet, already knowing the answer. It
was one of his favorites, and he watched it every
time it was on.

"You know it."

"Every time a human screams . . ."

"A vampire gets its fangs," he finished.

She turned to find him grinning at their little
Wonderful Life inside joke, flashing his very own
pointy white incisors.

He'd ditched the tie, tossed his suit jacket over
the back of a chair, and was now working to undo
the buttons down the front of his dark green shirt.

It amazed her that after all these years, she
never tired of watching him strip. The sleek lines
of his well-built body. The pull and release of hard
muscle under smooth skin when he moved. God,
he was gorgeous. Thank goodness he'd been in
such good shape when he'd been turned, otherwise he might have been stuck in the body of a
pudgy couch potato for all eternity.

The same could be said for her, of course. She'd
been born with the body of a supermodel and had
luckily died—and come back—before a lifetime of
Papa John's pizzas and Dairy Queen Blizzards
could change that.

She even adored his stubbled skull, which he

hadn't died with and had to trim daily. It made him look all sexy and dangerous. And the dangerous, at least, served him well in his job as a cop for the BPD—something she would worry about if she didn't know he could A.) take care of himself, and B.) recover in a matter of hours from almost any injury, even the most fatal.

The only reason he wasn't also covered from head to toe with tattoos was that they hadn't been as popular before his turning as they were now. Although there were times, while working under-cover, that he would get a design or two stenciled on his skin.

It was usually something scary and with distinct gang affiliations, like a skull with snakes and flames shooting out of the eye sockets. The ink completely disappeared each evening with the set-ting of the sun, and he would have to have them done all over again, but while they were there, she always had fun tracing the lines and colors and playing out a few bad boy sexual fantasies.

Slipping out of her dress and heels and jewelry and hose, she put on one of her long, satin night-ies, turning just in time to see Ian climb under the covers butt naked. While she'd taken the time to hang her gown back in the closet and put her ear-rings away, he'd left his clothes in a wrinkled pile in the middle of the floor. She would either pick them up in the morning or they would lie there until their housekeeper came in to clean up after the holidays.

"I don't know why you bother putting those things on," Ian said from where he sat propped up against the headboard by a stack of big, fluffy pillows. "I'm just going to tear it off of you as soon as the movie's over, anyway."

The stark white sheets were pulled to his waist, leaving his broad chest and mouthwatering six-pack abs bare. And her mouth did water at the sight—as well as his suggestive comment.

"Oh. So movie first, then making love to me, hm?" she said, feigning offense as she sauntered across the thickly carpeted floor, climbing the two steps leading up to the very tall, antique four-poster bed with its intricately carved headboard and lace canopy. "Nice to know where I fall on your list of priorities."

She perched on the edge of the mattress and began smoothing a bit of moisturizing cream over her arms and legs. Behind her, the bed shifted and Ian's warm lips pressed against her bare shoulder. She didn't actually need moisturizer, as her skin was as naturally—or *un*naturally, as the case may be—soft as a baby's bottom, but she liked the ritual and the fruity mango fragrance.

"Hey, it's Christmas. I'll only get to see Clarence get his wings five or six more times before he and George disappear again for another year."

"Uh-huh. And you won't dig out your DVD in June or July for a bit of a refresher?" she teased, not bothering to glance back at him.

"Maybe. Now come here."

She gave a yelp as he wrapped a strong arm around her waist and hauled her back against his chest. A minute later, she was tucked into his side and they were both settled in to watch the end of the black-and-white film.

No matter how many times she'd seen it, it

never failed to tug at her heartstrings in all the right places.

Help me, Clarence, please. Please! I want to live again. Please, God, let me live again.

She sniffled as George Bailey started running through town, wishing everyone and his uncle a Merry Christmas. His realization that his life really was a wonderful one, regardless of its various problems and pitfalls, made her eyes grow damp and got her every time.

And Ian knew it, flexing his arm to hug her closer and press a kiss to the crown of her head. She suspected this part of the movie put a lump in his throat, he was just too much of a man to show it. Otherwise, why would he bother watching it multiple times every year?

As the film ended with a cheerful chorus of "Old Lang Syne" and the credits began to roll, Ian reached for the remote and clicked off the TV, sending the room into almost total darkness. When it came to vamps, though, that just meant *all the better to see you with, my dear.*

Rolling toward her, Ian pulled her away from the headboard and onto her back, readjusting the covers so they weren't trapped between them. She turned her face into the curve of his shoulder, inhaling the warm, musky scent of his skin with a hint of citrus and spice that was uniquely his.

"What do you want?" she whispered, knowing he would know exactly what she was saying.

He settled more fully between her open legs, covering her from chest to ankle like a warm blanket . . . one much softer and more comfortable than the actual blankets.

"What do I want?" he repeated, taking her lead and following one of their favorite bits of dialogue from *It's a Wonderful Life*. "Why, I'm just here to get warm, that's all."

"He's making violent love to me, Mother!" she called out, even though they were alone in the house and there was no one else around to hear.

His lips curved up in a grin, revealing long, pearly-white incisors that made him look wolfish and dangerous and *hot*. A skitter of longing raced down her spine and into all of her naughty bathing suit areas.

"Not yet," he told her. "But I certainly plan on it."

Lowering his head, his lips grazed her collarbone while beneath the sheets his hands wandered in the very best way. As it always did, his touch melted her from the inside out. When his mouth started to move along her throat and the lobe of her ear, she knew her brain cells weren't far behind.

"Ian," she murmured as her eyes started to drift closed and her lashes fluttered when she tried valiantly to keep them open.

"Hmmm?"

"Do you think the others will get married?" she asked before rational thought could forsake her completely.

"Others, who?"

His mouth closed on the taut muscle running down the side of her throat and she gave a low moan. He very nearly threw her off her train of . . . Train of . . . Were they on a train?

He released her, and blood sluggishly returned to her brain stem.

Oh, right.

"Connor and Jillian. Sean and Vivian."

"I don't know." he mumbled distractedly against her skin, and he didn't sound as though he cared. "Why?"

"It's what people do," she said slowly, struggling to keep her mind on track.

His hands were traveling over her breasts now, his mouth threatening to follow suit as he suckled at the hollow of her throat. Angelina tipped her head back and hummed, letting her eyes slide closed as prickles of sensation began to unfurl all along her nerve endings.

"When they're in love. Vampire or human . . . or a vampire/human mix . . . you'd think that if they love each other, eventually they'd want to get married."

"Mmm-hmm."

Ian nudged a knee between her legs, urging her to part, to widen. And she did, welcoming him into the cradle of her thighs while she let her fingers trail over his bulging biceps and strong, expansive back.

"You love me, don't you, Ian?" she asked softly.

He raised his head, brows pulled down slightly as he stared down at her with intense dark eyes. "Would I be here if I didn't?" he responded.

Which was as close to *I love you* as Ian got—and not at all the answer she'd been hoping for.

Did eighty-some years of passion and dedication mean nothing to him? Or had she made their relationship too easy for him, so that he didn't think that vows or a true commitment were necessary?

Wrapping her arms around his neck, she held him close and brought his mouth down to cover hers. He kissed her, and with a sigh she kissed him back.

She wasn't so much hurt as . . . disappointed. Although he'd reacted almost exactly as expected to her gentle prodding, she had to admit that she'd hoped for more.

It was Christmas, a time when emotions tended to be softer and closer to the surface. Was it such a stretch to believe Ian might finally decide to propose tonight of all nights, even if it was prompted by her foot in the middle of his back?

Yes, she supposed it was. Because he was a vampire, and had been for so long, he didn't think of himself as partly human anymore, or consider that he needed to be tied by human traditions.

Ironic, since he was a cop, and spent nearly every night upholding human laws. Though she suspected that had more to do with the strong beliefs instilled in him as a child, long before he'd been turned. Things with Ian always seemed to be black or white, right or wrong, good versus evil. Plus, he was a rough and tumble guy; given his super strength and immortality, she was pretty sure he just liked to take names and kick ass.

But as his callused palms skated up her hips and over her stomach, dragging her nightgown right along with them, she wondered how things might have played out between them if she and Ian weren't vampires.

Would they be together at all? She certainly hoped so.

Would they be married?

Would they have normal jobs that were most often done during daylight hours, like maybe being school teachers or lawyers or store clerks?

What about children? Would they have just put their overly excited two-point-five kids to bed with promises of Santa Claus coming down the chimney to leave presents under the tree by morning?

It all sounded so wonderful. And she wanted it . . . well, the parts she could realistically have . . . vampire or not.

For the next half hour, while Ian did his best to turn her thoughts to mush, a small spot in the very back of her brain couldn't help but wonder . . .

What would their lives be like if they'd never been turned?

SIP TWO

Angelina woke up the next evening, expecting to find herself in her own house, in her own bed, wrapped in Ian's arms, just as she'd been when she'd fallen asleep the morning before.

But when she opened her eyes, her vision immediately focused and twenty-twenty perfect, she didn't see the delicate lace canopy of her bed at home. Instead, she was staring up at a dirty, no-longer-even-close-to-white ceiling. One of those pockmarked jobs with the removable panels like in schools and office buildings.

From there, her eyes slid to ugly, striped and peeling wallpaper in shades of buzzard-barf brown, booger green, and mucus yellow. Upon further consideration, she decided "ugly" was too kind a term; it was truly *hideous*.

She knew without looking, and without taking into consideration the condition of the walls and ceiling, that whatever bed she was in, the mattress was lumpy and saggy, the sheets scratchy and cheap. She just prayed they were clean—though judging by the rest of the room, that was one prayer destined to go unanswered.

For a second, her eyes squeezed shut at the thought. *Ick.*

She started to sit up, opening them again, only to jerk back in startlement when she found another person—a man—sitting at the foot of the bed, pulling on his socks and shoes. He turned slightly, enough for her to see the side of his face, and she let out a relieved sigh.

It was Ian. *Whew.*

At the realization, her heart slowed its rapid beat and her pulse returned almost to normal. She wasn't sure what they were doing in this cheap, grungy . . . motel room? . . . but if he was here with her, then she knew everything must be okay.

He stood and fastened the button of his jeans, tucking his shirt into the waistband. "You better get up and get dressed," he told her. "We've only got the room for an hour."

An hour? *Ewww*, they were in one of those disgusting rent-by-the-hour no-tell motels? *Ewwwww.*

She shivered, her skin literally crawling at the thought of all the bodies that had been in this room, on these sheets, doing all manner of ungodly acts. And what might be *literally crawling* in the sheets because of it!

With a sound of disgust, she leapt out of bed and reached for the pile of clothes on the floor only a few feet away. The carpet, too, was dirty and matted and . . . *gah*, she didn't even want to be *standing* on it in bare feet, let alone climb into clothes that had been lying on the soiled fibers for the last fifty-odd minutes.

What in God's name were they doing here? And how did they even get here, when the last thing she remembered was riding Ian like a hobby horse before falling quite comfortably asleep in her own much nicer, much cleaner, much more appealing bed.

She reached for the first item of clothing on the pile and shook it out. A white, sleeveless undershirt. Feminine only by its size and slightly tapered style.

This was supposed to be hers?

When was the last time she'd worn an undershirt? Umm . . . can you say *never*? Never in her life, either before her turning or after. Never, never, had she worn such a pedestrian garment.

So maybe these clothes weren't hers.

A giant mental block as tall and wide as the Great Wall of China went up in her head, refusing to let her wander down the path of whose clothes they might be if they weren't hers. *Shudders.*

Looking around the room, however, there were no other clothes that could be hers. No other personal items whatsoever.

Standing near the battered dresser and ancient, even more battered television set that rested atop, Ian crossed his arms and shot her an annoyed glance. "What are you waiting for? We've gotta get a move on."

The man glaring at her might look like Ian Hart, but he sure didn't sound like him. She couldn't remember the last time Ian had been so short or annoyed with her. Maybe because he never had.

This was more confusing than the moment she'd awakened from a deep sleep full of bizarre, vivid dreams to discover she'd died and been raised again as a vampire. It had taken her weeks to get used to the idea, and to learn to function as a blood-drinking creature of the night. Yet that experience seemed like a walk in the park compared to this especially strange *Twilight Zone* episode.

Since she didn't have much choice, she quickly shrugged into "her" clothes. Snug blue jeans, the white tank-style undershirt, and a plaid flannel button-down over that.

Really? Plaid? Flannel? Where was she going from here—lumberjack camp?

Apparently. Because her shoes were a pair of worn brown ankle boots.

"Don't forget your piece," Ian said, coming up beside her and handing her . . .

A gun. A big, black gun tucked inside a complicated holster.

What the *hell* was going on?!

She didn't own a gun. She didn't like guns. She'd never even touched Ian's gun in all the years he'd been carrying one.

But he was standing there, holding it out to her as though he expected her to take it. Then he handed her something else—a ponytail scrunchie.

"Remember to pull your hair back again, or someone will get suspicious."

Who? Of what?

She had to get a grip and figure out what was going on.

"Just . . . give me one more minute," she told him, her voice weak and scratchy, but as strong as she could make it at the moment. Then she darted past him and around the end of the bed, into the bathroom on the far side of the cramped room.

Giving herself strict orders not to look too closely at her surroundings, she stood in front of the sink and studied her reflection as best she could in the cloudy, dirt-flecked mirror.

She looked like herself. Same long, straight black hair. Same dark blue eyes, glittering back at her now like hard, multifaceted sapphires. The clothes obviously belonged to Lesbian Barbie, but she *wasn't* having an out-of-her-body-and-into-someone-else's experience.

So it must be a dream. A really lousy, unamusing dream, but a dream she knew exactly how to wake up from.

Pulling her hair back, away from her face, she fixed it into a sleek ponytail with the fabric band Ian had given her. Then she took a deep breath, squared her shoulders . . . and pinched herself.

She felt it, but it didn't particularly hurt. Worse, it didn't change anything. She was still standing in the grungy bathroom in her uber-casual, log-splitting attire.

Okay, well, she was a vampire, so she didn't feel pain the way normal people did. Closing her eyes, she picked a more tender spot—the soft skin on the inside of her upper arm—and both pinched and twisted. Hard.

Tears came to her eyes, but it didn't change her nightmare circumstances.

Dammit.

"Ang!" Ian called from the other room. "Let's go."

She didn't know what the big hurry was, but she couldn't leave until she'd figured out what was going on. Or preferably woke up from this god-awful nightmare.

Catching sight of a silver clasp on the shoulder holster Ian had handed her before she'd escaped to the Powder Room of the Damned, she grabbed it and did the only thing she could think of that would *wake her up!*

She shoved up her shirtsleeve and scraped the sharpest edge along the underside of her forearm as hard as she could. Sharp pain shot through her entire body, making her gasp.

Blood pooled along the cut mark before slowly running over the curve of her arm and dripping into the scratched porcelain of the sink basin.

Okay, so the blood was no surprise; vampires were filled with the stuff. But such a tiny pinprick shouldn't hurt this much.

Granted, it wasn't a severed limb; she wasn't going to die from the wound, and the pain was already beginning to ebb. But it shouldn't have felt like that at all. A cut like she'd just given herself should have registered as no more than a mosquito bite on her pain level radar.

On top of that, she hadn't woken up. The pain she shouldn't have felt in the first place hadn't sent her spiraling out of this nightmare and back into her nice, warm, comfortable reality.

Lifting her arm to her mouth, she licked the long cut to seal it. But the blood against her tongue didn't taste quite the same as usual. Oh, it tasted like blood, but it didn't burst in her mouth like an exceptionally fine wine. Didn't turn her warm and tingly as it slid down her throat.

And when she lifted her head to look at her arm . . . the slice was still there. Still open and red and . . . bleeding again.

Shit. Vampire saliva contained healing enzymes; it was how they kept victims . . . er, donors . . . from bleeding out, and sped up the healing of their own wounds. The cut should have been nothing more than a tiny pink scratch by now, but instead it was fresh and ouchy and flowing.

What the hell did that mean? Had she lost her mojo? Had she contracted some kind of bizarre vampire disease no one had ever heard about that slowed her healing or zapped her powers?

Or was *this* her new reality? Was she really here, in this motel room, in these clothes, living a life she wasn't sure she knew anything about?

Maybe she just needed to give it time, let it—whatever *it* was—play itself out.

Grabbing a wad of toilet paper from the roll on the back of the commode, she staunched the flow of blood on her arm. Wiped it away, tossed the tissue, grabbed another small bunch to tuck against the cut like a gauze pad. Then she yanked her sleeve back down and buttoned the cuff.

Before Ian could yell for her—or at her—again, she shrugged into the shoulder holster he'd given her. She only knew how because she'd seen him do it so many times, but the straps and weight of the gun still felt awkward and uncomfortable against her body, like a too-small bra she *really* wanted to toss in the fire—and not to make a political statement.

Well, what could she do? This was apparently her new persona: Paulina Bunyan, P.I. Or under-cover cop. Or rent-by-the-hour hooker for the nearest lumber camp.

Since she didn't know what else to do, she left the bathroom, her heart pounding in her chest as she shrugged into the navy blue parka Ian tossed her. Not a coat she would ever choose for herself, that was for sure, at least not outside of her usual space-time continuum.

He opened the motel room door, ready to step out, only to have a wide shaft of sunlight pour in.

Angelina shrieked and threw herself back, out of the way, rolling across the rumpled bed and landing on the floor on the other side, with the mattress and box spring acting as a shield. Her hands were lifted instinctively to cover her face and protect her exposed flesh, but also because she couldn't bear to see Ian catching fire and dying right before her eyes.

Only he wasn't screaming. She didn't hear the tell-tale sounds of popping and sizzling or his thrashing about, trying to stifle the flames that were licking at his flesh.

Lowering her arms, she poked her head up over the edge of the bed to find Ian . . . fine. Healthy. Nowhere close to being a crispy critter or pile of barbecue ashes. He was staring at her like she'd just sprouted horns and a set of bony wings from her shoulder blades, but was otherwise unharmed.

"What in Christ's name is wrong with you?" he snapped, both his brows and mouth pulled down in a scowl.

The question wasn't what was wrong with *her* but what was wrong with *him*. How could he be standing in a shaft of pure daylight and not be sizzling like a juicy steak on the grill?

Could it be because, in this reality, he wasn't a vampire?

It seemed too outrageous a possibility, but what other explanation could there be?

And if *he* wasn't a vampire, then . . .

She stood, slowly. Rounded the bed, slowly. Stepped into the shaft of sun, *slooooowly*.

No smoke. No burning sensation. Not even a tingle.

She took another step, and then another, until she stood smack-dab in the center of the doorway, every inch of her—hands and neck and face included—exposed to direct sunlight. It was warm, but not painful. The first drop of sun she'd felt on her skin in nearly a hundred and fifty years.

She didn't know whether to be excited about this turn of events . . . or horrified that she was apparently no longer immortal. And being no longer immortal meant that she was most likely very, *very* mortal. As was Ian.

"Are you all right?" he asked, his voice softer this time. He sounded genuinely concerned about her odd—to him, at least, she assumed—behavior. "I've never seen you act this way."

"Sorry," she apologized, stepping out of the motel room and letting him close the door behind them. "Just . . . jumpy, I guess."

Reaching into the inside pocket of his bomber jacket, he pulled out a pack of smokes, stuck one between his lips, and lit the tip. After taking a couple of deep puffs, he blew out smoke and moved to the driver's side of an older model, nondescript gray Ford Taurus. He clicked the button on his keychain fob to unlock the doors, then opened his and climbed in.

Not knowing what else to do, she followed suit on the passenger side. He started the car and cranked up the heat, but for a few minutes, only cold air blew out at them, making her teeth chatter.

"Can't blame you for the nerves," he said, rapping his hands on the steering wheel.

Curls of smoke started to fill the inside of the mid-size sedan and Angelina wondered how long she could hold her breath to keep the poison from entering her body. Ian's smoking had never bothered her when they were both immortal, because although it could be stinky, he'd always been careful to keep from blowing it in her face. And even if he did, it wasn't going to harm either one of them.

But now, if they were mortal (and judging by the fact that she was outside while the sun was still up without becoming a one-woman bonfire, that seemed to be the case), everything could hurt them. Somebody could run up to the car window right now and shoot her in the head. They could get in a car accident and have all of their appendages torn asunder. Secondhand smoke could even now be filtering its way through her system and blackening her lungs.

Oh, God! There were so many things to worry about now. Germs and disease and acts of God. A paper cut could do her in, where before having an entire tree fall on her would have only flattened her and put her in a maple syrup mood for a while.

She tried not to panic, but in order to avoid that, she was pretty sure she needed to take deep breaths, and that would involve inhaling cigarette smoke that would likely kill her in ten to twenty years. Which might not sound so bad to the average *homo sapiens*, but to her—vampire her—ten to twenty years was a catnap, the blink of an eye!

Just when stars began to dance in front of her eyes and she could feel herself turning blue, Ian ran the window down on his side of the car, and the gray cloud hanging over their heads began to dissipate, forced out by the slowly warming air blowing from the dashboard fans. She sighed in relief.

Putting the car in gear and backing out of the motel parking space, he said, "This case is starting to make me as nervous as a roach in a room full of exterminators, too. If something doesn't happen soon, I'm going to *plant* meth on one of the little bastards just for an excuse to bust them."

He pulled out of the motel lot and onto what looked to be a much busier main drag. She had no idea where they were, and even fewer clues about what was going on, so she was doing her best to pay attention to what he was saying *and* take note of her surroundings.

They were apparently both law enforcement officers of some kind; when she was alone, she'd look for a badge and try to find out for what branch or department. They were also apparently on some kind of drug case, one that was dragging and putting him on edge.

Okay, fine. Although she wasn't sure what the heck she was supposed to do or what sort of cop she'd be. She was a girly-girl, not a tomboy, and had never *touched* a gun before, let alone handled a firearm in such a way that she could point one at another person or—God forbid—use it.

All she could do, she supposed, was hope she figured out how she'd gotten here and how to get back before a situation arose that put somebody— her, Ian, or anyone else—in danger.

"And Ellen's acting weird, too. I think she's suspicious that all the hours I say I'm working might not actually be work related."

Angelina knew better than to ask who Ellen was. It might be tricky, but she was going to have to act like she knew who everybody was and what was going on until she started putting all the pieces together on her own.

So she said nothing, and let the awkward silence build between them until he pulled to the curb in front of a tall, slightly run-down, redbrick building. A wooden sign with spray paint residue in places identified it as BRIARVIEW APARTMENTS.

The car idled while they sat there, and finally she asked, "Why are we here?"

He shot her another one of those half-confused, half-annoyed glances. "I told you, I think Ellen's starting to suspect something's up. I promised I'd be home tonight for dinner with her and the kids before we go back out on stakeout. We've got the graveyard shift, so I'll pick you up again around ten."

Angelina understood all of the words he was

using. That was to say, her mental dictionary applied definitions to each and every one.

So why was it, then, that she was having so much trouble making sense of them as a whole?

Who was Ellen, and why was he rushing home to eat dinner with her? Why did he care if she was getting suspicious? And while they were at it, *suspicious of what?* and *what kids?*

Then her gaze flitted to his left hand, where it rested on the steering wheel.

He was wearing a wedding band.

She glanced at her own ring finger.

And she *was not.*

All of her fingers were conspicuously bare, which was odd enough for Vampire Angelina. But this wasn't just a case of under accessorizing. No, the fact that Ian was wearing a wedding ring while she wasn't was . . . not good. *Sooooo* not good.

She swallowed hard, her own suspicions beginning to build, as well as a sinking knowledge of who Ellen most likely was.

A lead weight pulled her heart down, down, *down* so far she was afraid it was going to disappear into the gaping black abyss of her shattered soul.

Ian was married, she realized.

But not to her.

SIP THREE

Angelina lost track of how long she cried after getting out of the car and making her way stiffly up the three flights of stairs to her apartment. Her apartment in this reality, anyway. She'd only found it by looking for her name on the row of mailboxes in the lobby, and the key had been in her coat pocket.

But once inside, she hadn't paid much attention to the dark, spartan interior, the proof of her poor housekeeping skills, or the fact that she hadn't bothered with a single sign of Christmas cheer, even though the rest of the apartment building was decorated with lights and garlands and a tree in the entry. Instead, she'd fallen back against the door, sunk to the floor, and sobbed.

Sobbed and sobbed and sobbed. Until her nose ran and her breath hitched. Until her chest ached and she thought she might throw up.

It was hard enough being thrust into a world and existence she didn't understand, but to find out the man she loved was married to another woman . . . ?

And that she was *the other woman.* A home-wrecker. A whore. Human Angelina was having an affair with a married man. A man she *had* to have known was married when they first got involved, since they were also partners on the job.

As guilty and disgusted with herself as she felt over that, she was equally disgusted and angry with Ian. What was wrong with him? She never would have expected him to be a cheater—in any life.

Was he cheating on her back in . . . well, her real life? The immortal one. Had he ever?

She didn't know, though she wracked her brain to remember any suspicious activity on his part that might have hinted that he had a mistress. And if she ever got back there, she was damn well going to find out.

Once she was as cried out as she was going to get, Angelina climbed to her feet and made her way to the kitchen sink, where she splashed her face with cold water and dabbed it dry with a dish-towel. According to the clock on the microwave oven, she had four more hours before Ian would be picking her up again for their stakeout.

Stakeout of what, she wasn't sure, but she assumed she'd been a cop—and Ian's partner—in this life long enough that begging off because she'd discovered her secret lover was a jerk and she wasn't in the mood to go out again—let alone be anywhere near Ian in the next millennium—wasn't an option. She couldn't even call in sick because he'd just seen her and would know it was a bald-faced lie.

There was also a pretty good chance that she'd begun her affair with Officer Ian knowing full well he was already a husband and father. So what did that say about her?

Blowing out a heavy breath that ruffled her bangs, she started moving through the apartment. Nothing looked even remotely familiar, and she wondered how long she'd been living here. Well, residing; she didn't consider this much like living.

Everything was dark and dreary. The carpet, the curtains, the sofa cushions were all faded and threadbare.

A ratty, dog-eared copy of Stephen King's *'Salem's Lot* sat on a low, scarred coffee table. This surprised her, since she'd never been a fan of the author's work before and made a point *not* to read vampire or paranormal fiction because so much of it was outrageously speculative garbage. Humans writing about vampires was like short order cooks lecturing on brain surgery. What the hell did they know about it?

Moving down the short hallway, she ducked her head into the tiny bathroom and noted a small array of toiletries near the sink. A single toothbrush, toothpaste, and a stick of heavy duty, androgynous deodorant. No sweet-smelling girly stuff for her, she guessed. Being a cop must be sweaty business.

She also must be lacking the personality gene now because the shower curtain was nothing more than a giant swath of plain white material.

At home . . . her other home, her real home, her vampire-occupied home . . . the guest bathroom was done in a bright flower motif while the

master bath was decorated entirely in seashells
and all things beachy. She and Ian found it both
ironic and amusing, since the beach was one place
they were never going to see, at least not in daylight. Moonlit walks in the sand were perhaps
doable, not that they'd ever bothered.

The bedroom, when she got there, wasn't much
better. Cramped and even darker than the other
rooms, it contained a lumpy double mattress with
sheets that looked as though they hadn't been
changed in months (*yuck*), a single dresser, and a
nightstand that held a chipped, shadeless lamp.

Didn't she have any self-respect as a human
being? How could she live like this, without color
or light or *hope*? She'd seen homeless shelters that
were less depressing.

Still, there had to be something personal lying
around. Some clue about her past, or her current
thoughts and feelings. Something that made this
place more than simply a place to crash when she
wasn't out screwing another woman's husband.

Twenty minutes later, she'd ransacked the closet
and under the bed, and was sitting cross-legged in
the middle of the bedroom floor, single lamp burning as brightly as it got while she read through a
shoebox full of newspaper clippings, photographs,
and assorted odds and ends. It was apparently her
version of a scrapbook.

From the shoebox, she learned about snippets
of her childhood, her high school graduation, her
enrollment in the police academy. There were a
few bits about old boyfriends and family members,
but nothing tantamount and nothing that stirred a
single memory in her brain. In the pictures, she

saw herself at different stages of her life, but she didn't remember a single one of them.

But at least now she had a bit of a better idea of what kind of person she was: how she lived, how she thought, how she acted. She might be a cop, which meant she had to be smart, strong, and independent . . . but she was also a lonely introvert.

The life she was leading here was so different from the one she was used to, it was like black and white. Even as a vampire who had to keep to nighttime hours, she'd always been outgoing, always had dozens of friends to keep her company and whom she could turn to if she needed to talk.

Boy, could she use one—or all—of them now. Maybe they would know what the heck was going on. How she'd gotten here, what she was doing in this alternate universe, and how long she was going to be forced to stay.

Was this all a dream, something she would wake up from in a few hours? Or was this her new reality, a very real new existence she was going to have to come to terms with because she was going to be stuck here forever?

The up side, she supposed, was that her definition of "forever" now was quite a bit different than it had been. Fifty or sixty years, tops, rather than the hundreds or thousands she'd learned to expect as an immortal.

Of course, time was relative. If she was unhappy, fifty years could seem like an eternity; whereas, if she was *happy*, a century could go by in the blink of an eye.

Pushing up from the floor, she felt every kink and cramp from being in the same position for too long—something that never would have happened before. She wasn't used to aches and pains, and judging from how uncomfortable they were, she didn't want to *get* used to them. But again— did she have a choice?

With less than an hour left before Ian showed up, she dug a fresh set of clothes from the dresser— another pair of jeans and a thick tan vee-neck sweater. Then she went for a quick shower, coming out feeling a little more human (har-har), and ready to face whatever nightmare within her current nightmare might crop up next.

She didn't know what their normal routine was—whether Ian came up to her apartment to get her when he picked her up for work, or if she met him downstairs. To be safe, she decided to meet him downstairs.

Since it was cold outside, and she could see that it was beginning to snow again, she remained inside the building's lobby, fiddling with the gun and holster that felt entirely unnatural tucked against her side beneath her ugly navy parka. She hoped to God she never had to draw it or she'd probably look like one of those bumbling, incompetent cartoon characters.

Within the next ten minutes, the gray Taurus pulled up to the curb and she ran out and jumped in.

Ian greeted her with a mumbled "Hey" as he pulled back onto the street.

"Hey," she replied. "How are the wife and kids?"

She regretted the snarky question the second it passed her lips. Especially since she didn't really *want* to know. Nor did she want him to know she was bothered by his marital status, not if she'd been having an affair with him for . . . who knew how long without voicing her annoyance.

He turned a fraction in her direction, his expression clearly stating she was treading into "nagging bitch" territory.

"You're going to start this again?" he asked.

His tone was short, as though they'd had this argument more than once before. And they very well may have. Wasn't like she'd remember one way or the other, right?

She pinched her lips to hold back any kind of response, since she wasn't sure what kind of response she should give. Should she fly off the handle and jump into a fight they'd obviously repeated ad nauseam, or should she keep her mouth shut? She honestly didn't know how Human Angelina would react, and she didn't want to do or say anything that would arouse Human Ian's suspicions.

She did know what Vampire Angelina would do if she found out her lover was secretly married, though, and took at least a modicum of comfort in running through the gory scenario in her head. She rarely flashed fang in anger, but for something like that, she'd go postal as only a super-strong, undead creature of the night could.

"Look," Ian continued, unaware of the bloody and painful demise his alter ego was currently suffering in her mind. "We've been through this before. *You're* the one who took off after graduation. I was ready to marry you and settle down straight out of high school, but you wanted to experience freedom for a while. *Find yourself.*" He sing-songed the words with obvious scorn. "So fine. Good for you. But I'm no monk, Ange, as you well know. So in the meantime, I hooked up with Ellen. She got pregnant, and I did the right thing. Doesn't mean I love her the way a man should love his wife. Doesn't mean I didn't still care about you. That's just the hand life dealt me."

She wondered if that was true, that they'd been involved once before—in love, even?—and she'd walked away. Innocently enough, of course, but if she'd loved Ian so much, maybe she should have stuck around and married him herself while she first had the chance.

She certainly wouldn't be in the mess she was in now, if she had. But then, hindsight was always twenty-twenty, wasn't it?

The slick polyester of her overstuffed coat rustled as she crossed her arms over her chest and scrunched lower in the seat. "It doesn't make what we're doing right," she muttered.

"No," he agreed, and she was mollified to hear the slightest hint of guilt in his tone. "But I couldn't leave Ellen now if I wanted to. It would hurt the kids too much, and you know damn well her father would have my ass. Mayor McCheese already thinks he owns the police force and everyone on it, starting with me."

She didn't know that; didn't even know who his wife's father was—although from his derisive nickname for the man, she assumed he was a high-up political figure in the Boston area, possibly even the actual mayor.

But the kid part she understood. It sounded as though, even if Ian wasn't the greatest husband in the world, he was a dad who loved his children. That was something, wasn't it?

The problem was, she didn't want to think about his having kids . . . not with anyone but her, at least. She'd gotten over the fact that, as vampires were unable to procreate, she and Ian were never going to have children of their own. So to come here and find that he *did* have kids, but with another woman . . . She pushed the knowledge aside, buried it deep and pretended her heart wasn't aching painfully in her chest.

"And you're the one who came back here," he added. "Came back, started hanging around, joined the force to be closer to me. You started this. If you're tired of it or starting to feel guilty, then you need to be the one to leave, but don't foist it all on my plate and make me the Number One Bad Guy."

She didn't know what to say to that, so she said nothing. As usual, she was discovering that there were a lot of gray areas to this story. When it came to her current existence and her relationship with Ian, she apparently wasn't a hundred percent innocent, and he wasn't a hundred percent evil.

Not that knowing that made her feel a heck of a lot better.

They drove in silence for a while longer, going deeper and deeper into what looked to be a very bad part of town. Run-down houses and broken-down cars lined the streets, most of them tagged with names or symbols or gang signs.

Street lamps were burned out, casting everything in dark shadows, but she could still make out the occasional human form. Hookers in short skirts, despite the frigid weather, and fake fur coats pounded the pavement looking for dates. Drug dealers sat on porches or stood in doorways waiting for customers. Junkies and the homeless littered the ground, passed out after shooting up or emptying a bottle.

The whole thing gave Angelina the creeps, and she wanted nothing more than to go home to her pathetic little apartment and lock herself safely inside. It might not be in the best neighborhood, but it was a far cry from this.

Unfortunately, she was supposed to be a cop. She was supposed to not only be used to these kinds of conditions, but willing to charge in and maintain law and order when the *dis*order and *un*-lawful stuff got out of hand. Too bad she felt about as well-trained to be an inner city cop as a fish on a unicycle.

Steering one-handed, Ian crept down a couple of side streets, then pulled into a long, rutted dirt alley between two houses that looked to be abandoned. All the windows were either broken or boarded up. There were no lights burning inside either, and the yards were about six summers past well tended.

He pulled to a stop a couple of yards from the end of the alley and cut the engine, plunging them into silence and almost total darkness. Other than their breathing, the only sounds in the dead, squalid night was the occasional bark of a dog or the faraway squeal of brake pads.

She wanted to ask what they were doing there, why they'd just . . . stopped, but worried it would make her sound stupid and make *him* think she'd flown even farther from the cuckoo's nest than he already did, since she was supposed to be up on their case load and already aware of their plans for the night. So she sat there. Silent, bored, and growing colder and more antsy as the seconds slowly ticked by.

How did Ian do this all the time? Even in their other life, he was an undercover detective, working stings and stakeouts one after another. She'd never thought about it before, but she wondered if he ever got as bored with it as she was now.

Shifting in her seat, she waited, fidgeting both for something to do and in an attempt to keep warm. She knew they were supposed to be watching for something, but she wasn't sure what, so she didn't know where to focus her attention.

Then Ian sat up, going on full alert. "Here they come."

Angelina straightened, straining to see what Ian did. A second later, a group of people came into view strutting down the sidewalk on the other side of the street several yards away.

A handful of men dressed like extras in Michael Jackson's "Thriller" video—brightly colored, out-of-style leather and chains, not rotting flesh. Each had an arm slung around the shoulders of a young woman. The men looked cocky and arrogant, to say the least.

The women . . . she couldn't put her finger on it, but the women looked odd. Drunk, maybe? Or high? They weren't stumbling, exactly, but they were moving stiffly, almost robotically, their expressions glazed and blank.

They climbed the steps of a run-down house directly across from where she and Ian were parked. The guy in the lead opened the front door, holding it while the others passed. As they did, each of the other men lifted a hand and high-fived him.

She couldn't see their faces, but she could see the leader's. He was grinning like an idiot playing with a light switch. And when he did, when his lips parted and the whites of his teeth appeared . . . he flashed fang.

SIP FOUR

Pulse pounding, Angelina sat up even straighter, focusing every ounce of her attention on the house across the way and its new inhabitants.

This was who they were staking out? *This* was the group Ian thought was running a meth lab?

Oh, they weren't drug dealers. Far from it. But what they were was much, much more dangerous.

Before, she would have smelled them a mile away. More than that, she would have sensed them. A buzz under the skin or a tickle in her brain like the beginnings of an ice cream headache that warned her another vampire was in the vicinity.

But because she was now a damn, useless *homo sap*, she had none of the essential, life-saving spidey senses that came with being a vampire.

Whipping her head around, she glanced at Ian, who was staring dead ahead at the supposed meth house. He had a small pair of binoculars out now, and was peering through them, watching for . . . she didn't know what.

What she did know was that the people in that

house weren't cooking up illegal drugs, but they were doing something just as wrong. The women who had gone inside weren't drunk or high or anything like that. They were human females who had been mesmerized by the male vamps, and were probably even now being sucked dry of their bodily fluids.

With luck, the vamps wouldn't kill them, but would merely drink enough to satisfy their thirsts, then send the girls on their way. Dazed, confused, dehydrated, and memories of being human Slurpies wiped.

But this was a nest. A group of rogue vampires living on the fringes of society—mortal and immortal alike—and well outside of the law.

It had taken centuries, but vampires had finally managed to integrate themselves with the human race. Were they completely and readily accepted? Of course not. There were still people who lived in fear of the "bloodsucking monsters" walking amongst them. There were even some who lobbied for their extermination (legally) and hunted them (illegally). For the most part, however, they'd done a pretty good job of blending in.

Even this group would be all right, flying under the radar, if they hadn't somehow called attention to themselves. She hoped they weren't killing people in their attempts to feed. Bad part of town or not, that just wasn't a smart move. But having the police on their tails, thinking they were mixing up drugs in the basement and selling them on the street wasn't much better.

Angelina wasn't worried about the nest, though. There was a good chance none of them were boy scouts, and it was more than likely that some or all of them were flat-out bad asses.

No, the thought that had her heart racing and her blood running cold was that this nest could very well be a huge danger to the cops. To Ian.

Ian thought he was staking out a bunch of drug dealers. Big deal. Run-of-the-mill street thugs with juice in their veins and maybe some heavy firepower. He had no clue that the men he was watching could leap small buildings in a single bound . . . lift a Buick and toss it to the other side of town . . . squeeze the life out of a person twice their size one-handed.

If they carried guns, it was just for show and convenience. To really kill—and if they were cornered, she had no doubt that's exactly what they would do—they would simply tear out their opponents' throats. And while a human could sometimes survive a bullet wound, there was no coming back from a ravaged jugular or worse.

"I can't tell what they're doing in there, can you?"

Ian's voice broke her train of thought and made her jump. He lowered the binoculars and she quickly swiveled her head back around to face forward, as though she'd been paying as much attention to the house across the street as he was.

Damn this human form, she cursed herself. With vamp eyesight, she could have seen through the windows even in pitch black and known what they were up to. With vamp hearing, she could have rolled the car window down and heard them as clearly as though they were sitting in the back seat. And if necessary, with vamp speed and strength, she could have zipped across the street, broken down the door, and taken out at least half of them before they'd even know she was there.

But in this weak, vulnerable, *useless*, mortal body, she could do none of those things. And she couldn't even tell Ian what she knew because . . .

Because in this reality, she wasn't sure whether or not people knew vampires existed. If they'd merged into society or not.

Because she didn't know how Ian would react to such a revelation. Would he take it in stride? . . . Be horrified? . . . Think she was crazy and report her to their captain or request a new partner?

No. This situation was too dangerous, too important. She couldn't take the chance that one of the latter would happen, and then that something bad would happen to Ian—something she might possibly prevent.

At the moment, she didn't know how she would manage that, given—*yoo-hoo*, no Super Vamp superpowers. (She'd truly never appreciated the damn things until they went bye-bye.) But at least with her knowledge of what was going on and what the gang members in that house really were, if she stuck around, she might be able to circumvent certain events.

She may not be able to stop a bullet or keep Ian from continuing to surveil the nest, but maybe she could convince him that the group wasn't doing what he thought they were doing and that they were a lost cause. Or maybe she could somehow make contact with the nest's leader and convince him to move on to . . . bloodier pastures.

Again, her lack of immortality would make that

difficult. No way was a big, bad vampire leader going to listen to or be intimidated by a little human female. Even if she did carry a gun—one she didn't know how to use.

But maybe there was a small chance that her knowledge of their existence and what they were doing in that abandoned house would be enough to make them nervous and get them to pull up stakes.

Ha! Poor choice of words; she'd be sure to phrase things differently if she ever found herself face to face with Thriller Boy.

Dropping her head to her hands, she clamped her eyes closed and let out a low groan. What a mess. Or as Ian—her Ian, Vampire Ian—would say, this situation was definitely fubar.

"What?" Human Ian sat up in his seat and grabbed the binoculars, once again staring straight ahead at the supposed meth house. "Did you see something?"

"No, nothing." She shook her head, raising it at the same time.

He was so intent on catching those guys doing something drug related. But he could sit there until the sky turned green and he still wouldn't get what he wanted. She had to find some way to get his focus away from the nest and onto something else.

"You know," she began slowly, racking her brain for something, anything logical that might convince him the Thriller gang was a lost cause. "Maybe we're barking up the wrong tree here."

He lowered the binocs and fixed her with a narrow, knit-browed gaze. "What do you mean?"

"How long have we been sitting on this group of miscreants?" she asked, trying to make the question sound offhand and rhetorical, even though she really did want to know the answer.

And did people use the term "miscreants" anymore? She'd have to be careful of her vocabulary or it might set off more bells and whistles than her little fear-of-the-sun dance had earlier that afternoon.

"Six months," he supplied.

Six months? Geez, Louise. Talk about a waste of police presence. They'd have been better off staking out the local Krispy Kreme for sugar junkies looking for their next high.

"Right," she said instead, as though she'd known it the whole time. "Six months. And we've caught them doing exactly nothing we can book them on. No cooking, no dealing, not so much as jaywalking or littering."

Oooh, look at her, sounding like a real live Police Woman. Living with a cop for the past eighty years had apparently paid off. Just call her Cagney. Or Lacey. Or . . . whatever.

Of course, she was grasping at straws and could only hope she really *did* sound like she knew what she was talking about without saying anything that wasn't true or accurate.

"Yeah. So?"

"So maybe we can't catch them at anything because they're not *doing* anything."

If possible, his brows and the sides of his mouth dipped even lower. Now he wasn't just confused, he was heading into pissed. Ian never had handled being told he was wrong very well.

"Come on, Ian. If that were a drug house, we'd have seen traffic pouring in and out of there all night. Strung-out junkies looking for their next fix, dealers hitting the streets with pockets full of product. I hate to say it, but I think this is a big, fat waste of time. Those guys are nothing more than wannabe hoods out for a good time with a couple of working girls. Still illegal, granted, but not quite Mr. Wizard setting up the meth lab you were hoping for."

She could tell she'd hit at least a couple of nails on the head because Ian's scowl was lessening and he was rubbing the spot between his eyes.

"Shit," he muttered.

"What?" she asked, her own eyes widening slightly as she worried she might have taken a wrong turn somewhere along the way in her impassioned speech.

"You're right," he said, and she breathed a huge but silent sigh of relief. "If they were cooking up meth in the basement, we'd have seen signs of it by now. But *something's* going on with those guys, I know it. I can feel it in my gut."

Angelina licked her lips, her own stomach going tight. She'd rarely known Ian's gut to be wrong, and it wasn't off base this time, either. He sensed something wrong about the bad eighties throwbacks because there *was* something wrong with them. Just not anything he could fathom or handle on his own as a mortal.

"Let's get out of here," she told him, hoping that if she could get him away from this place, she could also distract him enough to give up on his odd obsession with the group of vampires. For good measure, she rubbed her hands together and blew on them, letting him know how cold and uncomfortable she was.

After another few seconds of contemplating, weighing his desire to stick around and catch the vamps doing something he could nail them on against the futility of wasting any more time with the group, he huffed out a breath and cranked the engine.

Between the warm air pouring out of the vents and chasing away the chill that had soaked nearly to her bones, and the respite of seeing Ian walk away from a situation he couldn't truly comprehend or handle, Angelina had never been so relieved in her life. She sat back in her seat and began to relax, tension seeping from her muscles and nerve endings like steam from a pot of boiling water.

They drove back through town, the silence inside the late-model sedan growing with each passing mile. She could tell by Ian's knuckles turning white around the steering wheel and the sporadic tic at his jaw that he was anything but calm, anything but happy with the decision to end their surveillance. She could only hope that the farther they got from that house, the less preoccupied he would be with it and the people inside.

When they got to her apartment building, rather than pulling up in front to let her out as he had the last time, he turned into the small reserved parking area and nosed into an empty spot. She opened her door to get out, alarmed when he shut off the engine, pocketed the keys, and did the same. Stuffing her hands in her coat and hunching her shoulders from the cold, she watched him round the trunk of the car.

"What are you doing?" she asked, afraid she already knew the answer.

"Going inside."

She swallowed hard, not quite sure how to feel about his response.

On the one hand, it definitely wasn't a good idea for him to come up to her apartment. There was too much history between them, and they'd done too much wrong already.

On the other, this was her Ian. She didn't care what world or what reality they were in, he'd always been hers. In her mind, in her heart.

Even now, standing outside in the frigid night air when every bit of her should feel like it was in deep freeze, her body was humming, turning warm and molten with wanting him. She'd only been here—wherever this was—a day, but already she missed him.

Oh, literally speaking, they'd been together more than they'd been apart. But sitting in a car next to Ian, wondering how much of him was the same person she'd lived with and loved when she'd had fangs and known how to use them wasn't the same as *being with* him. She missed touching him, kissing him, looking into his eyes and seeing the utmost love and devotion shining back at her.

At that moment, she would have given almost anything to be back in her house, in the bed she shared with Ian, contemplating the next thousand years of their lives together instead of standing in the cold on a strange street, in front of a strange building, where she lived alone in a strange apartment, with no particularly inviting prospects for her future.

Licking her lips, she shifted uncomfortably, not quite able to meet his coffee-brown gaze.

"I didn't invite you," she felt inclined to point out, even if her voice was thready and weak and she wished she had . . . or could, without being eaten up by guilt.

One side of his mouth quirked up in a sexy half-grin, as he brushed past her and walked slowly toward the entrance of her building. "You never do."

SIP FIVE

They were in her apartment, toasty warm now with their coats and shoes off. Ian had helped himself to a beer from her fridge and was leaning against the sink, one arm angled behind him with his hand resting on the edge of the counter.

She stood opposite him, hands clenching and unclenching behind her back and swallowing reflexively as she tried not to drool. How could she be so turned off by the dynamics of their relationship, yet so turned on by him at the same time?

Human Ian wasn't quite as tall or muscular as Vampire Ian. Being turned did that to a person—honed and accentuated their build, their features, their inner beauty.

But Human Ian was certainly nothing to sneeze at. He was still ripped with a capital *R*. Bulging biceps. Broad, well-defined chest beneath an olive-green, long-sleeved cotton shirt. Flat stomach leading down to narrow hips and a first-class ass covered by a pair of faded but snug blue jeans.

She couldn't actually see his butt at the moment, but she'd had plenty of time to study it as she'd followed him into the building and up the stairs to her apartment, so she knew what she was talkin' about.

In addition to his fine physique, she was glad to know the rest of him was unchanged by his mortality, as well. He still shaved his head, still had a small, blond soul patch just below his bottom lip, still had a small silver hoop in his left ear, and could still melt her insides like butter at ten paces with a single glance from his dark chocolate eyes.

That hot gaze was raking over her now, sending her butter from merely melting to sizzling. She could feel her chest hitching as she struggled to breathe, her belly and lower slowly winding like a watch, tighter and tighter.

He took a pull from the bottle in his hand, then set it on the countertop behind him with a clink and pushed away, moving forward, closing in on her. There were only about three of his long strides separating them, but still he reminded her of a jungle cat, quietly and intently stalking its prey. And she *was* the prey, standing immobile, watching his progress, waiting to be pounced upon and swallowed whole.

Her tongue darted out to lick dry lips. Her hands behind her back fisted until the fingers tingled.

Yes—No. Yes—No. A game of tug-o-war was raging in her head, pulling her in too many directions, scrambling her brains.

She wasn't stupid; she knew right from wrong.

She also knew that this wasn't her reality, not really. She didn't know what it was—a dream? A nightmare? A rabbit hole she'd accidentally fallen through like Alice in Wonderland?

But she knew him. She knew herself. And she knew what they had together in the real world, in *her* reality.

Was that enough to assuage any guilt she might feel after the fact, after she gave in to the rabid pulse beating under her skin and the intense passion battering her soul?

He stepped close, crowding her. His firm body leaned into hers from chest to thigh, burning her like a furnace. She tried to breathe, to draw air into her lungs, but didn't want to press herself any closer to him. As it was, her nipples had come to attention inside the cups of her bra and she could feel the hard ridge of his erection nudging her from behind the fly of his jeans.

"I know you're still mad at me," he said softly, his hand coming up to frame her face. The pad of his thumb ran back and forth across her lips, sending tiny shockwaves rippling through her system.

She jerked her head. "I'm not mad," she told him.

And it was true. She was confused, torn, but not angry.

His lashes fluttered, his eyes growing shuttered. "You know how I feel about you," he murmured. A statement, not a question. "You know I can't let you go."

If she decided to leave, there wasn't a damn thing he could do about it, but right now, she definitely didn't want to leave. Maybe she should. If she were stronger, maybe she would. But at the moment, he was her only link to normality, the only familiar thing in a world where everything she knew had been turned upside down.

When she didn't respond, he took her silence as acquiescence and kissed her. His body pressed even closer to hers, pushing her back into the edge of the counter while his hands bracketed her hips and his mouth covered hers.

His lips were warm and soft at first, brushing over hers in feather-light touches. She stood perfectly still and let him, let her eyes drift closed as sensation bombarded her.

A second later, he traced the line of her mouth with his tongue, urging her to open. And she did. He swept inside, tasting her, claiming her, rocking her back until she wasn't sure her feet were still on the ground.

She lifted her arms, running her hands over his shoulders and the nape of his neck. She loved the feel of his stubbled skull beneath her fingertips, smooth in shape but rough in texture.

He deepened the kiss while she continued to stroke his sexy dome, then lifted her to perch more comfortably on the counter rather than at an odd angle against it. It also put his groin smack-dab at her center, and the two thick layers of denim they were both sporting might as well have been nonexistent.

She raised her legs and looped them around his hips, crossing them at the ankles. The action dragged him even closer, grinding their pelvises together and putting him right where she wanted him, *needed* him most.

He tugged at the hem of her sweater, pulling it up and over her head. Her arms floated back down to his neck and his mouth back to her lips as soon as he tossed the garment away.

His palms flattened on her bare skin, spanning her waist and trailing upward to cup her breasts still inside her bra. He used his thumbs to tease the peaks through the lacy material and she moaned, groaned, tightened her legs around his hips.

Letting her urge him on, he slipped his fingers inside the bra from the top, tugging until the material rested beneath her breasts along with the underwires. They felt full and tender, and when he released her mouth to kiss a trail down to one swollen tip, she nearly shot out of her skin.

Her head fell back, and she had to use her hands to prop herself up on the counter or she would have melted right into the Formica. His tongue licked and circled one taut nipple before taking it into his mouth to suckle gently.

He kept at it for several long minutes while she tried not to orgasm right then and there. Then, just as he lifted his head and she thought she might get a small respite from the waves of pleasure washing over her body, he settled in to torture her with the same treatment of the other breast.

She let him go for . . . well, as long as he wanted, because it wasn't like she had the strength or will to pull away, even if she'd wanted to.

But she did manage to lower her arms and work

her fingers into the waistband of his pants to pop the button and lower the zipper only slightly. She didn't go straight for the prize at the bottom of the cereal box. Oh, no, that would be too easy and bring things to a crashing finish much sooner than she suspected either of them would like.

Instead, she loosened his shirt and started sliding it up, over his washboard abs, the light covering of rough hair on his sculpted chest, his smooth back and bulging biceps. When she hit his chin, but kept tugging, he was forced to release her nipple—*whaaaa!*—and raise his arms over his head so she could yank it off completely.

He stood back for a second, breathing heavily, and she was able to admire (read: drool over) his amazing physique. He was a god, a work of art. If he'd been molded out of clay to represent every woman's image of perfection (read: favorite wet dream), he couldn't have *been* any more delicious.

For the first time, she also noticed that this Ian had tattoos. Not temporary ones he'd gotten for a particular job that would soon fade away, but the permanent kind that weren't going to fade while he slept.

And they were hot.

Wanting to feel them, see them up close, she grabbed his arm and tugged him slightly sideways, lowering her head to study the intricate designs.

Around his right biceps were three intertwined strands of barbed wire done in solid black. It was sexy and dangerous and sent a zing of arousal heating her blood and swelling between her legs.

Turning him the other way, she found the

image of an angel on his left biceps. Looking more enticing than angelic, the depiction on his arm wore a long, Romanesque gown and had dark, flowing hair that fell to her waist, ruby red lips, and sapphire-blue eyes. With a start, she realized the angel looked remarkably . . . like her.

Her head jerked up to meet Ian's gaze. He was watching her intently, waiting for her to finish her slow perusal of his ink. But her surprise wasn't reflected in his own brown irises, only a deep knowing and passion and . . . love.

Her lungs hitched, and she swallowed hard, blinking back tears.

Oh, my God. He might have married another woman, but he'd had *her* likeness tattooed on his body. Angel . . . Angelina. She wondered if his wife had ever asked about it—and what his answer had been.

Ian's voice was gravelly and tight when he said, "What—are you trying to decide on my next bit of body armor?"

She blinked again, this time in confusion.

"Me?" her voice squeaked out.

One dark brow shot up and he shrugged a broad, bare shoulder. "You picked the first two, why not the third?"

Emotion slammed into her with all the impact of a freight train careening down the tracks at full speed. Her heart stuttered to a stop behind her rib cage. Her lungs froze mid-breath, then felt as though they were shriveling like empty party balloons. And a warmth started low in her body only to spread out in every direction like the rays of a blazing-hot sun.

It was a warmth she recognized with some astonishment as love. Pure, unadulterated love for this man, mixed with equal parts adoration and devotion.

She tried to swallow, but her throat was tight, her eyes quickly growing damp and losing focus. Turning slightly to the side, she sucked in several much-needed breaths, hoping she wasn't on the verge of hyperventilating.

Spotting her purse . . . well, a purse; she didn't actually recognize it, but assumed it must be hers, since it was in her apartment and she presumably lived alone. She grabbed it, dragged it closer, and rooted inside for what she knew had to be there.

Ah-ha! Her hand closed around a tube of lipstick. She didn't care what color it was, she popped the cap and smeared a layer on her mouth without bothering with a mirror.

Ian's brows crossed. "What are you doing?"

"This," she said, then leaned forward and pressed a kiss to his firm left pec, just over his heart.

When she moved away, he was staring down at the bright red puckered lip marks she'd left behind. His gaze lifted to hers, a question clear in his eyes.

"That's what I want you to get next," she explained, the wispy words little more than a whisper. "My kiss directly over your heart."

For a beat, he didn't say anything. Then his

Adam's apple bobbed as he swallowed hard and his own eyes flickered with a dozen different emotions all at once.

A second later, he stepped into her, backing her up and taking her mouth with a stark desperation that matched her own. She welcomed him into the cradle of her thighs, wrapping her arms around his bare back. He nearly crushed her in a similar embrace, holding her so close to his chest, she could barely breathe.

Not that she cared. Vampires or no, neither of them seemed to need oxygen at that moment. They only needed each other.

They continued to kiss, lips and teeth and tongues ravaging while their hands made short work of the rest of their clothes. In the time it took her to unbutton his jeans and lower the zipper carefully past his burgeoning erection, he had hers undone and whisked down her legs. Pants, underwear, shoes, socks . . . all were yanked off and dropped to the linoleum floor.

Pushing his own denims down past his hips, he lifted her, spread her legs even wider, and entered her in one fierce, swift motion. She gasped into his mouth at the sharp penetration, but was more than ready for it. She was so wet, they might as well have been making love in the shower.

And then her gasp gave way to a long moan as he began to thrust. No preliminaries, no pretty words, just the frantic grinding of his pelvis into hers while she clung to him, scratching his back, biting his lips and tongue, digging her nails into his buttocks to urge him on.

He drove into her until the edge of the counter scored her skin and the back of her skull cracked into the cupboards. But she didn't care. She wanted him this way—hard and fast and mad with lust. Wanted him so crazed, he couldn't see or hear or think about anything but her.

Judging by the pounding of his heart, the heaving of his chest, and his staccato grunts of pleasure, she was getting her wish. And the end, when it came, was cataclysmic.

A volcanic eruption, atomic explosion, and dead-center lightning strike all rolled into one. With a near-roar, Ian gripped her hips and plunged into her like a pile driver one last time, shuddering, shaking, spilling inside her.

The second he started to come, she followed him over, her entire body convulsing and squeezing around him until she was drained and limp. A cattle prod couldn't have prompted her to move a muscle, unless it was the deeply internal ones still flexing around him with the sweet, uncontrollable aftershocks of a ten-point-five orgasm.

She didn't know how long they remained propped there, pressed together like hot, sweaty pancakes, completely unmoving, the only sounds in the apartment that of their ragged, mingled breathing. Ian seemed to recover first, kicking off his boots and pants with jerky movements, then lifting her up to drape bonelessly across his chest and shoulder. He carried her out of the kitchen and down the hall to her bedroom, throwing back the covers with one hand and tucking them both up to their chins.

As Angelina snuggled closer to his naked warmth, she knew it was wrong, that it wouldn't last. But it felt *so* right. And as long as he was here with her . . . as long as *she* was here, in this reality . . . she intended to enjoy every minute.

SIP SIX

The nice, warm cocoon of pleasure and contentment surrounding Angelina lasted all of about two hours. After resting for a bit, they woke up to make love again. More slowly this time before drifting back to sleep.

But the next time the mattress shifted, Ian wasn't rolling toward her, wasn't reaching for her—he was getting out of bed and going in search of his clothes.

She didn't get up with him, instead pretending she was still asleep. Listening to the sounds of his moving around her apartment, while in her head, she thought, *This is how it must be between us. This is how it's always going to be.*

They would work together, pretending nothing was going on between them. They would come back here or go to some seedy motel for a couple hours of hot, secret sex. And then he would sneak off to return to his wife and his real home where he'd built a life and a family. One that didn't include her.

From the other room, she heard the front door open and then close, and knew she was alone.

Was this really how she wanted to live out the rest of her life? she asked herself as she slowly drifted back to sleep.

Provided this was her reality now, that she was stuck here as a human being rather than going back to that other world where she'd been immortal and more in charge of her life than she was here, was this how she wanted to spend the next twenty, thirty, fifty years?

She wasn't sure, but judging by the ache in her chest and the heaviness lower, in her belly, where she suspected her conscience took up residence, she thought the answer might be no.

Sometime later . . . she wasn't sure how long . . . the low peal of a phone ringing woke her. She pushed out of bed, naked and groggy, going in search of the annoying noise.

It wasn't the phone in the bedroom, which meant the call wasn't coming in on her land line. And the only cell phone she knew about was the one she'd had in her coat pocket while she and Ian had been on stakeout.

Shuffling into the other room, she located her parka and wrestled with the bulky material until she could pull the small phone free.

"Hello?" she mumbled after flipping it open.

"Angie?"

A woman's voice calling her by an unusual name—she never went by Angie . . . or at least she hadn't in her vampire life—caught her off guard. Holding the phone between her shoulder and ear, she went to the kitchen and started gathering her discarded clothes, stepping into the pieces one by one.

"Yeah," she responded, even though it felt odd to answer to such an unusual name.

"It's Ellen," the voice on the other end said. "Ellen Hart."

Oh, God. The last name wasn't necessary. The minute the woman identified herself, Angelina knew exactly who she was talking to: Ian's wife.

How had Ian's wife gotten her number? Were they friends? Did they have backyard barbecues together? Did she attend their children's birthday parties?

Or were they casual acquaintances, familiar with each other only because she and Ian were partners?

Until she knew for certain, she had to be careful of what she said and how she acted.

Filling the awkward silence when Angelina didn't know quite what to say, Ellen asked, "Is Ian with you?"

Shit. Talk about a loaded question. If she said yes, would it clue Ellen in to the fact that her husband was having an affair? Or if she said no, would that put Ian in an even more precarious position because he'd told his wife he was going to be on the job with his partner—a.k.a. The Other Woman?

"He said he was going out to sit on a drug house or some such, and I just assumed he would be with you, but I haven't been able to reach him."

At the mention of a drug house, Angelina's blood went cold. She'd thought she'd turned Ian away from any interest in the vampire nest, or at least given him a reason to reconsider that they were cooking up drugs inside.

But even if she hadn't, why would he go back there alone? What did he think he could accomplish on his own?

"Are you two together on a stakeout or something?"

Jesus, how was she supposed to answer that? If she lied and said they were, Ellen would want to speak with Ian. But if she told the truth, the woman would only worry and possibly call around to other places and other people trying to track him down.

Worse than scrambling for the right thing to say to her lover's wife, though, was the fear that Ian had gone off on his own and gotten himself in trouble. Not with drug dealers or manufacturers, but with *really* bad guys. Bloodsucking bad guys, in the truest sense of the word.

"Not right this minute," she found herself murmuring, trying to keep her tone calm and steady. "We've been sitting on these guys for a while, though, on and off, and we've got a motel room down the street where we take turns resting while the other one of us keeps an eye on the house. He's there now, but he probably turned his phone off so it wouldn't wake him up."

Lie, lie, lie. And she wasn't even sure it was a good one.

"I can tell him you called when he gets back, before we switch off again, if you want, but it may not be for a couple more hours."

Ellen was quiet for a few seconds, then she

seemed to relax. "Okay. It was nothing important, anyway. I just needed to talk to him. Thanks, Angie."

Angelina managed to keep her voice level and composed until they'd said their good-byes, then she shoved the phone back into her coat pocket and hurriedly climbed into her boots and shoulder holster.

She was not a cop, not really. She might have a badge and gun, but the brain in her head was lacking the proper knowledge to use them effectively. Not that her ignorance was going to stop her from faking it or doing whatever she had to do to save Ian's life. If all else failed, she just had to point and shoot, right? Point and shoot and pray.

Provided he was actually in trouble at all. Maybe he was just holed up in another sleazy motel room, three-timing his wife and two-timing her.

She almost hoped that was the case. Not because she liked the idea of him being a complete and total womanizer, but because it would at least mean he hadn't done anything stupid like walking into a den of vampires and getting himself taken hostage . . . or worse.

Hitting the front door at a dead run, she raced out of the apartment building and started punching the button on her key chain fob the minute she reached the parking lot. She had no idea which vehicle was there or even if the keys in her hand were hers. But she was making an educated guess and hoping like hell she got one right.

One of the cars beeped and she hit the button again . . . and again until she spotted a set of headlights flashing against red brick.

Her car, it turned out, was a dented white Acura

with a bad case of tinworm. It actually pained her to unlock the driver's side door and climb in, knowing that her other ride—the one she'd enjoyed, but obviously taken for granted in her previous existence—was a sleek silver Mercedes with heated seats and a gray leather interior.

As she cranked the ignition and the engine barely managed to catch, she wasn't sure this pathetic POS even *had* heat, and the interior looked like something that had been pieced together from the corpses of other junked vehicles. Hers, it seemed, was the Frankenstein's monster of average American sedans.

Forget about pimping my ride, she thought with derision. *Somebody douse it with gasoline and light a match. Please!*

But she had more important things to worry about at the moment than how she looked driving down the street in the Uggo Mobile. Like whether this hunk of junk was going to get her all the way to where she needed to go, and just what the *hell* she was going to do once she got there.

She wasn't entirely sure where she was going, but with only a few wrong turns, she found herself on the bad side of the tracks, rolling past rundown houses and dark alleys that looked moderately familiar only because of the time she'd recently spent with Ian in these same areas.

Following the grid of streets, she turned up one and down another. Back and forth, crisscrossing, until she *knew* she was in the right place.

She slowed her speed, narrowing her eyes and searching the dark, unlit yards on both sides of the street for the abandoned house where she prayed she would *not* find Ian at the mercy of a bunch of bloodthirsty vamps.

When she found it . . . or thought she did, anyway—all of these clapboard houses with their peeling paint, broken windows, and splintered porch steps looked disturbingly similar—she slammed on the brakes, pulled to the curb, and cut the engine. For several long minutes, she simply sat there, watching the house for signs of inside activity.

What she wouldn't have given at that moment to have her vampire superpowers. Super night vision, so she could see through the window at a hundred yards as clearly as though she were standing in front of them. Super hearing, so she could listen for movement and voices, even hear what the occupants were saying. And most important of all, that super sixth sense that would allow her to *feel* another's presence, knowing if someone was sneaking up on her, or even how many people might be inside before she went in herself.

Taking a deep breath, she opened the car door and stepped out, facing the fact that she would just have to do what she could with her five average, everyday, *pathetic* human senses. That, and a handgun she wasn't entirely sure how to use without shooting herself in the foot.

She unsnapped the holster, anyway, and removed the firearm, opening and closing her hand around the butt of the gun in an attempt to get a feel for it and work up her confidence in carrying the thing. Or, God forbid, having to aim it at someone.

Of course, aiming a gun at a vamp wasn't going to do her much good. Even if she pulled the trigger, she couldn't count on a bullet slowing one of them down any longer than if she were using marbles and a slingshot. If she could manage to tap the heart or head, *maybe* it would buy her a little time. A few stunned minutes before he recovered, then came at her with a vengeance.

And that was *one* bad-ass vampire. If she could manage to hit *one of them*...when there were probably three or four more who would be on her like lions on a baby gazelle.

She wished, more than anything, that she had some backup. Cops were supposed to have backup, right? Or at least have backup available.

But she hadn't been in this body long enough to figure all of that out. She didn't even know where the precinct was that she and Ian worked out of, let alone how to radio in to ask for help. And even if she did...

Oh, yeah, she could just picture that. Calling in, asking for more officers to be sent to her location to help her break into a suspected drug den because she suspected her lover...er, partner... was being held by a gang of vampires.

Even if she didn't mention that last part, even if she trailed off at the "suspected drug den" part, they would be hella surprised when a bunch of supposed meth cookers and dealers they'd thought would be a piece of cake to bring down sprouted fangs and started tossing them around like bits of fireplace kindling.

Which meant she really was on her own, in every sense of the word.

Slipping across the street, she climbed the porch as quietly as possible—which wasn't easy, considering the loose and splintered boards that made up the crooked front steps. Peering in the front window, she saw nothing, heard nothing. Just black, empty space.

She abandoned the porch and moved around the house, slowly, silently, looking for all the world like a burglar, she was sure. Thank goodness this was a bad neighborhood, where no one was likely to call the police. She doubted they'd even *notice* her, no matter what kind of crimes and misdemeanors she was up to.

Tiptoeing into the backyard, she spotted a small window near the ground. A basement window. And on the other side of the glass, a low, flickering glow.

Dropping down to her hands and knees, she inched closer, practically pressing her nose to the filthy glass pane to get a better look inside.

At first, she couldn't tell what she was seeing. Then, as her eyes adjusted, she realized that the flickering light was a couple of candles burning on a low table off to the side, barely illuminating the figures in the room.

Of course, vampires didn't need light to see; like all nocturnal creatures, they had perfect night vision. But because they had opted for candles, she could make out four vampires milling about the room.

Two leaned against walls as if they didn't have a care in the world. One was chewing his thumb nail, the other slapping a wicked-looking knife rhythmically against his thigh.

Another stood almost in the center of the room, arms crossing his chest. And the fourth—the one she'd originally identified as the most Thriller-esque, the leader of the group—was pacing back and forth.

Between the two non-leaning vamps was an old wooden chair, and tied to the chair was a man.

Ian.

Her heart plummeted at the sight, falling to the bottom of her stomach and making her want to retch.

He was wearing nothing but jeans and a sleeveless, formerly white undershirt, and was beaten and battered. One eye was sickeningly red and swollen shut, the other not too far behind. Blood, both fresh and dried, trickled from his nose, mouth, and temple. There were cuts and abrasions on his arms and probably every inch of the flesh she couldn't see.

His arms had been wrenched behind him at what looked like a painful angle, then secured with a bit of dirty rope, and his head lolled to the side, chin meeting his chest. She didn't know if he was conscious or not, but at this point, she didn't really care. She just wanted to *get to him.*

For a second, she considered bursting in on them. Kicking in the window and jumping inside. But though that might give her the element of surprise for all of half a second, it wasn't going to buy her any real leverage. The vamps would be on her before she hit the ground.

So even though it went against her basic instincts to get to Ian by the fastest and most direct route possible, she made herself back away from the window and round the house the way she'd come.

Re-holstering her gun, she made sure the flaps of her coat hid it from view, then climbed the front steps once again. This time, she didn't worry about being stealthy as she raised her hand and rapped on the door.

She honestly wasn't sure what the heck she was doing. All she knew was that if she sneaked in and tried to take the vamps by surprise, she and Ian would both end up as human Slurpees.

So she was going in another way. Not necessarily a smarter or better way, but "Avon calling!" was about the best she could come up with on the fly.

After letting the seconds tick by with no footsteps sounding in the background or angry voices heading in her direction, she put her hand on the knob and twisted. The warped wooden panel stuck and she had to add the sole of her boot and her body weight to the effort.

The panel flew open with a jerky *whomp* and slammed back against the wall, sending Angelina stumbling gracelessly inside. Yeah, making a silent break-and-enter wasn't on the day's agenda. And if the vamps hadn't heard all that commotion, there was something wrong with them. A stone-deaf grandma would have heard her entrance, even over the triple-decibel volume of *Wheel of Fortune*.

Bracing herself for a confrontation at any moment, Angelina scoped out her surroundings. Peeling wallpaper, threadbare window treatments, and a couple of broken, lopsided paintings (of the garage sale, not museum, variety) made up the first room of the house.

The floorboards were bare and weathered, nearly as uneven and splintered as those on the front porch, and grime as thick as sawdust on the floor of a good ole boy honky-tonk covered every surface. Cobwebs filled the corners and dangled from the ceiling. Mouse, or maybe rat—she really didn't want to think too hard on that one—droppings and the occasional vermin-shaped skeleton littered the floor.

Okay, she didn't know how long this place had been sitting here abandoned, but it kind of put the need for manufacturing haunted houses at Halloween into the "obsolete" category. Hell, this one even came with its own scary-ass coven of vampires, who would gladly jump out at unsuspecting victims . . . and then give them more than they'd paid for by sucking them dry.

And the smell . . . Well, she really didn't want to think too much about that, either, but if trick-or-treaters were looking for a bit of reality in their holiday festivities, then the scent of cat urine mixed with Eau de Rotting Corpses should do it for them in spades.

Careful *not* to take a deep breath, she slowly made her way into a narrow hall where a stairwell led to the second floor and then broke off in opposite directions to another room and the back of the house. She figured her best bet at the basement was toward the back of the house, so she turned left and opened her mouth to begin her ruse.

"*Hel-lo-o!*" she called out. Not too loud at first; she wanted to come across as normal and natural as possible. "Hello? Is anyone here?"

Step by step, she moved through the house, listening for any sign of the occupants she knew were somewhere below. And then, out of nowhere, a hand grabbed her by the upper arm and spun her around.

She slammed into a hard wall of chest covered in squeaky red leather, and above her ear, a low, menacing voice whispered, "What do you think you're doin' pokin' around my pad, sweet thang?"

SIP SEVEN

The vampire's fetid breath heated her cheek and ruffled her bangs.

And how did she know he was a vampire, other than through her previous deductive reasoning? Well, the fact that his breath had the metallic tang of blood—mixed with a heavy dose of some sort of strong, hard liquor—was a pretty good giveaway.

Her stomach tightened. She hoped the blood she smelled wasn't Ian's . . . and that Thriller-vamp didn't intend to add hers to the cocktail.

Even if Ian had been bitten, provided he hadn't been drained to the brink of death or fed afterward from one of the immortals' own veins, he'd be okay. Woozy and dehydrated, but okay.

After processing those bits of information, Angelina's attention turned to the viselike arm cutting into her diaphragm and the granite wall of inhuman flesh at her back. Judging by his choice of words—*pad? sweet thang?*—she suspected this guy was a neo-vamp.

Not one of the older generation, turned eighty,

a hundred, even *hundreds* of years ago, but one turned probably within the past couple of decades. Which meant that he wasn't stuck in the eighties because it was his favorite era so far; he was stuck in the eighties because that's when he'd been turned, and he wasn't far enough away from it yet to let go, move on, embrace his new existence, and blend in.

His more recent introduction to immortality might also explain the nest and the bullying behavior. Often new vamps operated on a power high for a while and went off on dominance binges, overwhelmed by all of their newfound strengths and feeling the need to throw their weight around. Usually, a run-in with an older vamp who could kick the newbie's ass without so much as ruffling his hair took care of that PDQ.

So either this guy hadn't yet come across another vamp who'd been around the block a few thousand more times than he had . . . or he was just a plain old run-of-the-mill flaming asshole.

Keeping all of that in mind, she forced herself to relax and feign complete and total innocence.

"I'm so sorry," she said, letting her voice go thin and shaky. "I didn't mean to trespass, but I've been visiting my mother, who lives down the street, and her cat got out. She's really upset about finding the poor thing, so I've been going around the neighborhood, looking for it, and I thought it might have gotten in here somehow."

Given the broken windows, abandoned appearance, and odor of cat pee permeating the house, it was entirely plausible. Although she had no doubt that any small domestic animal who made the mistake of wandering into this place likely wouldn't last very long before becoming a four-legged appetizer. Rogue vamps like this weren't exactly known for their discernment when it came to feeding patterns.

"Have you seen him?" she asked, twisting slightly in an effort to break the vamp's hold—but not struggling, not acting as though it was anything but a normal response to wanting to face the person you were talking to.

She was careful, however, not to make actual eye contact with the six-foot-four fangster. Not all vampires had the power to hypnotize humans; it was a trait that took some time to master, but she wasn't taking any chances.

Rather than grabbing her again or throwing her through the nearest window, the tall, cocky vampire's mouth widened into a smirk. Closed lips, no sign of fangs. He was playing it smooth. But then, he didn't know that she already knew what he was and was more than familiar—intimately familiar—with his kind.

"Sorry, sweet thang," he oozed in a voice that ran down her spine like Tabasco sauce. "I haven't seen your pussy. Yet."

Oh, yeah. A Mensa member with a witty-slash-creepy double entendre comeback. It was all she could do not to roll her eyes and knee him in the marbles.

Vampires might have superpowers, but none of them were located in the family stones. One well-placed kick and she could have this guy on the floor, squealing like a sissy. And it was tempting, very, very tempting.

Pretending she didn't catch his subtle threat, she asked, "Would you mind if I looked around a bit? Momma's cat is kind of skittish, and I'm afraid he might be hiding in a closet or the basement or something."

As soon as she mentioned the basement, she knew she had him. His tall frame relaxed into an overconfident, I've-got-her-now stance.

One corner of his mouth lifted even higher. "Yeah, sure, sweet thang. Make yourself at home."

He stayed where he was, waiting, letting her take the lead, and then following a few feet behind. She moved back down the hall and checked the other rooms downstairs first, then headed carefully up the stairs to the second floor.

She was half afraid of falling through the rotting boards, straight to the basement far below. Which was her true destination, anyway, but she worried that if she made a beeline for Ian, the gang leader might get suspicious.

So she took her time, pretending to be nothing more than a helpless young woman in search of her mother's runaway feline. She looked in closets, behind window drapes, under broken, rodent-infested pieces of furniture, all the while calling for the imaginary pet: Fluffy.

If the situation hadn't been so dire, she would have laughed at the ridiculousness of it all. But it was a necessary façade. And she could only hope that the minutes she wasted wandering around was actually buying Ian some much needed time to rest and recover from whatever this group of vampires had already put him through.

Because she'd bet her badge and every one of her memories of being immortal that Mr. Big Bad Leader here gave his minions an order not to do another thing with Ian until he got back. He was too arrogant not to want to be present and in control, taking an active role in the torturing of an innocent human, bound and gagged and helpless.

A flare of anger shot through her as they trailed back downstairs. Oh, yeah, they were going to pay for that. All of it.

And not just what they'd done to Ian—though that was bad enough—but for everything she was sure they'd done to countless other victims over the years. All she needed was a nice, flaming ball of sunshine that would turn them into nothing more than a meal for the nearest ShopVac.

She glanced toward one of the broken windows, wondering how many more hours they had to go before dawn. Too many, she was afraid. And, silly her, she'd forgotten to pack her blowtorch.

Just as she'd hoped he would, when they returned to the main floor, Leader of the Pricks held up a hand and pointed her toward the back of the house. "The basement's this way."

Said the spider to the fly. Never mind his blatant disregard for the kitchen or anything else that lay beyond the basement entrance where a cat might be hiding out, he wanted her downstairs as soon as possible.

Since that's what she wanted, too, she let him usher her through the open door and down a narrow set of rickety steps. Only whatever light they already had burning down there cast any illumination on the stairs and kept her from tripping, falling, and breaking her neck before the Break-dancer Boys got the chance to do it for her.

She knew Thriller-boy's letting her wander around on her own wasn't going to last, but it still came as a surprise when he cracked her in the middle of her back with the flat of his hand hard enough to send her flying through an open, door-less doorway. The air flew from her lungs as she stumbled forward, tripped into Ian's slumped form, and sent them both crashing to the ground with a splintering creak of wood and a heavy thump of bodies.

Excellent. Though the assault did catch her slightly off guard, she wasn't quite as dazed as she let on, and couldn't have planned the fall better if she'd choreographed it herself. Keeping her head down, she gave it a small shake and made a sound somewhere between a whimper and a moan as though she was stunned, confused, maybe even in-jured.

She was down on the earthen floor—at least she thought it was earthen. Either that or the dirt was so thick and hard packed that it might as well have been. While she was draped half over a nearly un-conscious Ian, she did her best to loosen his bonds. The nice thing about bullies was that their muscles were usually bigger than their brains, and this group of vamps was no exception.

Because The Four Stooges were so tough, intim-idating, and self-assured, the ropes they'd used on Ian were mostly for show. They were wound tight around his wrists and ankles, but the knots were something a four-year-old could undo. And she was no four-year-old.

Then, as she continued to pretend her equilibrium was off, she made a point of using the chair, specifically the chair's legs—to push herself up, using all of her weight until she heard a nice, satisfying crack. Two of the legs broke off, sending her back down to the ground.

She groaned, playing her part to the hilt. And she must have been doing a good job because the vampires laughed like hyenas, enjoying her apparent weakness and the prospect of having a new victim to toy with until dawn.

Before trying to push herself up again, she leaned close to Ian's face. She knew he was still breathing, and she even thought he was awake, just out of it from the abuse he'd suffered.

"Can you hear me?" she whispered.

With his mouth still covered by a strip of tape, he blew a heavy breath out through his nose and gave a low groan. She took it as a yes.

"Good. Get ready. As soon as I can get the jump on these guys, we're going to make a run for it."

She barely got the words out before a big hand grabbed her by the back of the head, tangling in her hair and yanking her to her feet. But hopefully Ian had heard her. And hopefully he would have enough strength left to move under his own steam when the time came, because she didn't think she could kill, hurt, or distract four vamps *and* carry Ian out of this basement fireman-style.

Climbing to her feet, doing her best to keep Alpha Dick from scalping her, she was careful not to let him see the chair legs she was still holding, one in each hand. A.k.a. wooden stakes, asshole.

He spun her around, pulling her against him and leaning down to spew his hot breath all over her face. Lips pulling back from his teeth, he snarled at her, making no effort to hide his long, pointed incisors.

She let her eyes go wide, pretending to be shocked and frightened while really she was using her peripheral vision to scope out the rest of the room and peg the other vamps' locations.

"You picked the wrong house to go pussy-hunting in, sweet thang," he leered.

"Oh, I've got the right house," she said, after a beat of letting him believe she was frozen in fear. It was his turn to look surprised and confused, and before he could get two of his three connective brain cells working, she added, "And you're actually the pussy I was looking for."

With that, she brought her right arm up with all her strength, driving the chair leg through his leather jacket, between a couple of his ribs, and straight into his heart.

His eyes flared in stunned disbelief, and a second later he poofed. In slow-motion, she would have seen his skin disintegrate, followed by the stark white of his skeleton until he was nothing but a pile of dust on the already dirt- and dust-covered floor.

But it all happened too fast for the human eye to register, and she did have more important things to worry about. Confusion bought her enough time to spin on the other vamps and catch one of them with the remaining stake, but that left two more fangsters with a grudge to deal with. They came at her in a lurching rush, and she had mere tenths of a second to figure out what to do next—make a grab for the two stakes that were no longer sticking out of the dusted vamps' chests or head for Ian.

She headed for Ian. If nothing else, she could use her body to protect him.

He was coming around, thank goodness. Moving slowly, stiffly, he had his arms in front of him now and his legs untied.

Grabbing the chair, she flipped it and broke off the remaining two legs, then smashed the spindle back against the floor, leaving the pieces in hopes that Ian would catch on to exactly what they were fighting here, and put two and two together to get four: four wooden stakes, four dead bloodsuckers.

But either he was still too groggy, or his psyche just wasn't letting him go to that vampires-are-real place in his head. Which left her on her own to deal with the two vampires closing in on her while Ian used the wall to push himself to his feet and peel the tape from his mouth.

The stakes in her hand slowed them down a bit. Instead of rushing her, they were now stalking her one step at a time. Careful to keep them directly in front of her, she hugged the wall and walked backward, circling the room.

"Start moving slowly toward the door," she told Ian when she reached him, "and stay behind me."

Bodies pressed together, heart pounding in her chest, they moved like molasses out of the room and up the stairs to the first floor of the house. The whole while, the two ugly-ass vamps hissed and threatened and kept their razor-sharp fangs unsheathed and in full view.

Funny how fangs had never scared her before, not when she had a set of her own to flash back. But given her current, regrettably mortal state, those razor-sharp incisors might as well have been cobras ready to strike.

As they reached the top of the stairs, Angelina pitched her voice over her shoulder. "Can you run?"

"I think so, yeah," he said.

The words were shaky and weak, which didn't exactly fill her with confidence, but she would just have to hope for the best.

She gave a quick nod, even though she wasn't sure he could see it. "When we hit the front porch, I want you to take off to the right as fast as you can. My car is just down the street."

Announcing your plans to the enemy wasn't exactly Rule Number One in the "Urban Warfare Handbook," but in this situation, she didn't have much choice. Besides, if all went well, the two Lurches beading down on them would both be lawn fertilizer before they got halfway to the sidewalk.

Floorboards creaking beneath their feet, she and Ian made their way through the house. Whenever possible, he used the wall to support his weight, and she could hear the thumps of his steps, the slide of his body.

She could also hear the two vamps in front of her huffing with fury like bulls preparing to charge a red cape. The veins in their throats pulsed in time with the anger rushing through their bloodstreams, and she knew that if she didn't kill them right the first time, she probably wouldn't get a second chance. These two had blood in their eyes, and even without her vampire sixth, seventh, and eighth senses, she could smell the violent death that awaited her and Ian at their hands.

The front door squeaked on its hinges as Ian opened it, but instead of following him through, she stopped, buying him precious extra seconds. The vamps continued to creep forward, but she widened her stance, making sure they got a good look at the business ends of the chair legs she was still sporting.

"Don't let my size or the fact that I have breasts fool you, boys," she told them, listening as Ian limped as quickly as he could across the decrepit porch and down the steps. "I know what you are, and I know how to make you cry for your sires."

That gave them pause. It didn't send them running in the opposite direction—unfortunately— but it did keep them from coming any closer.

Once she thought Ian had put enough distance between himself and the house, she started moving again. Slowly, one step at a time, backing across the porch.

She reached the steps and knew that every moment now was critical. The two vamps came through the doorway and spread apart, flanking her, poised to attack.

Her first instinct was to glance over her shoulder to see where Ian was, make sure he was safe, that he was far enough away, and gauge how fast she would have to move to reach him. But the minute she turned her head, she knew the vamps

would be on her like ants on a lollipop. All she
could do was strike out as hard and as fast as possible, then haul ass.

Steeling herself for what was to come, she prepared to do just that. But on the next retreating
pace, her heel went through the rotting wood of
one of the steps and she lost her balance, falling
back. Her arms flailed and she let out a shriek of
surprise. Then the air left her lungs completely as
she hit the ground with a thud.

Just as she'd known they would at the first sign
of weakness on her part, the two remaining vamps
from the nest attacked. They covered her, hissing
and spitting, going for her neck.

But she still had the stakes, and she used them.
She nailed one in the side—the best she could do
with her arm pinned and at the wrong angle. He
grunted and rolled off of her, the piece of wood
pulling from his body with a soft squish.

"Ang!"

She heard her name, closer than she would
have liked, and cocked her head on the grass to
see Ian coming back—to rescue her.

Dammit!

"No! Stay back!"

She redoubled her efforts to loosen her foot
from the broken board and hold off the vamps,
but it was already too late. The second the unin-
jured vamp heard Ian's call, he jumped up and
headed for Victim Number Two.

"Shit," Angelina swore. With a mighty yank, she
pulled her leg free and spun to her stomach on the
ground. She didn't have time to aim, to stand,

nothing. All she could do was pull back her arm and launch a stake like a dagger.

It hit its mark . . . but well away from the bull's eye and without nearly the force needed to bring the vampire down.

He stumbled, groaned, but didn't let it stop his forward momentum. Another few feet and he'd be on Ian, who was standing on the sidewalk, ready to fight, ready to use whatever strength he had left to defend himself and protect her to his dying breath.

Which was exactly what she was afraid of.

She sprang to her feet, only to be hit from behind and knocked to the ground by the other vamp—the one she'd stuck and then (stupidly) forgotten about. The asshole straddled her, pressing her into the dirt and grabbing her by the hair to yank her head back. *The better to bite you in the jugular, my dear.*

Fuck that. She still had a stake in her hand. The wrong hand, but that was easily remedied. Getting at a decent angle to dust the bastard was a little more difficult, but after a short struggle, she managed to buck him off slightly and roll to her side.

Good enough. Hauling back, she staked him. Dead center, straight to the heart. A shocked expression crossed his face, and then he disintegrated, covering her with a fine layer of vamp ash.

She didn't waste time brushing it off, but leaped to her feet and turned for Ian. Her heart seized when she saw him on the ground, held down by the last vicious, bloodsucking vampire.

She started forward, but wasn't fast enough.

Full throttle might as well have been slow motion. Her feet felt like they were mired in quicksand, like she was on a treadmill instead of solid ground, running as fast as she could but getting nowhere.

And then the vamp leaned down, pressed Ian's face away from him, and sank in his fangs.

"Noooooooooo!" She screamed at the top of her lungs, the sound ripping through the night air, going on and on and on.

At a run, she fell on the vampire, using her body weight to drive her stake into his back, through his heart, and out the other side. He *poofed* in an instant, sending her sprawling onto Ian's bloody, unmoving form.

Tears rolled down her cheeks as she searched him for signs of life. His neck was a mess. A giant red, ragged hole stood out on the left side, where the vamp had torn into him. Not just two small puncture marks, but a big, gaping wound.

God, could he even survive this? It looked as though his jugular vein had been severed completely, blood still spurting.

Even as a vampire, it would have taken some time, but as a human . . . Fear clutched her stomach, made her mouth go dry.

She covered the gash with her hand, doing her best to shrug out of her parka and use it to staunch the flow, as well. Then, digging into the pockets, she found her cell phone and dialed 9-1-1.

After she dropped the phone and continued to apply pressure to his neck, she started patting his face in an attempt to wake him up.

"Ian. Ian, can you hear me?" She fought to keep her voice steady and not let panic take over, but could feel the warmth of his life's blood seeping through the layers of her coat and between her fingers.

Suddenly, he jerked, his eyes flying open, but they were wide and unfocused.

Her heart lurched in her chest, hopeful. "Hold still, baby," she told him, tears clogging her throat. "The ambulance is on its way."

She stroked his face, his slightly stubbled head, the unmarred side of his throat. He struggled to raise his arm, grappling for her, and she quickly took it, twining the fingers of her free hand with his. His mouth opened, as though he were trying to speak, but all that came out was a sick, gurgling sound and a bubble of red that seeped slowly from one corner.

"No." She screwed her eyes shut, silently begging him not to die, hoping his injury wasn't as bad as it seemed, even though deep down she knew . . . *she knew.*

In the distance, she heard sirens, and prayed they were for him, prayed they would reach him in time.

"Hang on, Ian," she whispered. "Just hang on. Please. I love you. I love you so much."

His lips continued to work, still trying to form words, sounds. The thin trickle of blood grew thicker, running down his cheek toward his ear.

With a gasp, his body arched off the ground, and she clutched his hand even tighter. He coughed. Once, twice, spitting blood as his eyes slid closed.

And then he was still. So still.

"No. No," she railed, voice watery as she began

to cry. Her eyes filled, clouding her vision. "Please, God, don't take him. Please, don't."

If she were still a vampire, this never would have happened. She could have taken out those low-rent assholes in the basement and gotten Ian out without another scratch.

If Ian were still a vampire, he never would have been hurt like this, never would have been abducted to begin with. And even if he had, he would have been able to fight back, to heal.

She hated this life. Hated being a human, hated that Ian was human. She didn't want to be here when her old life was so much better. When she could have Ian to herself, alive and well and immortal.

In a flash, she remembered the last time she'd been with Ian in their old life . . . the night they'd watched *It's a Wonderful Life,* and she'd wondered, *What would their lives be like if they'd never been turned?*

And now she knew. It wasn't better. It wasn't Ward and June Cleaver and happily-ever-after; it was atrocious. The most horrific of nightmares that she would give anything to wake up from.

She wanted to go back. She didn't know how she'd gotten here in the first place or why she was suddenly playing the part of Georgette Bailey in *It's a Terrible, Horrible, No-Good, Very Bad Life,* but she wanted to go back.

Letting her head fall to Ian's still, unmoving chest, she closed her eyes and let the grief pour out of her in great, wracking sobs.

Take me back, she thought.

She knew it was useless and wasn't even sure who she was trying to ask for such an impossible favor, but she couldn't seem to stop herself.

"Help me, Clarence, please," she begged, falling into the ever-so-familiar dialogue from Ian's favorite movie.

Please! I want to live again. I want *him* to live again. *Please, God, let me live again.*

SIP EIGHT

I want to live again!

Angelina sat up, the scream ripping from her throat and shattering her own eardrums. Her eyes were open—she thought—but everything around her was dark. And tears, great, fat rivers of wetness rolled down her cheeks.

"Ang! Angelina, wake up!" Hands shook her shoulders and she whipped around, trying to make out where she was and who was with her.

A second later, a light flared and she found that she was in her room. Her *real* room, and Ian was beside her in their big, soft king-size bed. She inhaled sharply, the air getting stuck in her lungs for a moment before rushing out on a sob.

"Oh, God. Oh, God, Ian." She launched herself at him, hugging him so tight she nearly crushed his sternum. And then she jerked back, eyes wide.

Running both her gaze and her hands over his magnificent body, she checked him everywhere. His face, his throat, his chest, arms, stomach . . . his throat again, both sides.

He was perfect. More than perfect, he was completely unharmed. No blood, no bite marks. Not a scratch or a bruise or even a tattoo.

But just to be sure . . . She grabbed his lips and pried them open.

"Excuse me?" he mumbled past her awkward hold.

Fangs. Beautiful, dangerous, pointy-tipped fangs.

She felt for her own needle-sharp incisors with her tongue, then double-checked with her fingers.

"Oh, God. Thank You, God."

Ian's brows knit. "Are you okay? You're acting really strange."

She nodded, but had one more terrible, horrifying thought.

"Pinch me," she said.

His eyes narrowed even more. "What?"

She lifted her arm, gesturing to the sensitive flesh at the inside of her upper arm. "Pinch me," she told him again. "Really hard. Please."

He looked as though she were asking him to go vegan, but did as she asked. With two fingers, he reached out and squeezed a thin bit of skin, adding a twist for good measure.

"Ouch!"

At her cry, he let go immediately, face coloring slightly with remorse. He opened his mouth, and she knew he was about to apologize for hurting her, but she didn't want his apology. That pinch of pain was the sweetest, most wonderful thing she'd ever felt.

And so was . . . Bringing her arm to her mouth, she used the tip of one fang to slice open her wrist. Not deep, but enough to draw blood.

For a moment, she watched the thick red fluid bead on her skin, then leaned in and licked it off. Mmmm, it tasted wonderful, the way blood should to a vampire. And her saliva worked exactly as it was supposed to, sealing the wound almost instantly so that the cut was no more than an angry pink line marring her flesh.

Lifting her head, she smiled so wide, she thought her face might break. "Oh, Ian, I love you!"

She threw her arms around him, knocking him back against the pillows. He hit with a *hmph* as she landed on top of him, his hands going automatically to her waist.

They were both naked beneath the covers, the same way they always slept. The knowledge made her grin even as she kissed him stupid.

When she came up for air, Ian was staring at her funny. "Are you sure you're all right?"

She nodded vigorously. "I've never been better, believe me. I've never been so happy to see you, or to be in this room, or to know that we're going to live forever and you're stuck with me, whether you like it or not."

Straightening slightly, she arched a critical brow. "But don't think that means I'll be a pushover. I'd better be the only woman in your life—today, tomorrow, and for the next thousand years. Otherwise, your forever is going to end a lot sooner than mine."

That odd expression crossed his face again and darkened his chocolate-brown eyes. Lifting a hand, he cupped her cheek, and stroked her with his thumb.

"When I look at you, there are no other women. There never have been."

Emotion clogged her throat, and her lashes grew damp again. Because she didn't think her mouth would work well enough to form words, she used it to kiss him instead.

What started as a soft brush of lips quickly turned into something deeper and more passionate. She stroked his chest, luxuriating in the rock-hard pectorals and pebble-tight nipples, the ridges of his ribs leading down to his six-pack abdomen.

His growing erection brushed between her legs as he grasped her hips, and she teased it, rubbing her warm, wet folds back and forth across the tip. He groaned, fingers flexing before he did a bit of teasing of his own by cupping her breasts and flicking the turgid tips.

She gasped, throwing her head back and letting her lashes flutter closed as desire swamped her. The sex between them had always been good—better than good; it made triple-X skin flicks look like *Pride and Prejudice* on Valium.

But after what she'd been through—dream, nightmare, Dickens's "Ghost of Christmases to Come"—she didn't even care, as long as it was truly over. After what she'd been through, having him belong to another woman and then die in her arms, being with him this time was somehow . . . different.

Hotter and more tender, deeper and more meaningful. She never wanted to leave this bed again, never wanted to stop touching him, kissing him, reminding herself of how much he meant to her.

Whatever had happened, it had cleared her head like a bucket of ice water, putting everything into crystal clear perspective. She didn't care about a ring or wedding vows. They were all ribbons and bows on a package that was already so perfect, it didn't need wrapping.

Ian's fingers slipping between her legs to part her slick folds slammed her back down to earth and reminded her that there would be time to analyze her dream-slash-otherworldly experience later. Much . . . later.

She tipped her head back, letting Ian kiss her throat. Her long, loose hair brushed the small of her back while he trailed tiny little sucking bites along her flesh, his fangs scraping, but never breaking the skin.

Wrapping her fingers around his thick, rigid penis, she centered herself over the plum-shaped head. With the prick of his teeth at her jugular, she lifted his wrist to her mouth, biting down just as she lowered herself onto his pulsing cock.

He filled her, stretched her. His blood in her mouth, his fangs piercing her throat completed her. The sensations made her body sing, like she was clutching the frayed ends of a live wire in her bare hand.

They fed while they moved, long, deep pulls to match the long, slow strokes of their bodies. But as the flow of their blood slowed, the speed of their bodies increased until they were bucking against one another.

Their mouths met, breaths mingling. She could taste the tangy flavor of her own blood as she twirled her tongue around his, and knew he was tasting the very same thing.

Grasping his hands, she twined their fingers, then bore him back on the bed, pinning his arms on either side of his head. Her knees clamped tight to his hips as she rode him, faster and faster, racing toward completion.

The room filled with both the sounds and scents of their mating, their passion seeping into every pore of her skin and muscles and bones. It didn't just warm her, it turned her into a blazing furnace of lust and need.

She met every upward thrust of Ian's hips with a driving rhythm of her own until they were sweating, pounding, gasping, groaning. Almost without warning, the orgasm hit, rocking Angelina to her core as she screamed Ian's name. A second later, he clutched her hands hard enough to break bones and came with a ragged shout.

Collapsing across his chest, she reveled in the warmth of his skin, the heavy beat of his heart beneath her ear, and the feel of her tender internal muscles rippling around him.

Five, maybe ten minutes later, he shifted with a moan, rolling her onto the mattress. She expected him to leave her there and return to his back, putting a few inches of space between them as their ardor cooled and they tried not to slip into a complete comatose state.

Instead, he moved with her, covering her body so that his weight pressed her down. Not crushing, but definitely reminding her of why they didn't make blankets out of sandbags and cinderblocks.

The man was two-hundred-plus pounds of pure, mouthwatering muscle.

He wasn't trying to smother her, though, or go for round two. He was reaching past her, stretching until he could pull open the top drawer of the nightstand and dig inside.

A second later, he leaned back, propping himself up on one elbow while he stared down at her. One hand supported his head, the other placed a small, square box on her stomach, just beneath her breasts. It was wrapped in pretty red, metallic paper and topped with a perfectly tied bow of thin gold ribbon.

Angelina's fingertips went cold while her heart struggled to pump blood through her veins. She licked her lips and swallowed past her suddenly dry throat.

"What's this?" she asked in a voice that sounded sandpaper rough.

"I was going to wait until later to give it to you. Till we were downstairs near the tree, doing the whole Christmas breakfast, exchange-of-gifts thing."

"What is it?" she asked again, afraid to get her hopes up. Almost afraid it was another dream. Or worse yet, a dream within a dream, like that movie *1408* where poor John Cusack thought he'd escaped the evil hotel room and had a shot at happily-ever-after only to be sucked right back into his homicidal nightmare reality.

One corner of Ian's mouth tipped up in a grin. "Open it and see."

With shaking fingers, she lifted the box, untied the ribbon, and removed the lid. Inside was another box, this one black velvet, slightly rounded on top.

Her heart kicked against her ribs, and the nervous chill in her hands spread to her lips, along with a tingling numbness. Taking the ring box out of the gift box, she pulled back the lid . . .

And sucked in a breath at the most exquisite diamond solitaire she'd ever seen. It sparkled like the North Star, even in the dim light of the room and through the sheen of tears filling her eyes.

Brushing his lips against her temple, Ian whispered, "Will you marry me?"

She blinked, trying to clear her vision. Looking from the ring to Ian's soft sable eyes and back, she managed a weak, "Are you serious?"

He inclined his head, his face a study of solemn lines and firm features. "I want you to be with me till death do us part." One of his dark brows winged upward and his lips softened in amusement. "And considering just how long that could be, I think you know I'm not kidding around here. So if your answer is yes, put the damn ring on your finger. If it's no . . ."

He flopped back on the bed, splaying his arms and legs as though he were about to be drawn and quartered. "Just stake me now and get it over with. Put me out of my misery."

She knew he was only teasing, but considering what she'd just been through—or just dreamt she'd been through—she didn't find it funny. In fact, it sent a shaft of fear so deep into her soul, she wasn't sure she would ever shake free of it.

Flipping over onto his chest, she kissed him hard, then met his steady, somewhat confused gaze. "Don't say stuff like that. Ever. Don't even joke about it."

Grabbing the ring, she tossed the box aside and slipped it quickly, firmly onto her left hand. "Yes, I'll marry you. If you'd asked me a hundred years ago, my answer would have been yes. If you asked me a hundred years from now, my answer would be yes. And if you never asked me . . ."

She brushed his mouth with her own, then followed the contact with her thumb, tracing the supple line of his lips. "My answer would be the same. In my heart, I'm already your wife, and you've always been my husband. For me, there will never be another."

Emotions, tender and strong, flashed through his eyes a second before he drove his fingers into the hair at the nape of her neck and pulled her down for a long kiss full of love and devotion.

When he released her to catch her breath, he murmured, "You know, you might have mentioned all that before. Do you have any idea how intimidating it is for a guy to go ring shopping and work up the courage to pop the question? Half the time, I swear it would have been easier to spend the night in a tanning bed."

Feigning annoyance, she rapped him in the chest with the back of her hand—and made sure to use the one with the giant, three-carat diamond on it. "Oh, stop whining, you big baby. I'm worth it, aren't I?"

Growing immediately serious, he framed her face with his hands and pulled it close to his own. "You are worth *everything*, Angelina. I love you more than life, more than eternity, more than a nice, warm glass of O-positive after a long night of resisting the urge to chomp on dirtbags before tossing their asses in jail."

When she chuckled even through the glimmer of tears filling her eyes and throat, he winked at her and pressed her knuckles—ring and all—to his lips. "And now everyone will know you belong to me."

Angelina cocked her head and offered him a watery smile. "Was there ever any doubt?"

He smiled back, flashing straight white teeth and a set of sexy, spiked fangs. "Nope."

And then he kissed her, reminding her that the life she led with the man she loved was a wonderful one, indeed.